THE
MISTRESS

BOOKS BY JILL CHILDS

THE
MISTRESS

JILL CHILDS

bookouture

Published by Bookouture in 2020

An imprint of Storyfire Ltd.
Carmelite House
50 Victoria Embankment
London EC4Y 0DZ

www.bookouture.com

ISBN: 978-1-83888-969-2
eBook ISBN: 978-1-83888-968-5

For Nick

PART ONE

LAURA

CHAPTER 1

I didn't turn up uninvited. He summoned me, with a text. The last thing on my mind was killing him.

My hands shook as I got ready. Not too much make-up; just a little eyeliner, a hint of blusher and lipstick. He didn't like painted ladies. That's what he called them. He laughed, quoting someone. Shakespeare, maybe. It usually was. That was Ralph all over. He didn't just teach literature, he lived and breathed it.

When he made love to me, it wasn't just the two of us between the sheets. We were Romeo and Juliet. Troilus and Cressida. Antony and Cleopatra. He let slip little lines, little phrases from all the poetry stored in that handsome head. *A lass unparalleled*. Or, *she makes hungry where most she satisfies*. I learned them by heart and googled them after he left, marvelling at how much he knew. He made me feel like someone special. Someone beautiful. Someone else.

I parked the car in the next street, to avoid notice. It was a warm night, but I pulled on a wide-brimmed hat that shielded my eyes, and strode briskly, head low, down the road and along to the house.

His street was deserted. The pavement was littered with spilled blossom from the spindly trees, as if I'd missed a wedding. It was still light and next door's curtains were open, offering me a wide view of their sitting room. I took it all in with a quick glance, making sure no one had seen me, then strode past.

He'd left the gate open. He always did when he expected me because of the way it creaked. I slipped through like a shadow and crept down the path to the front door. It gleamed in the mellow evening light. Black and recently re-painted. Helen had organised the painter, of course. She organised everything, including Ralph. He joked about it sometimes, if it came up. Not quite poking fun. He respected her too much. It hurt to admit it, but I could tell there was feeling there, even now. Not love, exactly. Certainly not passion. A grudging admiration. A sense of duty.

He'd once read out a poem of his at the school writing group about Odysseus and Penelope, a love poem of sorts. That was in the early days, when I was still trying to resist him. But thinking of nothing but him. My breath catching in my throat like a teenager when I went up to the Upper School, his territory, for a meeting. My senses so keen as I walked through the corridors, scanned the main hall from the first-floor windows, that I thought my sexual longing for him must radiate from me like nuclear energy, illuminating me for everyone must see. The pain of disappointment if I headed back to my classroom, back to the Lower School, without even seeing him, was just as visceral.

His poem asked who was the real hero – Odysseus, waging war with a sword, or Penelope, waiting for him so faithfully, weaving and unravelling and again weaving to preserve her honour?

I asked him, afterwards, as we gathered up our coats, keeping my voice low, pretending not to be leaving with him but knowing, we both knew, that he'd hurry after me and walk by my side to the Lower School car park, chatting as we walked.

I asked, 'What inspired you to write that?'

He smiled, his eyes crinkling, his gaze so direct, so full of feeling, that it made me shudder.

'What do you think?'

And I saw in a moment that it was for me, his lyrical, passionate poem. It was a salute to my chastity, to my struggle to stay faithful to Matthew, the boyfriend who'd left me nearly two years earlier and broken my heart. I realised then that when he looked at me, he saw something no one else saw. He saw the real me.

The following week, when he walked me down to my car after the group and asked me out, yet again, for a drink, I was ready. I blushed and couldn't meet his eye and said, 'Yes.'

What made me think of that, now? I ran the palm of my hand over my eyes, drying them and saw a streak of light flash across the glistening paintwork, a reflection from my watch, and stood still for a moment, concentrating on my breathing, trying to steady myself.

I didn't know what to expect. I didn't know why he'd texted me. I was hollowed out. I hadn't eaten – I hadn't really eaten for weeks – and my hands, clenched into fists at my sides, shook. The tablets the doctor had given me to help with anxiety – we both knew she meant depression – gave me mood swings. Weepy one moment, enraged the next. I wasn't myself. At school, people were starting to notice.

I swallowed, took a deep breath, then raised my hand and tapped with bare knuckles on the wood. The gentlest tap, for fear of waking Anna. Just as he'd taught me.

CHAPTER 2

We bumped against each other as he shut the door behind me and we were crammed, for a moment, in the narrow hall. Awkward. He was so close, I could feel the heat of his body, radiating outwards towards me. His lifeforce. I reached out and put my hand on his lower arm, feeling the warmth of his skin through his cotton shirt sleeve.

He jumped as if I'd given him an electric shock and pulled his arm away. My insides contracted. It was still there, the bond between us. Why else would it affect him so powerfully? But he looked haunted, his face closed as he turned from me.

My legs shook. I realised too how much I'd pinned my hopes on the possibility he'd changed his mind, that he realised what a fool he'd been to let me go and wanted me back.

He said, 'Drink?'

He led me through the hallway – past the narrow table with its neatly stacked mail and framed photos and the cellar door tucked under the stairs – and into the kitchen. My heels clip-clopped across the floor tiles and I tiptoed, trying instinctively not to make a sound. In the kitchen, I leaned against the counter, *her* kitchen counter, and watched him, learning him all over again. The way he ran his fingers through his hair when he was nervous, the breadth of the shoulders beneath his shirt, shoulders I'd so often clung to when we made love, his particular smell of male sweat and fresh laundry and shower gel. Ralph. I bit my lip.

He poured us both a glass of red wine and handed me mine. Shiraz, his favourite. He'd had it ready, there on the counter with two glasses. I wondered if Helen had bought it in her weekly internet shop.

I turned, nervous, and made a show of looking over the two neat shelves of recipe books there. They were ordered by region: Chinese, French, Italian, Middle Eastern. Each small section was arranged alphabetically, by writer. Helen, ever the librarian. How did he stand it?

I turned back. The kitchen clock on the wall behind him said nearly quarter past eight. They kept it five minutes fast, always. All the little things I knew about them and their life together. My insides tightened and coiled and I drank the wine, more quickly than I should.

'Where is she?'

He looked at the floor. 'Some school thing. A talk. About happiness, actually.' He gave a dry laugh.

We'd once had sex right there on that neatly scrubbed kitchen table where they sat each morning for breakfast. It turned him on, the thought of how much she'd disapprove, not only of the infidelity but of how unhygienic it was.

'So…' I tried to sound nonchalant – just another ploy to make him want me again. 'Where do we start?'

He answered without looking at me. 'We need to talk.'

'We do.' My fingers gripped the stem of the wine glass. For weeks now, some of the most painful weeks of my life, he'd ignored my texts, refused to answer my calls, avoided me in the school corridors, however desperately I'd tried to stalk him, trailing him from class to class. I knew his timetable by heart.

He drank a gulp of wine. 'I know you're hurt. I'm sorry, really. I never meant—'

Something inside me clenched. 'You never meant what?'

He paused and finally slid his eyes round to mine. They were wary and perhaps sheepish.

'I'm sorry, that's all. About what happened. But you've got to stop.'

I couldn't answer. *That was it, was it?* After all he'd said. How much he loved me. How right we were together. I was so sure he'd leave her, in the end, leave her for me. I bit down on my bottom lip.

He couldn't look me in the eye. 'I know you're angry. I get it. But you're just making things worse.'

'For you, maybe.' I had nothing more to lose.

He shrugged. 'Please. It's over. I'm sorry but it is.' He shifted his weight, his eyes looking across sightlessly at the cooker on the far side of the kitchen. 'It's not just about hurting me. Or Helen. It's about Anna too.'

I snorted. 'You should have thought about that before. What you've done isn't just wrong, it's illegal.'

He drank the wine. 'I'm not doing anything with… honestly, it's not what you think…' He trailed off, embarrassed.

'Stop it, Ralph. I know exactly what's going on.' I set down my wine glass and closed the gap between us, forcing him to look at me. 'And I'm not bluffing. You know that, don't you? I'm serious.'

His eyes widened. What had he expected? That I'd shut up and go away and let him carry on? I shook my head.

'I'll do it, Ralph. I will. I'll tell everyone. I'll write to the governors. It'll finish you. Don't you see? Not just with Helen. You'll never teach again.'

'They'd never believe you.' His eyes were uncertain. 'You've no proof. You can't have because it's not true.'

He looked so anxious, so vulnerable. A shock of hair spilled forward over his forehead and, without thinking, I lifted my hand and tucked it back. How many times had I done that in the past? It wasn't over. It couldn't be. We were too good together.

For a moment, neither of us moved. I saw myself reflected there in his brown eyes. Part of him.

Suddenly, I leaned in and kissed him on the lips. It wasn't planned. It just happened. Gently at first, then harder. His lips parted under the pressure and my tongue slid into his mouth, searching for his. I fumbled to touch him and ran my hands down his chest, feeling his warm, smooth skin through his shirt.

He put his hands on my shoulders, holding them, and murmured, 'Laura.'

I flushed. He wanted me. I could feel it. That was the real reason he'd asked me to come. He was just confused, held back by some misplaced idea of duty to his family and shame for what he'd done. He deserved better.

I surged with a sudden sense of my power over him, the hope that I could pull him back to me if I just kept going, if he let himself surrender to me. I wasn't lost. I could still make him mine again. It wasn't too late to cauterise the pain of the last few weeks.

I pressed against him a second time, my lips finding his. This time, he barely resisted. He let me kiss him, let me tease him with the tip of my tongue, then, finally, he shifted his weight, slid his hands from my shoulders to the small of my back, pulling me close, and kissed me back. I trembled, triumphant as well as excited. He wanted me. I was right, all along. He was mine for the taking.

Our kissing, sweet at first, became intense. I tugged at his shirt and slid my hands underneath the cotton. His skin was warm and familiar. He shuddered at the touch of my fingertips.

He pulled away a second time, less certainly than before, and looked down at me, safe now in the circle of his arms. I ran my tongue round my lips.

'Oh, Laura.' He sounded agonised.

I pushed against him, then smiled. His eyes were easy to read. He was too far gone, I could tell. No turning back. Whatever resolve he'd had, whatever plan to resist me, it was too late. It wasn't over, this passion of ours, far from it. I would win yet.

I took control, seizing his hand and leading him through to the sitting room. I pushed him back onto the settee, scattering its neatly arranged cushions, then straddled him. He moaned and closed his eyes, his head falling back. I started to unbutton his shirt, kissing my way down his chest, my heart surging.

*

Afterwards, I slumped on top of him. My legs, bent on either side of his, were stiffening. My face pressed into his sweaty, cooling neck.

He whispered into my ear, 'Laura?'

'Hmm?' My lips kissed the skin close to his mouth, breathing in his familiar smell. He moved his arms from round me and my back, naked and suddenly exposed, chilled. He shifted his weight, trying to lift me off, trying to move.

'Oh no, you don't!' I tried to pin him down, playful.

He didn't seem in the mood. Stronger than me, he pushed me to one side and I fell onto the mess of cushions. I watched, defeated but happy, as he got to his feet and padded across the room. My eyes drank in the contours of his body, the narrow hips, the long sweep of his spine, his buttocks.

I lay back, reliving the feel of his hands on my body. I imagined Helen sitting primly in this very spot later this evening, watching television, drinking tea, with no idea what we'd done here.

My body slowly cooled. I heaved myself to my feet, pulled on his large, crumpled shirt, discarded on the floor, and went in search of him.

'Ralph?'

The kitchen floor was hard and cold under my bare feet. He was standing there in the shadows, just inside the doorway, hunched over his phone, thumbs tapping.

He turned, then started when he saw me.

I smiled, cheeky. 'Hey, you. What're you up to?' I stepped towards him, imagining how alluring I must look, feeling the soft fabric of his shirt brush against my skin as I moved.

He dropped the phone on the kitchen counter as I reached him.

I pressed myself against his side, tilting my face to his. 'Ready to go again?'

He couldn't look me in the eye.

'We can't...' He hesitated. 'That wasn't meant...'

He pushed past me, embarrassed, heading back into the dingy hall. I grabbed at him.

'Wait. Ralph. What?'

He pulled away. His skin was slick.

My heart fluttered with panic. 'Ralph, I love you. Don't you know that?'

He shook his head, his face miserable. 'Laura, I'm sorry—'

I raised my voice, willing him to stop and listen. 'Is it what I said before? About telling people what you've done? I just can't bear it. That's all.'

He twisted away. I had the sense he wanted to shake me off and escape upstairs. I lunged at him, pushing him backwards and his back banged against the wooden panelling below the stairs. His abrupt change of mood frightened me, just when I'd let myself hope.

He rallied and grabbed my wrists. 'Shh! Keep your voice down.'

Anna, of course. He was worried about disturbing her, his innocent princess. Asleep upstairs in her perfect bedroom, all pink and frills.

'You miss me too. I know you do. Don't lie.' My voice became a shriek as I lost control. 'That's what drove you to do it, isn't it? What you did.'

He pulled a hand from my wrist and tried to put it over my mouth, to shut me up. I twisted and grabbed his hair, kicked out at him. It was brutal, I was brutal, but something exploded in me, feeling him use his strength against me, the hands struggling to restrain me, when just a short time earlier, they had been caressing me.

Even fighting him made my heart pound. Our naked bodies slapped against the hall wall, twisting, slippery with sweat, limbs knocking. It was as if we were two halves of the same whole. I felt it again as powerfully as I had when we'd made love, lost in each other. As if we'd never been apart.

He rallied and tried to push me away and I pressed back, kicking out at his ankles, lunging at him with strength I didn't know I had.

It happened in a moment. One second, we were locked together, wrestling in the narrow hallway, fighting with raw passion. The next, I shoved him away, hard, and he lost his balance, then fell heavily against the cellar door. It gave way under his weight and he plunged backwards into the darkness. His eyes were wide with shock, his arms flailing, as he struggled to regain his footing, slipping on a mess of buckets, brooms and boxes cluttering the top of the cellar steps.

He toppled sideways and disappeared from sight. Sickening bangs and thuds, muffled and quickly fading. I screamed, picturing his grasping body bouncing helplessly down the concrete steps. Then, finally, a dreadful silence.

For a second, I didn't move. I couldn't. I couldn't even breathe.

A sudden noise at the far end of the hall. I twisted to look. The front door was thrown open. Helen stood there. Her jaw slackened in disbelief as she stared at me, frozen in the dark hall, wearing nothing but her husband's shirt, my terrified eyes on hers.

CHAPTER 3

Helen didn't move. Her eyes were glassy. Her body looked rigid with shock. The house sucked itself empty of air, of sound, of life.

The moment stretched, unbearable.

Finally, Helen jolted into motion. Her handbag fell from her shoulder and landed with a thud as she kicked the front door shut and sped towards me with hurried strides, electrified by the panic on my face.

'What?' Her voice was hard and thin. 'What happened?'

I couldn't speak, just tore my eyes from her face to look again into the dark vacancy beyond the open cellar door.

She pushed past me and waded into the debris at the top of the steps, groping for a light switch just inside the doorway. At once, she let out a high-pitched cry, so primal it made the hairs on the back of my neck bristle. Her horror echoed, bouncing off the stone.

I pressed behind her, shaking, straining to see. The single, dusty lightbulb in the cellar below gave a faint light.

Ralph lay, crumpled and motionless, at the foot of the steps. He looked as if he'd hit the concrete head first, his neck tilted at an awkward angle. His limbs spilled in a heap, one leg bent under his body, the other trailing. I reached for the white-washed wall to steady myself.

Helen flew down the steps, hurtling into the cellar and collapsing over him, running her fingers over his chest, then higher, to his neck, with frantic, clumsy movements. For a moment, she seemed to be strangling him, then I realised why she was pressing her fingertips into his flesh. She was searching desperately for a pulse.

I imagined the marks rising on his skin, white, then red, where her fingers probed. She twisted suddenly and reached for his wrist and her fingertips circled it, again searching for life. My heart stopped, watching, waiting.

Another cry, desolate and heart-rending. '*Ralph?*' I gripped the doorframe, my knuckles whitening. Sharp flares of pain stabbed my stomach. I crumpled, bending forward, my eyes fixed on Helen, a shadowy shape in the gloom.

She crouched over him, her legs drawn up, sinking her face in his side, her arms spread across the broad bulk of his body. She was wailing, a low guttural howl of misery and pain from deep inside her as she cradled him and rocked herself to and fro.

His hand lay limp, palm up, on the concrete floor. The fingers that had written so much poetry, which had caressed me, curled uselessly into the air.

My knees gave way and I sank abruptly onto the top step. I drew the edges of the shirt around me, shivering now, and put my face in my hands. Everything smelt of him. My palms. The shirt. *What had I done? Dear God, what had I done? How could it be?* This man who, just minutes earlier, had been strong and pulsing with life, how could he be gone?

I rocked myself backwards and forwards, nauseous, copying her rhythmical movement instinctively, without knowing why.

The soft wailing continued to rise from below, bouncing round the hard walls. She was keening, burying herself in his body.

I stuttered, 'I'll call someone.' I struggled to find breath. 'An ambulance.'

She lifted her head and stared up the steps. Her eyes shone, ghoulish in the gloom. She seemed to be struggling to place me, to remember who I was, to assemble in her mind what had happened and why I was also here.

I said, 'He fell against the door. It just—'

'How?' she breathed. 'How could you?'

My insides froze. She turned back to Ralph and lay across him, trying to kiss his forehead, his cheek. I couldn't bear to look but I couldn't tear my eyes away. She pushed her hand into his curled one and held it. Then she pushed back and got to her feet, looked around.

I was hunched forward, my body shaking so hard, my feet teetering on the concrete steps. I could hardly bear my own weight.

'Or the police?' My thoughts were wild. *Who should I call?* 'Maybe.'

'No!' She snapped up her head and gave me a look of disgust, taking in my naked legs, my hands, clutching the folds of her husband's shirt round my chest. A shirt she may have chosen, washed and ironed. 'Don't you dare.'

I shrank back into myself. I thought of her daughter, asleep upstairs in her bedroom. Of Ralph's reputation at school, ruined. Of the scandal once the circumstances of his death became known. It would all come out, just as I'd threatened. About me. About *her*.

'It was an accident.' I saw him again, clawing the air as the door gave way, his eyes wide. 'He fell.'

She blinked towards the top of the steps, replaying what had happened in her mind.

'Why?' she whispered. I didn't know if she was struggling to make sense of the accident or of his betrayal. She'd never suspected an affair, Ralph had told me. She'd trusted him.

Her eyes landed again on me, huddled on the top step, tugging on the shirt to cover my bare thighs.

'Our daughter…' she said. 'She mustn't know.'

Anna. I swallowed and tasted bile.

Helen twisted back to Ralph's body, taking possession of it, cradling it in her arms. She reached up and tugged an old sheet down from a shelf, a dust cover perhaps, shook open the folds and stretched it over him. I sat, horrified, watching, listening to her sobbing, powerless to act.

Time stretched.

Somehow, shivering, I pulled myself to my feet and made it back to the sitting room. Everything was still. I forced myself to gather my scattered clothes and get dressed, then sat on the end of the settee – I don't know for how long – looking blankly into the empty room, trying to breathe. We'd been here together, just a moment ago. He'd made love to me. I'd felt him come back to me. I pushed my knuckles against my mouth and bit against them, trying to stopper my own grief, struggling to keep myself sane.

Later, I rummaged in the kitchen cupboards and found a bottle of gin. I swallowed a slug myself, barely aware of the taste, just the burn on my throat, then went back to the top of the cellar steps.

She was still bent over his covered body, motionless, her face resting on his chest. I shuddered. He must be cooling. Stiffening. I couldn't look. My stomach heaved.

I said, 'I think I'd better call someone now.'

'Wait!' Her head jerked up. 'Wait. We mustn't wake Anna.'

I stared down at her. The shock was playing games with her mind. It was over, for all of us. Anna too.

I shook my head. 'She's going to find out. We have to…'

She closed her eyes. She seemed older than the woman who'd appeared in the doorway earlier. Drawn. Haggard. Her breathing was ragged. She looked as if she were struggling to rally her strength, to regain control of her shattered nerves.

She muttered to herself, '*Think.*'

My eyes strayed to Ralph's protruding leg, his foot sticking out from the cover. The bare skin was puckered and shrivelled in the cold. The gin rose in my stomach.

I made it to the downstairs toilet before I vomited. My face was almost in the bowl, my eyes staring at the toilet brush in its holder. Pristine. A neat plastic case, oozing blue disinfectant, hung down from the rim. When I closed my eyes, everything swirled. I was a speck of dust, spinning through time and space, in free fall. *Dear God, what had I done?*

*

When my stomach was empty and I was retching nothing but acid, I crawled out on my hands and knees, like a dog. My head throbbed.

I pulled myself up the edge of the kitchen counter and splashed cold water on my face and wrists, took some sips from cupped hands. It was nearly dark outside. Through the window, the shapes and colours of the garden fence, the roses climbing their trellis, fused with my reflection, a pale, ghostly face with wide, frightened eyes staring back at me.

I couldn't face going back to the cellar steps. I took the second door out of the kitchen back into the sitting room.

I jumped. Helen was sitting there, a solid shape, silent and motionless in the gathering gloom. She was still wearing her cardigan and clumpy shoes. She perched on the very edge of an armchair, her back erect. Her hands were clasped tightly together, the knuckles blanched. Her forehead was tight with concentration. She was deep in thought, or perhaps praying. For strength, perhaps? For resolve.

I hesitated. I didn't know what to say.

Her lips twitched. She was muttering to herself, lost in her own world.

I took a step further into the room and she looked up, startled, then pointed me to the armchair opposite.

I opened my mouth to say again, 'We need to call the police,' then thought better of it, sighed and closed it again. I could give her time, if she needed it. I couldn't refuse her that.

I sank into the chair and observed her. His wife. My rival. He'd wanted to leave her – he'd always said so. He just couldn't bear to hurt her. It would kill her, he'd said. And there was Anna to think about, too.

I shook my head. It already seemed a long time ago, our battle for Ralph. Now, we'd both lost, after all. I clasped my hands in my lap. Clammy palms. My body wouldn't stop shaking. My head ached. Nausea rose again and I swallowed it down. I needed to get home, to crawl into bed, to sleep. If I could ever sleep again.

I thought about everything that would unfold once I called the police. Sirens. Banging at the door. Long hours at the station. Questions. Statements. Harsh lights and bare, chilled rooms. I couldn't bear it. My head swam. *Maybe she was right to hold off. Maybe there was another way.*

Ralph. Lying dead in the cellar, just feet from me. And it was all my fault.

After a while, Helen opened her eyes, turned and looked out of the window. She rose to her feet, switched on a standard lamp and drew the curtains, leaving a crack between them for the light to show.

'They can't know what happened.' Her face was stony. 'No one must know.'

'That he's –' I hesitated – 'gone?' It was impossible to say *dead*. 'They'll find out.'

She turned dead eyes on me. 'Maybe. Eventually. But not yet. And not what happened.'

I blinked. Was that it, then – she wanted us to somehow keep secret how he'd died? So no one found out, not even Anna, that their happy marriage had never been what it seemed?

I didn't know what to say. She suddenly seemed so hard, so determined, as if she were daring me to disagree.

She said coldly, 'You owe me that, at least.'

'But I don't even know how—'

'Do what I tell you. No questions.' She got to her feet. Her hands were fists at her sides. 'He's heavy. I'll need help.' She hesitated. 'It might keep you out of prison.'

She led me stiffly back out of the sitting room into the hall. Her manner had changed. She held her grief in check, her movements mechanical and efficient. I couldn't imagine what it cost her.

At the cellar door, she turned back to me. 'Wait here. I'll call when I need you.'

She disappeared, her footsteps echoing as she hurried down the steps.

I shrank back against the wall, steeling myself, trying not to think of his prone, twisted body. This man who was always in motion, always full of passion, of life. My stomach twisted and heaved again and I put my hand to my mouth, tasting acid. My face was chill with nervous sweat.

Muffled sounds drifted up the steps. Her shoes, sharp on the cement floor. Her laboured puffs of breath. The tug and scrape of a heavy object. The rustle of thick plastic. I closed my eyes, trying to block it all out and shuddered.

Finally, she came heavily back up the steps and appeared in the doorway. She was panting slightly, her hairline slick with sweat.

'Don't think about it. Just do it.'

She was thinking aloud, talking to herself as much to me. I thought, how little I knew her, this woman married to the man I loved. I'd tried not to think of her much, unless I really had to. She was just another school mum, lining up at the gate at half past three. Just another volunteer in the school reading programme, sitting in the Lower School library, listening to children read, one by one. She'd had to be. It was too painful to think of her as anything more.

She seemed to focus again on my face, remembering I was there, and her expression hardened. 'If you try anything, I'll tell them it was you. You pushed him, didn't you? What were you doing? Fighting?' She despised me, I heard it in her voice. 'No point denying it. Your skin under his fingernails. Your DNA all over him. It's manslaughter, if you're lucky.'

Lucky? I shivered.

She said, 'I'd gladly see you rot in jail. Believe me. But it's Anna…' She swallowed. 'They'd drag us all through the mud. Your sordid little affair – which meant nothing to him, by the way – splashed all over the papers. A teacher, hitting on another teacher, while his seven-year-old sleeps upstairs? Did you stop to think how she'd suffer? They'd crucify you. Ralph too.' She paused. Her mouth trembled and, for a moment, she looked about to break down. 'I'll grieve… but not now. I can't afford to. That comes later.'

A vein pulsed in her neck, a sign of the effort it took her to hold herself together, to keep herself in check. Once she could speak again, she stabbed at me with her finger.

'Listen,' she said. 'This is what you're going to do. You're going to shut up and do exactly what I tell you.'

*

The cellar stank of mould and turpentine. I blinked, willing my eyes to adjust to the gloom. The concrete floor felt tacky underfoot, the sole of my shoes sticking slightly to the surface when I moved.

I tried not to feel, not to think, just to do, as she'd told me. Anything else was impossible. But the thought kept breaking through. *This was Ralph, this weighty, inert body, encased now in a massive plastic zip-up bag, a surfboard cover. This was his flesh inside.*

He used to surf when he was younger. He'd told me *she'd* never been interested. I tried to imagine when and where he'd bought a surfboard and this bag for it, where he'd travelled. Somewhere sunny where he'd bronzed as he surfed, strong and muscular. I swallowed hard, feeling her waiting, glaring at me.

I crouched where she'd pointed, at the bottom of the steps, and looped my arms around the end of the cover. The plastic was cold and slippery. When I tried to lift, the hard shapes inside shifted. *Feet. Ankles. Knees.* I dropped them with a start as if they were burning hot.

She raised her eyes.

I stuttered, 'I can't…'

She shot me a poisoned look. 'You'd better.'

I bit hard on my lip, bent down again and threaded my arms under his legs, inching forward until I was grasping him higher, taking the weight of his thighs and hips. Helen, her face set hard, shuffled towards me from the other end, her arms encircling the bag. His head and shoulders, his chest.

'Okay? Now move. Small steps.' She was already panting.

I closed my eyes and teetered backwards, my heels bumping into the bottom step. Ralph, raised from the floor now, sagged between us. Together, we crept upwards, heaving him, one step at a time. First me, steadily rising up the narrow steps, all my energy poured into my straining arms, into trying not to stumble, then Helen coming jerkily after me. The only sound was our own heavy breathing and low, visceral grunts.

In the hall, we set him down, as gently as we could, on the floor, just feet from the front door. I collapsed back against the wall, sweat dripping down my back, and closed my eyes, seeing spangles. My chest hurt. My muscles ached. I just wanted to get my breath back and then sleep. To wake in the morning and find all this gone. To have Ralph alive again.

Helen's bony fingers dug into my shoulder. I forced my eyes open. Her face, thrust into mine, was flushed, her hair in clumps.

'I'm going upstairs to check on Anna, then we go. Don't leave anything behind.'

I blinked. 'Will she be all right on her own?'

'She'll be fine. Thank you for caring.' She gave me a sour look. 'The hatchback's right outside. I'll check the coast's clear, then we move him.' She hesitated. 'We need to be quick. We can do it if we work together.'

I took a deep breath, then forced myself to nod.

CHAPTER 4

It was nearly ten o'clock by the time we got Ralph into the back of the car and set off.

Helen sat straight, her back rigid, hands gripping the steering wheel tightly, eyes fixed on the road ahead. The satnav had calculated her route, out to the coast. Thirty-eight minutes. For once, there was so little traffic that it might actually be right.

I twisted away from her and watched passing, empty pavements, trying not to think about the load in the back. The only voice was the mechanical female tone of the satnav, reeling off instructions.

'In eight hundred yards, turn left.'

I thought, *I've killed someone. Ralph. I've killed Ralph.*

The satnav said, 'Now turn left.'

Helen turned the wheel.

I thought, *It was an accident.*

The satnav didn't care. 'Now take the right-hand lane.'

What was I doing? My stomach heaved with a fresh surge of panic. This was madness. Why was I letting her take control like this, letting her bully me?

'Prepare to take the second exit.'

I sat there, numb. *It was too late. All too late.*

I knew where we were heading. I recognised it from the satnav's map. I'd been there before. With Ralph.

As we approached the coast, the line of shabby wooden boathouses came into view, running along the back of the shingle beach. My face glowed hot, remembering the last time I'd been here. Ralph and Helen had access to a friend's sailing dinghy, stored in one of the boathouses. Months ago, before Christmas, Ralph had taken me out in it. He said he'd told Helen he'd promised to check over the sails and lay it up for winter. In fact, we took blankets and a bottle of champagne and he took me right out to sea, then furled the sails and we floated together, naked, drinking and making love and drinking some more until the wind turned and the chill across the water finally forced us to put our clothes on and head back to the shore.

Seeing it again, now, his death seemed impossible. I would wake up tomorrow and this would be nonsense, all of it.

Ralph would be there at school, an elusive, charismatic figure disappearing into a classroom to share his passion for Shakespeare or Keats or Milton and Anna would be out in the playground at lunchtime, chasing her friends or playing hopscotch, hair flying, not a care.

Helen turned into the shadowy, deserted car park and came to a stop at the far end, close to their friend's boathouse. She climbed out and opened up the back.

I forced myself to follow her. Already, she was rummaging inside, dragging her dead husband towards the lip. The wind, rough with salt, whipped across my face as I helped her.

We worked in silence, carrying the bulky surfboard cover across the shingle to the edge of the water and dumping it there. Freezing water seeped into my shoes. She headed back at a run to the boathouse and unlocked the double doors, then together we pulled the dinghy across the stones to the edge of the water on its metal, wheeled frame.

She climbed inside and I handed her the mast, then watched, uselessly, as she set about attaching it and trimming the sails. Ralph lay on the beach beside me. Near enough for me to reach out with my toe and touch him. *It wasn't too late. I could still turn and run, call the police and tell them everything, beg for mercy.*

I thought about what she'd said. Manslaughter. She was right. I'd killed him, however it had happened. They'd send me to prison for years. I shuddered, trying to imagine being locked up in a small cell, at the mercy of hardened criminals. I'd never survive.

Helen's movements were quick and sure. She seemed an experienced sailor. I thought of the shock on her face when she'd stood, frozen, in the doorway, staring at me in horror. Then, the desperate pain of her weeping. Now, she was pouring every ounce of her strength into holding herself together, into coping. Into stopping herself thinking about the fact that her husband, the man whose bed she shared every night, the father of her child, lay cold in our makeshift body bag on the wet stones at our feet.

Once the sails were secured, she bent forward over the side of the dinghy and gestured impatiently to me to drag the surfboard bag closer over the loose stones, to lift one end – I imagined his head and shoulders, stiff now – and help her heave it on board. We managed it together, both sweating and grunting.

Finally, she drew the dinghy clear of the frame and together we slid it deeper into the water until it rocked and swayed on the waves. I took off my shoes and tights and splashed through the shallows, pushing the dinghy ahead of me as far as I could. My feet ached in the ice-cold water, my arches stabbed by stones sticking out of the sand.

As soon as the dinghy was properly afloat, she gestured to me to grab the rubber handle on the side and pull myself on board. I fell head first into the boat, then shuffled sideways to sit on a coil of rope, keeping as far away as I could from the surfboard bag, my wet feet stinging with cold, my hands thrust into my pockets, and watched her manoeuvre into the wind, catching the force of the night breeze and taking us steadily further out onto the black water. *Please, God. What had I done?*

The weak lights of the coast shrank to points. Darkness pressed down on us, broken only by the dim glow from the dinghy's small, mounted lights. One, near the rim where I was sitting, spilled over onto the water, illuminating the black waves which were now whipped high by the wind. The dinghy bounced and splashed its way forward. Another light, fixed to the mast, glistened in Helen's eyes. Her expression was intent. She was clearly concentrating hard, lost in her battle to keep us stable in the gathering swell.

Finally, she tied off the sail and clambered the length of the dinghy, gesturing to me to move forward and take my place at Ralph's feet. My hands were numbed by the wind. My body shivered so hard with shock and cold that I stumbled and swayed as I crawled into position, keeping low.

I strained to see in the darkness. Helen unzipped the surfboard cover and peeled it from the top of his body, drawing out his head and shoulders, wrapped in the sheet. I blinked, trying to make out what she was doing as she bent low over him in the deep shadows. I had the sense that she was clasping him to her chest, lowering her face to his for one last kiss.

I turned my eyes away and peeled off the rest of the cover, drawing it from his body like a second skin, then lifted his feet and heaved them up, pushing his legs and raising his hips to the height of the dinghy's rim. Helen straightened up, lifted his shoulders and chest and, panting, raised them too.

He lay there for some moments, balanced on the edge, a bulky line between the two women who'd loved him most in this life, until Helen signalled to me and we put our shoulders to him and pushed. He flopped over the top, falling with a sudden splash into the blackness beyond. The dinghy blew forward, the waves surged and we were left, the two of us, staring down into nothing but the vast, empty darkness of moving water.

CHAPTER 5

We stowed the dinghy back in the boathouse, then drove off with a crunch of gravel, the heater turned up to maximum. The houses above us, high on the bluff, proud of their views of the sea, were in blackness but I sensed eyes watching us from their windows. Knowing eyes. I thought, *This is how it will be.* This constant feeling of fear, of being watched, of guilt. *This is how I'll live, for the rest of my life, after what I've done tonight.*

Beside me, Helen was shivering violently. Exertion, perhaps. Or delayed shock. The engine strained and the heater blew out dust as it struggled to generate warm air.

Neither of us spoke on the drive back. I rocked myself, arms wrapped round bent legs, my feet resting on the lip of the seat. Now and then, I glanced across at her. She seemed to have collapsed into herself, as if she'd borrowed energy to take control in the way she had, to do what she thought needed to be done, and was now in debt.

It was nearly one o'clock in the morning by the time she turned into their road, parked outside their home and switched off the engine. For a moment, neither of us moved. I thought of Anna, alone inside, and prayed she hadn't woken.

There was a period of silence. Then she said, without turning to look at me, 'I'll never forgive you. Don't get some idea we're bound together by this. We're not. I'll curse you till the day I die.'

I didn't answer. How could I? I clenched my jaw, eyes staring sightlessly at the bumper of the parked car ahead, trying to keep control of my senses.

She said in the same dead voice, 'If you fall apart, if you breathe a word of any of this, I'll take you down. You understand? I'll say you forced me to help you. That you threatened Anna.'

I couldn't speak.

She twisted to face me, her mouth hard. She loomed so close that I smelt her breath, stale now, saw the map of jagged red lines across the whites of her eyes.

'He was my husband. We loved each other. And you destroyed him. Don't ever forget that.'

CHAPTER 6

My own flat, poky compared with their home, was silent and thick with shadows as I let myself in. I stripped off my clothes and put everything in the washing machine, then started a hot cycle, not caring whether the young man downstairs could hear me. I ran a hot bath and poured bubbles in. All I wanted was to block out what had just happened. Then to sleep for as long as I could.

I rummaged in the bathroom cabinet for the tablets the doctor had prescribed after Ralph left me, took a couple, then dug out a bottle of malt whisky, left over from Christmas, and poured myself a large measure. It burned its way down the back of my throat. I lowered myself into the bath, shivering despite the scalding water, and tried to lie still, to relax, to let go.

When I closed my eyes, Ralph was there. His face, shocked, eyes wide, as he fell backwards through the open door. The stillness as he lay, his body twisted so awkwardly, at the bottom of the steps. Only hours ago, I'd kissed his lips, slid the tip of my tongue into his mouth. Now his body was drifting, lifeless, under the waves, starting to rot. *Those were pearls that were his eyes.* He used to quote that. One of his favourite lines.

I put my soapy hands to my face and started to cry, noisy, uncontrolled sobs. I pressed a fist against my mouth to stop myself from screaming. How would I survive this? How would I live without him, with no hope of ever seeing him again? And with the guilt, the horror of what we'd done? I thought about her. Her battle to force herself to set aside her grief and manoeuvre the dinghy out into the blackness, to cover up what her husband had been, for the sake of her daughter.

Her steeliness frightened me. I knew then that I'd do as she'd instructed, somehow, God only knew how. I'd get up the next morning, dress and go to work, as she'd told me I must. At school, I'd try to behave as if everything were normal. If anyone remarked on how pale I looked or saw the way my hands shook, I'd look rueful and say I had a sore throat, I must be coming down with something.

I'd lie and lie and lie, as if my life depended on it.

CHAPTER 7

For several days, life staggered on. I went through the motions at school, teaching, marking, sitting through meetings in a daze. In the playground, I searched the wheeling clouds of children for Anna but never saw her. Every time I passed by the school library and spied the bent head of a parent volunteer I slowed to look more closely, but it was never Helen.

After school, once home, I locked the door behind me, ate as much as I could force myself to swallow down, then lay, shaking, in bed, wondering if Helen's shock and grief were as violent as my own.

There were moments that I almost forgot what had happened. Seconds, when, as I first came to consciousness in the morning, I felt normal, free from fear, safe. Then the memories came crashing back.

Then, at school, the gossip started.

Lunchtime. I came in from playground duty and made myself a cup of coffee in the staff kitchen, added a splash of milk from the communal fridge, took out my Tupperware box and headed for the table at the far end of the room.

Elaine Abbott, the Lower School deputy head, Hilary Prior and Olivia Fry were already there.

Elaine, middle-aged and always well-mannered, looked up at me as I joined. 'We're just talking about Ralph Wilson,' she said. 'Have you heard?'

My stomach tightened. My cup slipped as I set it down and coffee slopped over the edge. I fumbled for a tissue to mop up the ring and wipe off the bottom, then slid into a seat. 'Heard what?'

Elaine, looking hearty in a sports shirt and tracksuit top, leaned forward. 'He's disappeared.'

'Disappeared?' I fumbled the top off my Tupperware box and stuck a fork into my pasta salad. The flavour of red onion and pepper cloyed in my mouth.

She nodded. Her own lunchbox was empty, already pushed to one side. She nursed a mug of tea between her hands. The mug was her usual staffroom favourite, a present from a class, with a slogan in pink sparkly letters, *Teachers are like angels, they make miracles happen.*

'He's been off for days,' she said. 'Not answering his phone. Then the office finally got hold of Mrs Wilson and she's frantic. He's gone missing.'

Hilary Prior, an expert on all things marital since her own wedding the previous year, said in a low voice, 'Makes you wonder about his home life.' She gave a meaningful nod.

Olivia Fry, doe-eyed and slender, added, 'He's always been, you know, a bit of a charmer, hasn't he?'

What was that supposed to mean? I kept my eyes on my food. The pasta in my mouth seemed as solid as wood. I chewed and chewed and struggled to swallow. My cheeks felt hot.

Elaine drank her tea. 'The state of his marriage is his business. But it's not like him to stay off work for no reason. Sarah's furious.' Sarah Baldini, the head of Upper School, ran a notoriously tight ship. Elaine scraped back her chair and gathered together her box and lid, fork and mug, her eyes glancing across to the clock.

Hilary said, 'Sports club? On a Friday?'

Elaine shook her head. 'Fifth year revue. Can you believe it's come around again already?'

Hilary munched on a hummus salad roll and waited until Elaine had left before whispering, 'They've got the police involved.'

Olivia choked. 'The police? Why?'

'It's so out of character. You know, teacher, family man...' Hilary sounded knowing. 'He wouldn't just take off.'

I finally stabbed another forkful of pasta and dared to look up at them both, trying to sound natural. 'Who told you that?'

'Jayne. I was in the office this morning, photocopying. She got it from Matty.' She caught Olivia's blank look. Olivia had only joined the Lower School in September and was still catching up, especially with Upper School staff. 'Matilda Campbell in the Upper School office. Tall with long, dark hair? Very nice. Worth getting to know.'

Olivia, eyes wide, said, 'So what're the police saying? About where he is?'

Hilary pulled a face. 'No one knows. Watch this space.'

I packed up my lunch and just made it to the staff toilets before I was sick.

CHAPTER 8

That evening, I went online and started trawling for news. I couldn't find anything about Ralph that I hadn't read before. I tried not to linger over the articles I already knew so well. In those early weeks, when I'd first met him, I'd relished spending time at home in the evening, googling him, examining his face, his body, in private in the photographs posted there.

His picture on the school website, a black-and-white portrait of Ralph leaning one shoulder nonchalantly against a wall, his hands deep in his pockets, his hair flopping forward across his brow. Ralph the poet. The photograph of him on the community news website, standing on stage, surrounded by a glowing teenage cast. I loved that picture. He looked younger in it and desperately handsome. That was three years ago, before I'd really known him, when he'd directed a school production of *Romeo and Juliet*.

But about his disappearance, not a thing.

I didn't bother trying to cook. I couldn't eat. I sat, glassy-eyed, in front of the television for a while, taking in very little.

Ten o'clock. I should think about bed.

But I couldn't. I was too restless. Too haunted. I was frightened of the stillness of my own bedroom, the bed where Ralph had once made love to me, but where I'd also shed so many tears, first when he left me, then again when I discovered what he'd done. When I tried to doze, all I could see were images of his body, twisted and broken at the bottom of the steps.

*

Even as I got in the car, I was pretending to myself that I was just going out for a drive, just to be out in the world, surrounded by the living, to calm my nerves. When I came to his road, I slowed to walking pace. Coloured light from wall-mounted TV sets flickered through the gaps between closed curtains. Cars were neatly parked. Gates closed.

His house looked no different from any other on the street. The downstairs curtains were drawn, a fringe of light brightening the gap between them. I strained through the darkness, trying to see movement. Nothing. He'd paced there, just three days earlier, agitated because I was with him, because I wanted him and he knew he wanted me too.

A horn made me jump out of my skin. A car had slid up behind me in the road and was impatient, hurrying me along. I gathered speed and kept driving, this time heading for the coast.

My senses heightened as I drew close to the sea. Everything seemed more intense, more vivid. The sharp tang of salt in the air. The depth of the shadows. The ghostly outline of shabby huts and a scattering of abandoned cottages, derelict now, set here and there along the marshes, on land which was steadily eroding as the sea surged and encroached.

I parked the car outside the small parade of shops, a short walk from the entrance to the car park and the boathouses. A security light clicked on as I walked away from the car and I ducked out of the beam into the shadows, then wondered if that just made me look even more suspicious and if there were security cameras recording everything I did.

It was a mild evening but as I rounded the corner and entered the far end of the car park on foot, a salt-sharp breeze caught me from the sea, scouring my cheeks. Several vehicles were parked together in the darkness, noses towards the water. The stripes down the side of the nearest vehicle shone in the half-light. A police patrol car.

Heart pumping, I ducked my head and ran for the line of boathouses, trying to make myself invisible in the shadows there and take shelter from the wind.

I crept into the gap between the first two boathouses and stopped. My breath stuck in my throat. The beach was thick with shadow but as my eyes adjusted to the gloom, I made out two dark figures, stocky with equipment, their heads squared off by caps, sitting shoulder to shoulder on the wall, looking out to sea. Police.

I froze, frightened to move closer in case they heard me. They were speaking in low voices, a man first, then a woman. A silence, interrupted only by the wind blowing in from the water. The woman said something else, then laughed and got to her feet, shook out the dregs from a takeaway coffee cup onto the shingle and stretched her arms.

I pressed against the roughened wood of the boathouse for support and stared out towards the water. For a while, all I could see were strands of stray light bouncing off the surface, flashing on the sudden surge of foam each time a wave broke and hurtled up the beach, only to draw back with a grumbling clatter of loose stones. Then, lifting my eyes to scan the waters further out to sea, I saw the swinging light of a boat. My legs buckled and I grasped at the wooden wall to keep myself steady. A small motorboat or launch, bobbing there on the water.

The male police officer heaved himself to standing and they both turned and crunched back across the shingle to their car, their movements easy and relaxed. I kept to the shadows as they started the engine of their patrol vehicle and left.

When I looked out to sea again, the lighted boat had disappeared.

I sank to the ground and trembled on the stones, dizzy, wondering what they knew, what they might have found.

CHAPTER 9

I barely remembered driving home, just the sense of my heart pounding so forcefully that my chest ached and my breath coming short and hard as if I were running. This was it. I'd had the sense, until that moment, that it might still be possible to change my mind, to present myself to the police, to confess everything and have faith that they'd believe me, whatever Helen's version of events might be. They had to believe me. I had the power of the truth on my side.

But there on the shingle, frightened out of my wits at the sight of the officers, I realised it was too late. My moment to speak had passed. I was part of this now, whatever I thought and however it had happened. No one would believe me if I described it as a freak accident – our disposal of his body gave the lie to that. I was too wracked with guilt to be credible. It was a crime and I had to move quickly and protect myself as best I could.

At home, I ran up the communal stairs two at a time and fumbled my way into my flat, hands shaking. I switched on the bright overhead lights and started to search through cupboards and drawers, pulling out anything that connected me to Ralph. His deodorant and shaving foam in the bathroom cabinet, preserved in the hope he might yet stay another night. In the kitchen, the packet of fancy coffee he kept here for himself, already half-empty and becoming stale, and the oat biscuits he snacked on with cheese.

In the sitting room, I tore along the bookshelves, pulling out the paperbacks he'd bought me. There weren't many. Some volumes of poetry by writers I'd admitted I'd never read, novels he'd bought me because he wanted to share his love for them and which served as the basis of long discussions over drinks, over dinner, my eyes locked on his as he talked, our hands entwined on the table top.

In my bedroom, I rolled up the old jumper he'd once brought over here and I'd never given back. I pressed it to my face. The smell of him had already gone. In my bedside table, I rummaged through random scraps of paper bearing his handwriting, each one a memory, a torn-off shopping list for a champagne picnic, a cryptic, flirtatious poem he'd written for me soon after we'd met, a scribbled love note I'd come home to find on my pillow.

From the bottom drawer, I drew out the worn, leather-bound volume hidden under papers, an anthology of nineteenth-century poetry, and lifted it to my face. The musty smell of the pages took me straight back to our first days together. To the heady excitement and restlessness. It was one of his very first presents and the most precious. He'd had it for years, he'd said, turning the pages to show me his favourite. I shook my head and pushed it back into the drawer. That was one thing I couldn't just throw away.

I ripped the other pieces of paper to shreds, then bundled everything into a bin bag and took it outside to the back of the flats. Silence. The only sounds were my footsteps and the pant of my own breath. I hid the bag deep in the piles of residents' rubbish in the giant bins there. Another day and it would all go to the public waste dump to be incinerated.

Before I went to sleep, I sat up in bed with my phone and did the hardest job of all. I deleted every message from him, every email, every photograph and finally, deleted his number. By the time I switched off my bedside lamp and crawled down under the duvet, exhausted, I'd taken a step I could never have taken until now. I'd erased him from my life.

If Helen or any other piece of evidence led the police to my door, I was ready for them.

He'd probably done the same to me long ago. Tore up my little love notes and dumped them in some public bin. Deleted messages. Dropped the spare keys to my flat down some drain. If he hadn't before, his wife certainly would now. I wondered what else she'd find once she started emptying his pockets and clearing his study. I wondered how much she already knew about her husband's darkest secret which might now rise, blinking, to the light.

I barely left the flat that weekend. I hid, my curtains drawn, lying all day on the settee in pyjamas, tucked up in a blanket, watching TV. I couldn't eat.

At night, I struggled to sleep. Every time I closed my eyes, Ralph was there, waiting for me. Sometimes he hung in the sea, gently rocked by the current, limbs spread, hair floating. His eyes, open, fixed me with a look which was sometimes mournful, sometimes malevolent. *I'm still here*, it seemed to say. *You won't get away with it.*

CHAPTER 10

Ralph rescued me from myself. It was his doing, not mine. He pursued me. I was helpless to resist.

It began last September, not long after the start of term.

I'd stayed late at school, marking a pile of year three exercise books in the Lower School staffroom, writing positive exclamations illustrated with smiley faces and occasional sticky stars. A dirty cup, the coffee already finished, sat beside me. The staffroom was deserted. It was nearly five-thirty. Another half an hour and the school janitor would patrol the building on his rounds, switching off lights and closing doors.

I needed to go home. I just couldn't face the empty flat, not quite yet.

I rarely walked up the slope to the Upper School buildings. It was foreign territory, for me, populated by strangers. Some Lower School teachers like Hilary Prior, who seemed to know everyone, popped up at lunchtimes now and then to sit in the larger, better equipped staffroom there but it intimidated me. Everyone knew the hierarchy within school. Upper School teachers had higher status than we did in the infant school, however valuable our work. There was an unspoken sense of snobbery as if we, mostly women and caring for four- to eleven-year olds, were only capable of wiping noses, reading picture books and decorating paper plates whilst they, tasked with teenagers as old as eighteen, were practically university lecturers.

The janitor's heavy footsteps sounded down the corridor and I packed away the books I was reading and stowed them in my locker. A photocopied poster about the new teachers' writing group was pinned on the corkboard above it. I looked at my watch. It was just starting.

My heart thudded. *Maybe I could just have a quick look? I needn't stay.*

I hesitated, suddenly gripped by nervous excitement. I looked again at the poster, trying to work out where the classroom lay. I licked dry lips and tried to gather my courage. *Just do it. Why not?* It would while away an hour.

I got lost in the Upper School, taking a wrong turn in the maze of corridors that ran to and from the school hall. I was about to head for a stairwell and leave for home after all when a classroom door shot open just behind me.

'Looking for us?'

Ralph, of course. Ralph Wilson. It's strange now, looking back, to remember that there was ever a time I knew nothing about him. He told me later that he always kept half an eye out for me, that he saw me walk past, my face flushed, and guessed I might be lost.

All I knew then was that he was standing there at the door, a handsome, charismatic man, with an inviting grin on his lips. He was wearing a crimson corduroy jacket with black faux leather elbow patches and a grey, scoop-necked cashmere jumper. Behind him, half a dozen faces turned to me, teachers staying on after school, sitting in a loose semi-circle round his chair. Blank and uninterested features, for the most part, waiting for this little-known Lower School teacher to hurry up and join or to leave; either way, they didn't care, as long as I ended the interruption to the reading.

I shrugged and nodded, caught, keeping my eyes low and feeling myself flush as I scurried in and found an empty seat towards the back of the group. They were mostly Upper School teachers. Olivia Fry, her long legs delicately crossed, her long hair falling in a curtain down her back, was one of the few from Lower School.

Ralph settled again and carried on reading. It was one of his own poems, about love and time. I barely heard the words, it was his voice which entranced me, deep and mellow and dramatic. He didn't so much read as intone, like an old-fashioned stage actor. Something inside me twisted and knotted. When he finished, there was a moment's silence and he looked straight at me, his gaze direct and open, as if he knew me already and was just waiting for me to realise, to catch up.

As he followed me out of the classroom at the end, he asked, 'Do you write?'

I shook my head, embarrassed by his attention. He had such presence, such good looks, he daunted me. I worried too that I was already disappointing him. Olivia wrote children's stories, I'd heard her discussing them with Elaine Abbott in the staffroom, asking for permission to read them to the children in class.

He didn't look disappointed. He just smiled and held my gaze and I found myself smiling back, stupidly.

Another teacher, a bearded man who'd mentioned he taught physics, called over, 'Fancy a pint, Ralph?'

'At the Half Moon? Maybe. I'll catch you up.'

The men disappeared in a group, familial and collegiate. Olivia and another young female teacher followed along behind. I turned away, willing him to stay and talk to me, but feeling awkward. I was uncomfortable in groups.

'Well, thanks for coming.'

I nodded, hardly daring to wonder why he was still here, still smiling. His eyes were still on mine. My stomach contracted and – fearing it, fearing him – I turned and started walking away.

Abrupt. John Bickers, in my end-of-year appraisal in the summer, had said I was sometimes described as abrupt. I still wondered who'd said that about me. Hilary Prior, perhaps, so friendly on the surface but with a reputation for gossip and treachery? Or one of my more demanding year two parents?

John had been sitting in his office, his elbows on his desk, his hands raised into arched fingers, touching at the tips to form a bridge, and looked at me appraisingly. I knew that look. The kindly old head of Lower School. Seen it all before.

'We're all different, Laura,' he'd said. 'Nothing wrong with that. But best to fit in, you know, where one can. Makes for an easy life.'

Now, Ralph hurried after me and fell into step at my side. He held out his hand. 'Ralph Wilson,' he said. 'English. Upper School.'

His hand was warm and soft. I thought then, *a poet's hand*.

'Lower School, year two.' I hesitated, then grinned. 'Laura. Laura Dixon.'

He said, lightly, 'Well, Laura Dixon, come for a drink. Do you know the Half Moon? It's just around the corner. You'll have plenty of school chaperones. Come on, you know you want to!'

He looked disappointed when I panicked and said a hasty 'No, thank you.' I fled, shoulders hunched, along the corridor and back down to the Lower School car park, cursing myself all the way.

What was the matter with me? A drink wouldn't have hurt, would it? He was just overwhelming.

I thought about little else for the rest of the week, going over our short exchange in my head like a love-struck schoolgirl, thinking back to his poetry, his voice, his smile.

He said he thought then that he'd blown it, missed his one and only chance with me.

But he told me too that his spirits soared when I appeared again the following Tuesday evening. And the one after that.

Of course I was there. I counted down the days until Tuesday. I ticked off the hours to the end of the teaching day, hurried up the hill towards the Upper School classroom, then slowed, excited, shy, full of anticipation, as I approached the classroom and looked for the first glimpse of him, increasingly sure that, every time I glanced across at him, his eyes would be on my face.

His smile. It was utterly captivating.

Each time, he stole a word with me in the deserted corridor, once the others had headed home or to find the bar. We strung out the minutes, strolling together past empty classrooms, down towards the Lower School car park, relishing the tension, the flirting, the anticipation of what might be to come.

We fell into easy roles without knowing quite why. He was the admirer, the would-be seducer. I made a show of resisting him.

His enthusiasm was puppyish. 'One drink. We can join the others if you like. Or not. Obviously, I'd prefer not. Come on, Laura. Live dangerously.'

I longed to. It wasn't a lack of interest that made me hold out, it was the thrilling pleasure of being pursued with such determination. And trepidation, too. I sensed from the start that if I fell for Ralph, I'd fall long and hard. I'd lose myself all over again.

It was two years since Matthew had packed his bags and walked out on me, leaving me desperate and bereft. I'd finally adjusted to being alone. I'd learned to close myself off from other people, to protect and guard my heart.

I didn't want my heart broken into pieces again so soon.

But Ralph didn't give up. He charmed me. He persuaded me. And, I know now, he also lied to me.

CHAPTER 11

The Monday after Ralph's death, I dressed for school with care in my smartest dress and a pair of low-heeled shoes. My face in the bathroom mirror was pale and pinched. I outlined my eyes in kohl and tried to rub colour into my cheeks, darken my lips. *Painted lady.*

I practised in the mirror, thinking what to say if anyone asked. 'I've had the flu. Dreadful. Hardly been out of bed all weekend.' My eyes looked back at me, dull and lifeless.

The staffroom crackled with a low hum, an electric current of gossip, jumping from one person to the next.

Hilary Prior raised her eyes to me as I headed for my locker to gather the year twos' exercise books.

'Have you heard?' she whispered. 'Ralph Wilson. They're saying it might be suicide.'

I started. 'Who is?'

'The police.' She looked exasperated. 'Don't you remember? His wife reported him missing? Still no sign of him. Girl trouble, maybe?' She arched her eyebrows. 'Anyway, it's nearly a week now since he went out. That's the last she saw of him.'

The exercise book on the top of the pile in my arms slipped off and crashed to the floor. I stooped to pick it up, then tilted too far forwards and another three cascaded after it. Pages of crayoned drawings and unsteady lines of pencilled words flapped like dead fish.

Hilary ducked down beside me and helped me to pick them up, then stacked them back on the pile.

'His wife's in a real state. I mean… you wonder, don't you? Was he really so depressed he'd… you know? Awful.' She blinked. 'Wonder if they'll keep Anna home?' Ralph's daughter was in her class. 'Poor thing. What can you do?'

In the corridor, Elaine Abbott hurried to catch up with me before I turned into my classroom. Another ten minutes and children would start streaming in from the playground, pushing and scurrying, bustling with sports kit and bookbags, amid fierce adult cries – *Quiet, year two! Don't run!*

'John's composing a staff email,' Elaine whispered. 'Check your inbox. Should be there by morning break.' She looked round, unusually wary. 'Let him know if you have any concerns or see, you know, signs of distress in the children. I'm arranging support in school.' She sucked on her teeth as she turned away. 'Dreadful thing. Quite dreadful. Poor Anna.'

I set down the pile of books on my desk and sat heavily, looking out over the deserted classroom. In a moment, the day would rush in on me in all its noise and fury.

Split diagraphs and the eight times table. A playlet about the Great Fire of London. Models of seventeenth-century houses fashioned from painted cereal boxes, with straw for thatch.

Hilary's news had pulled the rug from under me. I sat in the silence, trying to stop trembling, trying to find calm. I had no idea if I could make it through.

To all staff, Lower School
Status, Confidential

Dear Colleague,

It is with great sadness that I am writing to you about concerns for our Upper School colleague, English teacher Ralph Wilson.

As some of you may have heard, the police are pursuing several lines of inquiry. I will update you when more
information is available.

Naturally, our thoughts and prayers are with Mrs Wilson
and their daughter, Anna, at this difficult time.

Miss Abbott has arranged for a counsellor, specialising
in loss, to be on call throughout the week. Please feel free
to refer to her any child who seems distressed by these
events or indeed to contact her if you also feel in need of
particular support.

This information is shared with you in the **strictest
confidence.** The heads of Lower and Upper School have
been authorised by the board of governors to speak to the
media. Please refer any inquiries to me or to Miss Baldini.

I was on outside duty at morning break. I read the email in
haste on my phone as I put my coat on.

As soon as I stepped out into the playground, swallowed up
at once by the shrieks and cries of Lower School children, Olivia
Fry, her coat unbuttoned, a scarf loose around her neck, came
across to me, a young child attached to each hand.

Her face was ashen, her voice a whisper. 'Have you seen?'

I didn't need to ask what she meant. The email, of course. It
was the only topic of conversation.

'Terrible.'

'His poor wife.' She slid her eyes away from mine as she spoke,
gazing out across the throng of teeming, screaming children,
running, tugging at each other's coats, swinging each other round.

Something in her tone, in her pallor, in the way she avoided
looking directly at me made me pause. What was it that made me
suddenly suspicious of her? *Had she also...? Olivia?* I shuddered,
remembering her at the writing group. The long princess hair. The

round eyes. Her voice, shy and slightly hesitant, as she started to read her children's story to the group and Ralph, sitting forward in his chair, his eyes on her face, encouraging her.

I turned my back to her, trying to find space. A small child, Emma Something in reception, barrelled into my legs and flung her arms around my thighs, hugging me for a moment's comfort before turning and spinning off again into the chaos of whirling children.

If I was right, was Olivia before or after me? Or during, even? Did she know, then, about Ralph and me? My mouth felt unnaturally dry. What if she told people? What if she told the police?

She stepped forward into the fray to separate two fighting year one boys and sent them off in different directions, on warning.

When she came back into range, I whispered, 'What's the latest?'

I meant, *have they found him, that floating, bloating, rotting corpse which once made love to me and perhaps to you too?* It was too horrible to mention.

She whispered back, 'They're searching the heath. He used to take long walks there, apparently.'

The heath? I blinked. I'd never known Ralph to walk anywhere, if he could help it. Then I thought, *that's Helen's lie. She's plotting to throw them off the scent.*

Bile rose in my throat.

CHAPTER 12

The police came, heralded by a second staff memo.

To all staff, Upper and Lower School

Police officers investigating the disappearance of our colleague, Mr Ralph Wilson, will attend school today to conduct
interviews. They have requested any member of staff who
feels able to share information about Mr Wilson – however
trivial – to access the link below to select an interview time.
Please endeavour to timetable these interviews in non-
teaching time but, if a clash proves unavoidable, please
contact Jayne (Lower School) or Matilda (Upper School) to
arrange temporary cover. The police emphasise that even
minor observations about Mr Wilson's recent behaviour and
state of mind may prove valuable. I'm sure we will all be keen
to assist them in whatever way we can at this difficult time.

Olivia Fry pushed me into it. She booked a slot with a Lower
School teaching assistant who'd also attended some of Ralph's
writing group meetings and suggested I should come too. No,
not suggested, insisted.

'What if there was something, some snippet of information,
that helped?' she said, cornering me in the Lower School playground when we were both on lunch duty. Her large eyes were

earnest and moist with emotion. 'It would be awful if we didn't. Think of his poor wife.'

I wriggled and squirmed. She had no idea how much I thought of his poor wife. Her face, stony and set, haunted me almost as much as the memory of her dead husband.

I shrugged. 'I'd be wasting their time, though. I hardly knew him.'

She pursed her lips. 'I know. I'm the same. But we must. We'll go together, get it over with.'

One of the girls came running over, unbuttoned coat flying, face blotchy with angry crying, demanding justice in some squabble with another girl. Olivia turned away from me to stoop to her and sort it out.

I broke the rules and strode quickly across the playground towards the school building and the staff toilets. The swirl of dodging, swerving children, the shrieks and screams blurred and shook. I was hot with fear. I couldn't do it. I couldn't sit in the same room as an investigating officer and feel their eyes on my face. I couldn't hold it together and answer questions. They'd know. I'd give myself away. Guilt would radiate from me in waves. How could they not feel it?

But how could I refuse to go along with the others without looking suspicious?

The night before the interview, I didn't sleep. I paced, numb, up and down the flat, frightened of closing my eyes. Sleep wouldn't come. All I saw that night was the knowing face of a detective, his eyes on mine, reading my mind.

CHAPTER 13

They let the police officers borrow Sarah Baldini's interview room, annexed to her office.

Three of us – Olivia, a plump, motherly teaching assistant and I – sat in a line on a row of chairs along the wall outside Sarah's office, hands on our knees, waiting for our slot.

My palms itched with sweat. I wiped them off inside my pocket every now and then on a clean handkerchief, fearful of giving myself away. Olivia too looked pale and tense.

The teaching assistant, who liked to chatter, made nervous jokes. 'I feel as if we've been sent for, stuck here, like this.' Awkward silence. 'This must be what the naughty boys feel like.'

The door opened and an Upper School teacher came out, the bearded science teacher who also attended the writing groups and always went cheerily to the pub afterwards. Now, he looked unusually solemn.

The teaching assistant whispered, 'How'd it go? What're they like?'

He shrugged. 'Good luck.'

Already a young constable with a clipboard had emerged from behind him and stood in front of us, checking our names and contact details on her list. She looked barely twenty, younger even than Olivia. Her hair was twisted into a tight bun at the back of her head, held with a dark net and about a hundred clips.

As we got to our feet and made to follow her in, my stomach fell away. My knees buckled and I dropped back down to my chair with a bump.

The teaching assistant, all mother, bent over me. 'You all right?'

I couldn't answer. My heart raced. My hands, gripping the sides of the chair for support, felt cold and slippery.

'You're white as a ghost.' The teaching assistant hesitated. 'Shall I tell them you're not well?'

She started to turn towards the office which had already swallowed up Olivia and the young constable. I shot out a hand to grab her arm and struggled to my feet.

'I'm fine. Sorry. Just got up too quickly.' I lowered my voice and managed to whisper. 'Time of the month, you know.'

She nodded and smiled and I managed to follow her in, my legs wobbling beneath me.

I saw at once, as soon as we entered the office, that it wasn't at all what I'd expected. My mind, playing tricks during the night, had conjured up a TV detective, a hard-bitten, all-knowing middle-aged man with a trilby hat and shabby suit and a cigarette in the corner of his mouth, a man who leaned forward, eyes appraising, perched on one buttock on the corner of his desk.

In fact, the office had most recently been used by the visiting trauma counsellor and was still set up as a sanctuary. The straight-backed chairs had padded seats and were arranged in a friendly circle around a low table which offered a box of tissues, a large jug of water with a tower of paper cups and a small vase of yellow carnations.

I almost laughed, thinking how scathing Ralph would be. How *petit bourgeois*. How touchy-feely. For a moment, I imagined how we'd chat about it, compare notes over a glass of Shiraz about the detective, standing there now, hand outstretched, to greet us. She was wearing a cheap navy blue trouser suit that shone with too much polyester. Marks and Spencer, probably. A plain white blouse. A discreet silver necklace. She was middle-aged but seemed already world-weary. Her face was carefully made up. Powder had settled in the creases which fanned outwards from the corners of her eyes and striped her forehead. Her lipstick, an oddly bright shade of red, needed freshening up. I felt the heady dizziness of relief.

'Detective Inspector Johns – Eileen Johns.'

She gestured to us to sit and there was a general scraping of chairs and awkward arranging of legs until we were all settled, we four, drawing a tight circle round the table. The young constable took a seat behind her boss and picked up a pad and pen to resume notetaking.

'Thank you so much for coming forward.' Her eyes darted from one face to the next.

My hands, loose in my lap, reached for each other.

'I understand you've requested an interview because you knew Mr Wilson and might have something to share with us. So, where shall we start?'

Olivia, of course. Sitting primly there, her hair cascading around her shoulders, her back straight. She started to explain to the detective about the writing group, about the fact we had chosen to come together because we'd been the three members of staff from the Lower School to attend and had much the same information to share. She spoke about his poetry, his talent, his natural charisma.

The detective nodded, listening, giving nothing away. The constable's pen scratched its way across the page.

Olivia seemed determined to take the lead, jumping in to answer the detective's questions as if we'd agreed that she would speak on behalf of us all. News to me.

The detective's eyes were bright. Clever, that much was clear. Taking it all in.

'How much did he disclose about his personal life?'

'Nothing directly. I mean, we were colleagues. We didn't share confidences.' She paused, as if she were searching for the words. Her hand reached for her hair, falling forward now over her left

shoulder, and flicked it back with a practised movement. 'But you
learn a lot about a person when they share their writing, especially
poetry. It's very intimate. I'd say he was clearly a romantic. He
seemed to adore his wife. And Anna, of course. His daughter.'

'Any hint of tension in his marriage, as far as you were aware?'

'Oh, no.' She looked shocked. 'Quite the opposite. Mrs Wilson
comes into school regularly to listen to the children read. We have
a lot of parent volunteers, all police checked, of course. It really
helps. She's a lovely lady. Very friendly. I didn't know them well
but they both seemed, well, very lovely people.'

The detective nodded and let the silence stretch a few beats
longer than felt comfortable.

'And Anna's a delightful girl. Very sweet-natured.'

I thought about Olivia's dig in the staffroom, about Ralph
being a charmer. No sense of that here, in front of this audience.
She made him sound as pious as a choirboy.

As I watched her, listening to her childlike, rather earnest voice
and the glow of admiration for Ralph which shone through her
description of him, I curled with dislike. There was something
artificial in the way she spoke. A performance. What was she up
to? I didn't know. The detective's face gave away nothing.

Behind her, the constable scratched away, to and fro across
the page, her bun immaculate. I wondered how long it took her,
with all those pins.

The teaching assistant, sitting between Olivia and me, nodded
with enthusiasm as Olivia spoke and breathed 'oh yes' and
'absolutely' from time to time.

When Olivia finally finished, the teaching assistant leaned
forward earnestly and said, 'I agree. Such a lovely man. I mean,
I didn't know him well, of course. I went along to meetings too,
when I could – not to read my own work, I don't have the gift,
but just to enjoy. And just listening to him read his poetry, well,
you could see he was a tender soul.'

I tried not to snort. *A tender soul?* Something else to make Ralph laugh.

The detective shifted her attention to me. Her eyes, meeting mine, froze me to the core. They were exactly as I'd feared, after all, just not in the body I'd imagined. They saw everything. They knew.

'Miss Dixon? What exactly was your relationship with Mr Wilson?'

I stared, transfixed, unable to speak. The constable's pen stopped scratching and she lifted her head to look at me. Everyone looked at me. My legs, planted squarely on the carpet, started to tremble.

'Miss Dixon?'

I opened and closed my mouth, but nothing came out. I was stricken. All I could see was Ralph's body, crumpled at the bottom of the steps. And Helen, crouched beside him in the gloom, her face pressed into his side, her sobs echoing round the bare, cold cellar.

CHAPTER 14

I licked my lips and tried to clear my throat. 'I hardly knew him. Really.'

My voice squeaked in my ears. *She would know, if she didn't already.* My thin little voice oozed guilt. She must smell it coming off me, as rancid as sour cream.

'I went to a few meetings, that's all. He was very friendly. He made everyone welcome.'

The detective didn't blink. Silence. The room seemed suddenly airless.

The teaching assistant jumped forward just as I reached out a hand and started to sway. She grabbed hold of my arm and threaded her other arm around my shoulders, sturdy and comforting.

'You're not well, are you?' She appealed to the detective. 'She's very hot.'

She lowered me to the floor and poured me a glass of water, then fanned me with one of the trauma counsellor's leaflets. Yellow letters on a blue background flashed in front of my face, back and forth as she flapped. *Having trouble sleeping? Feeling sad or depressed?*

'I'll be fine.' I sipped the cool water, focussed on the swirly carpet and concentrated on breathing. *In, out. In, out.* Gradually, I managed to recover myself. I scrambled back onto my chair, hoisted in part by the stout teaching assistant. 'I'm so sorry. I think I must be coming down with something.' I paused, gathered myself together. 'It's just so sad, wondering what's happened to him. And his poor little girl. Anna. I can't imagine—'

The detective nodded to the constable and she jumped up and handed round small printed cards. *Detective Inspector Eileen Johns. Investigating officer.* A list of phone numbers to call, including a hotline, a police email address.

'If anything else occurs to you, anything at all.'

The detective got to her feet and nodded, her eyes weary.

Outside, a young man was waiting, a new Upper School teaching assistant. He looked up, face anxious, as we came out of the office.

Cool air in the corridor found my clammy neck, face, hands.

Once we'd turned the corner and were out of earshot, the teaching assistant blew out her cheeks and said, 'Well! There we are then!'

I didn't answer. I wanted to quicken my pace and get away from them, to recover on my own, but my legs didn't have the strength to hurry.

The three of us walked down the corridor in step.

The teaching assistant said, 'You ought to have a sit down before you go back to class.' Her eyes were concerned. 'I've got aspirin, if you need some.'

Beyond her, Olivia was watching me, her eyes sharp.

CHAPTER 15

Eventually, after an extended absence, Anna came back to school.

Hilary was full of it.

'I told the class she might be feeling a bit S-A-D.' She did a good job of looking stricken, but I sensed how pleased she was to have a leading role in this tragedy. 'I'm not sure how much they really understand, you see. About grief. I mean, they're only seven.'

Olivia nodded. 'One or two may have lost grandparents.'

'Or family pets,' put in Elaine. 'The loss of an animal can be deeply traumatic for a young child.'

I tried not to roll my eyes. I could imagine how Ralph would feel about his loss being compared to a dead gerbil.

'John called her into his office this morning for a little chat,' Hilary went on. 'So thoughtful. She's very close to Clara Higgins. I've asked Clara to move tables so they can be together for a while.'

Elaine nodded. 'Clara's a sweet girl.'

'She goes home with Anna a lot, doesn't she?' Olivia said.

'All the time,' Hilary said. 'She's a single parent, Clara's mum. Works long hours.'

Elaine said, 'Wasn't there another Higgins girl?'

Hilary nodded. 'Isn't there one in Upper School? Or is she Hopkins?'

'I suppose Helen Wilson is a single parent too now, isn't she?' Olivia looked thoughtful. 'Wonder how she'll manage.' Elaine scraped back her chair and got to her feet. 'So sad.'

Olivia picked up her coffee mug, ready to wash in the staff sink before we all headed back for afternoon classes. 'Poor Anna. Who'd have thought.'

'We'll all look out for her. Of course we will.' Elaine reached across and patted Hilary's arm. 'And she's in safe hands here.'

I'd only become aware of Anna's presence at school recently, since the shock of discovering she was Ralph's daughter. She was only in year two and seemed a quiet kid. Thin and wiry. I sensed the same romantic dreaminess as her father.

That first week, once I knew she was back, I made it my business to look out for her. When I was on playground duty, which was some part of most days, I watched her every chance I could, scanning the swirling mass of running, screaming children, unbuttoned coats flapping. Clara Higgins, her best friend, was usually close at hand. They crouched on their haunches in corners together, heads almost touching as they whispered, or ran, hand in hand, weaving in and out of the manic chaos.

It wasn't easy to give her my full attention. I was constantly distracted by the more mundane playground tasks of adjudicating fights, scolding bullies and sending injured or badly behaved children to the office. I also had to fend off the attentions of a minuscule reception girl with a single long plait. Rosie, was she? Or Rebecca? She wasn't settling well and had taken to hanging around whichever teacher was on duty. She grasped my fingers in her tiny, warm hand and clung to them as if I were a lifeboat in a dangerous, tempestuous sea.

Anna seemed as lively since her return as any other child. Her features had always been a little pinched, but her colour was high and her hair, usually gathered into two stubby plaits, flew as she chased around, screeching, with Clara.

Every time I tried to wander over to where they were playing, dragging the needy reception girl after me, Anna and Clara darted off to another part of the playground, deep in some game of their own invention. It was like trying to lasso water. I'd just need to be patient and seize my opportunity once it came.

CHAPTER 16

Two months later

I straightened my skirt. I was wearing a dress today, just for him. In those two years after Matthew and before Ralph, I'd lived in trousers and shapeless jumpers. Then, meeting Ralph, I had wanted to emerge again, to come out of hiding from the world.

'Ah, she has legs!' He had reached for them when I slid beside him into the passenger seat of his car, ready to be taken out. He'd run a warm hand over the smooth mesh of my tights, from calf to my knee and a little further to my thigh. 'Orwell could never have written "Two legs bad!" if he'd seen yours.'

Then that smile. It turned me to liquid. Always.

Now, I bit down on my lip, took a deep breath and walked on, feeling his eyes, in a face enlarged to poster size and glued onto a black-edged board, follow me into the chapel.

It was a beautiful day. That was all wrong. The sun had no business shining. The bright light fell in multi-coloured shafts through the polished stained-glass windows and threw patterns across the stone flags underfoot. The rows of seats in the body of the chapel were filling quickly. There was a muffled sound of whispering and creeping, of people gathering on tiptoe, people who were afraid to be heard, who were frightened of causing offence.

I ran my eyes across the crowd. A lot of teachers from school were here, bunched together in knots of friends, hushed with embarrassment. The bearded science teacher and another I didn't recognise hung together by a row of seats as if they didn't know whether they were allowed to sit down there. Olivia, her long hair cascading freely down her back, was seated at the end of a full row of Lower School staff. I ran my eye along the row. Elaine Abbott, too. Hilary Prior. Everyone's clothes were unnaturally muted. Brown. Grey. Black.

Then I saw them. Off to one side, watching us all from their seats at the back, tucked away in the corner shadows. Detective Inspector Johns and a man – another detective, for sure. They sat very still, backs straight, heads slowly pivoting, observing everyone.

I stopped. A young woman in a black jacket, her face professionally sympathetic, stepped forward and handed me a thin paper booklet, mistaking my hesitation perhaps for grief or nerves. She gestured to the side.

'More seats upstairs,' she whispered, as if it were a sad secret.

I took her advice and turned, climbed a short flight of steep, winding stairs and emerged to find a small balcony six rows deep, the organ ranged behind it, overlooking the chapel. I found a place at the front and leaned forward, forearms resting on the polished wood lip. From here, in the cheap seats, I could see without being seen.

It was a comforting building. The far window was dominated by a vast cross, splintered into glassy fragments and buried within multiple shades of green and brown. It was a symbol which was vivid enough to signal its intent to churchgoers, but discreet enough not to offend those who didn't believe in any world after this one and preferred to see nothing but nature; grass and leaves and branches in the shapes and hues.

A bulky middle-aged man squeezed in beside me, a woman settling on his far side. He handed her a memorial booklet and leafed through his own in a flutter of pages. I looked at the one in my hand, already marked by my warm, sweaty fingers.

Ralph Edward Wilson. His photograph was printed on the front, inside a black border. The same portrait as the one at the entrance, glued to a board.

My eyes ran over the hymns and readings printed inside. Keats. Shakespeare. T. S. Eliot. Sarah Baldini was doing the Shakespeare. Poor choice. She might be a head teacher but she had a high, reedy voice. John Wilson was giving the tribute. *John Wilson?* I shook my head. Ralph's father was already dead. He didn't have a brother. *Some cousin, perhaps?* He'd never mentioned one. I closed the booklet and Ralph's eyes found me again.

Hey, they said. *Is this for real? All this fuss for me? I hope there's a chance of a drink afterwards. A good stiff one.*

I could almost hear him laughing.

Below, music started. A slow jazz number. The blues.

The final stragglers hurried to take their seats, forcing others to bunch up, to lift up coats and bags and lay them across their knees. The women in black jackets found spaces, here and there, and led people to them.

Helen. I took a moment to recognise her as she came into view underneath us and shuffled down the aisle towards the empty front row. Her head was bowed. Her shoulders sagged. She was wearing a long grey coat which flapped round her knees and leaning heavily on the arm of a stout, broad-shouldered man. The falling shafts of sunlight, thick with dancing dust, picked out strands of silver in his dark hair. They were a grotesque parody of a bride and father, walking down the aisle to a husband on their wedding day, their friends and family gathered to bear witness.

My breath caught in my throat. It was Helen, of course, but she looked so utterly different from the woman I'd known before. She looked, from the way she walked, the way the man supported her, the way people on the ends of rows glanced at her then looked quickly away, as if she'd aged a decade in a matter of weeks, desiccated by shock and sorrow. She was a widow. A grieving widow. And it was all because of me.

She reached the front and the man lowered her into a seat as if she were incapable of bearing her weight without him. The mournful music stopped and there was a general shuffling and coughing as a man in simple clerical robes – someone I'd never seen before and suspected Ralph, atheist to the core, would never have met either – appeared at the front of the congregation, opened his arms in a gesture of both welcome and blessing, smiled sadly and began to speak.

I closed my eyes and tried not to hear. I had no rights here, I knew that. I was an anonymous nobody. If I was in pieces with grief, deep in mourning, I had to keep it to myself. I wasn't his widow. But this Ralph, this loving father and devoted husband, this wasn't the Ralph I'd loved.

CHAPTER 17

The day I finally decided to say yes to Ralph and go out for a drink with him, I chose my clothes with care. At the end of the school day, I went to the staff toilets to re-apply my make-up in secret and spray my mouth with minty freshener.

Olivia, all long legs, glanced up at me as I walked into the writing meeting and found a place along the desks and – did I imagine it or did something in her face change? I felt suddenly hot as I sat down. The fat girl at school plastering on lipstick at the school disco and thinking the jock would suddenly notice her. Maybe he was playing with me, that was all. A bet, even. A private joke.

Then he walked in, his leather briefcase spilling papers, and his eyes scanned the room, then found mine and settled there and he smiled and I was beautiful again, shy and happy and glowing like a teenager and who cared what anyone else thought, let them, he was here and it was all to come.

That evening, he hung back as the others gathered up their jackets and coats and headed off to the Half Moon.

He batted them off. 'Maybe see you there.'

I hung back too. I knew. My whole body was primed and stiff with knowing.

He waited until the corridor was empty, then turned to me, his eyes searching.

'Let's go for a drink,' he said. 'Somewhere quiet.'

I went to find my car and drove up the hill to the turn-off for the Upper School buildings. He'd parked on the far side of the road there, waiting for me. He indicated and carefully pulled out in front as he saw me approach.

We drove in convoy through the suburbs and into the countryside. It was grizzly weather, already dark with the onset of winter and cold. When I turned, following him off the road into a shadowy, almost deserted pub car park, I sat for a moment, staring over the top of the steering wheel into the blackness.

What am I doing? A foolish question when I already knew.

He appeared at the side-window, physical and real, and drew me out of the car, walked me through the chill with my hand tucked into the crook of his arm, as if we were already an old married couple, and into the warm. It was midweek. He led me into the quiet snug and settled me into a table there.

'Let me guess.' He waved his hands about and pretended to be a stage magician reading my mind. 'Madam's tipple is, methinks… port and lemonade?'

I laughed. 'Not even close.'

'Guinness.'

I raised my eyebrows. 'Really?'

He disappeared and came back with two glasses of Shiraz. His signature wine, I soon learned.

'I'd get a bottle, but not tonight.' He nodded through the window at the darkness of the car park. 'We're driving. Next time.'

Next time. I smiled. It felt so thrilling and yet so easy, so familiar, right from the start.

He was good company. He sizzled. All I had to do was sit back and forget myself, to feel the wine thaw me out and to let my shoulders fall, to let myself laugh, to set down my own awkward heaviness and be someone softer, someone lighter. Someone more like him.

He crackled with life. Funny stories about his English students and his battles to make them read. About the tricks he played on them and the bets he struck with the boys who refused to study anything written before they were born.

He was edgy and flirty and intense and I stopped worrying about why I was there and where this might lead and whether this was really a good idea and all the other anxieties that had made me hesitate until now and I just let it happen.

At the end of the evening, when we got to our feet and made to leave, he stopped me in the shadowy porch and turned me to him, as gently as if I were china, then slid his arms around me and kissed me on the lips, reverently, chastely. His eyes glistened in the low light.

'Laura Dixon.' That voice, low and languid. 'What have you done to me?'

As if it were all my fault.

I drove home in a blissful daze, looking out at the dark, quietening streets as if I'd never quite seen them before. My body tingled. My lips still felt the pressure of his. My breath pulsed in shallow, excited bursts. I was alive. I was attractive. I was falling in love and, oh my, how madly.

My phone pinged just as I was putting my key in the front door of my flat. My hand fumbled with the lock. I didn't let myself check my phone, not at first. I wanted to savour the moment, to tease myself. Maybe it was an overdraft alert from the bank. An automatic reminder of some routine appointment at the dentist or the optician.

Smiling, I closed the door and took off my coat, hung it on a peg. Went through to my bedroom, my head buzzing with wine and adrenalin, and then, only then, took out my phone.

Safely home?

My smile broadened in the darkness. I dropped back onto the bed, phone in hand. I texted back in a rush, before my more sensible self could intervene and stop this new, reckless woman bursting out from nowhere:

Come for dinner. Friday night?

I hit send. I lay on my back, ears buzzing in the silence and stared at my phone.

Nothing.

I sat up and carried it through to the kitchen, keeping it close while I filled a glass from the tap and drank water.

Nothing.

I started to panic. What if I'd misread him? I'd made a fool of myself. *Oh, how embarrassing.* What if he told people? How would I face them at school?

I carried the phone into the bathroom and set it on the edge of the bath while I washed and cleaned my teeth. Nothing.

Maybe I should text again: *Only joking!*

My face in the mirror was tight with tension. He probably befriended every new writer. Took them for a drink. It was just his style. Chatty. Gregarious.

I was getting into bed, distraught, when my phone finally pinged. I snatched it up.

Love to. Hold the Guinness.

I put the light off and imagined him here, in the flat. He'd bring it back to life. His energy. His zest. I'd cook properly from one of my old recipe books. Something I hadn't done for years, not since Matthew left. And a decent dessert.

All I had to decide now was what to wear.

CHAPTER 18

They played jazz again at the end of the memorial service. The melancholy sax tore my heart out. The man whose hair was flecked with grey helped Helen to her feet first and led her out. Once she was out of sight, the mood changed. People stretched and chatted in low voices and made for the exit.

Upstairs, in the balcony, voices hummed around me. I folded the order of service in half and stuffed it into my bag, then followed the crowd downstairs.

Everyone spilled out, blinking, into the sunshine. The chapel was surrounded by gently sloping lawns with wide, well-tended rose beds. In front, curling to the front steps, was a broad, tree-lined drive where cars could deposit and collect the chief mourners and, in other more normal circumstances, the hearse.

As I emerged, the crowd was starting to thin. Some people were striking out in small groups towards the main car park at the other end of the drive, funereal coats, redundant in the warm sunshine, hanging limp now over their arms. Stragglers greeted each other and stood gossiping, grateful for the sunshine.

I scanned the faces. The people coalesced around different periods of Ralph's life. Family members, some who clearly met rarely, explained to each other in loud voices who was whom and exclaimed about the passage of time. Children, vaguely remembered in pinafores or short trousers, had transformed into unlikely adults. Adults, once vigorous, were now stooped and bald. There was no sign of *her*, at least. That would have been more than I could bear.

A car door slammed shut and an engine purred into life. I looked across. A shiny black car was sliding away. Helen gazed vacantly out from the back seat.

Elaine Abbott, always polite, waved me over to join the group of Lower School teachers.

'They're having drinks at a restaurant down the road. You coming? Hilary's got room if you want a lift.'

I hesitated. 'That's okay. I drove here too, actually.'

I didn't know whether to go on to the wake with them or not. Part of me wanted to see Helen; I didn't quite know why or what I wanted to say, but it seemed important. I needed to know how she was, if there was anything she needed to tell me about the police investigation, if she had any hint of what they really knew.

Hilary said in a low voice, 'Funny funeral with no body.'

'It wasn't a funeral. It was a memorial service,' Olivia corrected.

Hilary pulled a face. 'Same difference.'

Elaine said, 'Legally, he can still be declared dead, even without a body, if everything points to that. I mean, I don't want to be gruesome –' she looked around and lowered her voice – 'but frankly, even if they did find a body at this point, what kind of state…' She left the thought hanging.

'They can identify just about anything nowadays, can't they? Bit of bone. Teeth…' Hilary said.

'Do you mind?' Olivia pulled a face. 'It's not *CSI*.'

Elaine said, 'Anyway, that's why the investigation's so important. Once the police think they know what happened, they can make progress on a death certificate.'

'Even without a body?'

'Apparently.'

Olivia said, 'But they don't know what happened.'

Elaine shrugged. 'I'm just saying, once they do.'

Hilary said, 'Jayne says they searched all over the heath. Even dragged the reservoir. Didn't find a thing.'

Olivia looked sceptical. 'How would she know?'

'She got it from John Bickers,' Hilary went on. 'But the reservoir's very deep. They might've missed him. And, as you say, by now... What? Don't look at me like that. I'm just saying.'

Elaine shivered. 'Let's go. This is getting morbid. I'm just sorry for his poor wife. Imagine. Not knowing.'

Olivia said, 'I need a drink.'

'She'll get his death in service pay-out.' Hilary was unstoppable. 'That's something. And his pension, eventually.'

'Only once he's declared dead.' Elaine looked thoughtful. 'I wonder if Sarah Baldini could make discreet inquiries? Check that Helen can manage? It's not just her, is it? She's got Anna too.'

Olivia said, 'I'm glad Helen didn't bring her today.'

I sensed that she was picking up on an earlier conversation.

Hilary frowned. 'She needs to be told.'

Olivia said, 'I know, eventually. But she's only seven.'

Around us, the crowd gradually dispersed. Only the two police officers remained at the entrance now, standing there at the top of the steps, surveying the mourners. I tried to keep out of their line of sight, using Elaine as cover. Just seeing that female detective, Johns, made me nervous.

The three teachers set off together down the drive and I trailed along with them, half-listening as they gossiped about the other teachers, about which ones had bothered to come along on a Saturday and which had not, about Sarah Baldini's reading and the tribute that Ralph's relative, whoever he was, had delivered so badly that Elaine hadn't heard a word.

I gazed out at the grounds as we talked, at the memorial gardens with their small, solemn granite stones, some planted with flowers, one or two decorated with tethered balloons and streamers, as if they marked a recently lost child. It all felt unreal.

I kept repeating to myself: *that was Ralph's memorial. He's dead. Really dead. I'll never see him again.* Even now, it seemed impossible.

A large crow landed on the grass ahead of us and hopped across it, ugly and ominous. I let my eye be drawn. Something moved in the trees beyond. I blinked and narrowed my gaze. More birds, perhaps. A shadow stirred and I stopped. It was a man. He was too far away for me to make out his face, but he was tall with broad shoulders. I had the sense of him looking right at me. I let out a cry. *Ralph?*

As I gaped, he shifted sideways into the cover of the trees and disappeared. I shook my head and tried to calm myself down. I was being ridiculous. I was seeing things. *Not Ralph. It couldn't be. Too short. Too thickset.*

The other teachers paused, looked back at me. 'What?'

I nodded towards the trees. 'Someone was standing there, watching us.'

Olivia frowned and screwed up her features to stare. 'I can't see anyone.'

Elaine said, 'Trick of the light. That's all.' She reached out a plump hand and patted my arm. 'We're all a bit jumpy.'

Hilary said, 'Probably some poor chap caught short. I could do with a loo myself.'

Elaine said to me, her voice kind, 'Come for a drink. I'll come in your car, if you like. I know the way.'

I shook my head. 'Thanks but…' I hesitated. They were all looking at me, the three of them. Elaine seemed concerned. The other two had hard eyes. They didn't like me. I didn't like to think about it but deep down, I already knew that. I wasn't liked. *Abrupt Laura Dixon.* I'd tried to keep myself to myself. I'd tried not to mind. But now I was frightened of them too. I couldn't afford to draw attention to myself. I couldn't afford to let them suspect me. If the sharks came circling, who here would protect me from them?

I swallowed. 'I'm not feeling great. Sorry. I think I'll just go home.'

Back in the flat, I opened a bottle of Shiraz and drank a glass. I unfolded Ralph's memorial service booklet and pinned it on the fridge with the Shakespeare magnet he had given me, one of the small gifts I'd missed in my mad purge and couldn't bear now to throw away. His dead eyes followed me round the kitchen. The magnet read, *My heart is ever at your service.*

Not anymore, I thought. *Your heart's stopped, Ralph. Cold in the ocean. I stopped it.*

I switched the TV on and lay on the settee, my head on one padded arm and my knees hooked over the other, and worked my way through the bottle of wine. The TV picture blurred and swam. I thought about eating but I was empty, not hungry. An emptiness food couldn't fill. Hours slipped by. Outside, the light was becoming soft and mellow as the day drew towards its end.

When the early evening news came on, I struggled to my feet and swayed across the room to the window to draw the curtains. The wall propped me upright. I put my forehead to the cool glass, then squashed the end of my nose there too. I was too high up for anyone to see me.

I grasped the edge of the curtain and started to pull it across. Then stopped. A man was sitting on a wall near the bus stop, there, further down the road. His head was craning forward, over a newspaper, his face obscured.

I frowned, struggled to see. He looked familiar. *Not Ralph. Too short. Too stocky.* I stared again, hanging now off the curtain I grasped in my hand. *Was it him, that figure I'd seen in the shadows, in amongst the trees, as we left the chapel?* I shook my head and reached for the window frame, nauseous. I was imagining things. What would Ralph say? *Crazy loon.*

Maybe it's my guardian angel, I thought, *come to save me. Or the devil's messenger, come to drag me off to Hell for what I've done.*

My phone pinged. I went through to the kitchen to check the message, then stared at my phone. There was no listing there, just *Number withheld.*

It was a simple message. Two words.

Miss me?

I dropped the phone and staggered to the bathroom, acid in my throat, my outstretched hands banging against walls and doorframes as I lurched from one to the other.

CHAPTER 19

That first night, when Ralph came for dinner, I cooked salmon en croûte. Shop-bought pastry, ready rolled. Stuffed with butter and flaked almonds, currants and chopped ginger. I'd made it the night before, giving myself time on Friday evening to shower after school and get ready.

My hands trembled with excitement as I applied make-up. I nearly poked my eye out with the pencil. I tried on one outfit after another. Black trousers and black silk shirt. *Too tight*. Same trousers and purple frilly top. *Too low*. A shift dress. *Too short*. A woollen work dress. *Too frumpish*.

I settled on a red cotton button-down dress with bold yellow flowers. Wraparound to show off my waist but not too low over the bust. Confident. Casual.

I had a gin and tonic to steady my jangly nerves, then put out a bowl of crisps and paced in front of them, eating the overflow each time I passed the table. I soon realised I'd eaten so many, the bowl was half-empty. I topped them up and had another drink.

By the time the door buzzed, my head was floaty with gin. His picture on the security camera was too grainy to recognise but I pressed the door release, then ran back to the bedroom, worried now about my dress.

The face in the mirror looked panicked. The make-up was too heavy. I wasn't used to this. It had been a long time. I wasn't ready. What was I thinking? This was a big mistake.

A rap on the flat's front door made me jump. He must have bounded up the stairs, two at a time. I took a deep breath and tried to pull myself together. A dark shadow loomed against the wavy security glass. I put a sweaty hand on the lock and opened it.

Him. Really him. Clutching a gold bouquet of autumn flowers. That smile.

He held out the flowers and I took them, buried my face in the yellow and gold, hiding.

'Can I come in?'

I stepped to one side, so close to him in the hallway that I felt the heat from his body. He was slightly out of breath.

'Did you run up?'

He handed me a bottle of wine. Shiraz. 'I had to. I couldn't wait. I wanted to see you, Laura Dixon.'

He opened his arms and I stepped right into them, squashing the bouquet. I felt the hard muscle of his chest through his cotton shirt, let his arms enfold me. I found myself smiling, crazy smiling. I was happy. I was home.

He pulled away a fraction and looked down at me, still holding me loosely in the circle of his arms.

'I was worried.' His eyes read mine, relieved and perhaps amused. 'I wasn't sure.'

I nodded. I knew exactly. But it was all right. He was here and we wanted each other, we belonged together. Nothing had felt so sure for a long time, not for me. His arms felt safe, wrapped around me, and his smell enveloped me too, that heady, sexy mix of soap and shower gel and fresh sweat, tying my stomach into knots. Nothing else mattered. I didn't care that the salmon was drying out, that my head was already reeling with gin, that my body wasn't as lean and taut as it used to be, that the only crisps left in the bowl were the broken, salt-encrusted scraps of the packet end.

Being with him was enough. I was full of hope, full of love, full of craziness.

We made love for the first time that evening. Later, much later, after the salmon and the Shiraz – a bad choice for fish but that didn't stop us – he took me to bed. Well, to the floor in the sitting room. We discarded clothes, piece by piece, and he kissed every inch of me.

When I was dozing and already thinking how wonderful it would be to wake up next to him in the morning – to make love again, then sleep some more and finally, late in the day, go out for coffee and croissants, maybe in that café on the high street, full of loved-up sleepiness, huddling close together on our seats and clinging to each other as we ate, licking flakes of croissant from each other's fingers, my face scratched from his stubble – it was only after all these thoughts and dreams of what lay ahead that I realised that he was easing himself away from me.

I opened my eyes, feeling the draught down my side. He was looking for the bathroom, perhaps. Or heading to the kitchen for a drink of water.

No. He was gathering together his scattered clothes, turning his underpants the right way round, starting to dress. Getting ready to leave.

My stomach contracted. The woozy dreaminess disappeared in a second.

'Ralph?'

He crept across the floor and bent to kiss the tip of my nose.

'Gotta go,' he whispered. 'I'm sorry.'

I hesitated, watching his deft movements, seeing his naked body disappear under clothes and wondering when and if I'd see it again.

I twisted to look across the shadowy room to the clock. Half past midnight.

Why did he have to go? I was afraid to ask.

He was fully dressed now. Keys and coins jangled in his pocket as he arranged the folds of his trousers and fastened his belt, becoming his outside self again.

He sat on the edge of the settee to ease on his shoes and lace them, then stooped again to kiss me, on the lips this time. 'Parting is such sweet sorrow.'

I tried to remember how much wine he'd had. 'Are you okay to drive?'

He smiled. 'I'm fine.'

I blinked. He'd kept refilling my glass. My head was spinning. Had he been more careful about his own?

'Can't you stay?' I regretted it at once. *Too needy. Too begging. No, Laura. Don't demean yourself.*

He didn't look cross, just rueful. 'I wish I could. Believe me.'

I opened my mouth. I nearly said it out loud, this thought that had just rushed in like a tidal wave, *Is there something you need to tell me?*

I couldn't. I swallowed back the words. *Not now. Not like this.*

He whispered goodbye and disappeared, taking the air, the life out of the room. I listened as the door clicked shut behind him.

I lay there on the floor, my body cooling, too crushed for a moment to stir myself and crawl into bed. *Why wouldn't he stay?* Doubts gnawed at me. We'd talked so much – about poetry and film and teaching and school but very little about him, about his life. *I just assumed…* well, he'd seemed such a free spirit and so keen to pursue me.

I closed my eyes. I was imagining things. I should trust my heart, my instincts. He was a decent man. *My man.* I nodded to myself. He was just being sensitive, giving me space. That might be it. He was wary of rushing me.

I shifted my limbs, feeling the imprint of his fingers, his lips, still lingering there, and stretched, letting myself smile again.

As I finally stirred myself and went into the bathroom to drink some water, then clean my teeth, my phone pinged. I rushed to look, then sighed. It wasn't from him after all. There was no listing, just the words: *Number withheld.*

I opened it up to find a short message: *Missing you already. When can we meet again? X*

I hesitated, confused. *Who's this?*

Romeo. Password: salmon en croûte.

Wherefore art thou using new number?

Juliet hotline.

That made me laugh.

I put down the phone and carried on cleaning my teeth. My head was fuzzy with wine and tiredness but euphoric.

It was time to move on and to trust again. Time to forget those final, bitter rows with Matthew about 'needing his space' and 'feeling shut in'. To forget the silence after the door closed behind him, that final time. To forget the hurt and fear and the lifelessness of being alone.

I put away my toothbrush and picked up my phone again. *Juliet hotline.* Where did that come from?

It would be different this time. He wasn't Matthew. He was Ralph. He was special.

My fingers typed back: *Soonest. Miss you too. Juliet. xxx*

That's the thing about falling in love. By the time you realise, it's already too late.

I brimmed with energy that weekend, buoyed up by constant thoughts about Ralph. I cleaned the flat, imagining the next time he'd come round. That October was golden, mellow with warmth and fading sunshine. I went for a long walk by the river, seeing the dying trees, the squirrels, the light flitting across the water, with new eyes. Imagined having him with me. Imagined being happy together there, hand in hand.

I shopped and cooked, wondering what he most liked, and kept my phone close, in case.

On Tuesday, I dressed for school with care and found myself humming as I pressed through the day, the duties, the teaching, the lesson preparation. As soon as Upper School ended, I hurried up the hill towards the writing group classroom. I'd hardly eaten. My stomach was too knotted with excitement. I scurried down the corridor. The classroom door stood open as people wandered in, chatting. I hurried inside and found a seat in the circle, then dared, at last, to raise my eyes properly and search him out, knowing his eyes would already be doing the same.

He wasn't there.

I breathed deeply and steadied myself, trying not to let the anguish show on my face. Others took their seats. The science teacher with the beard stepped to the front.

'I'm afraid Ralph can't make it this evening, folks. Family crisis. He sends his apologies. So,' he looked round the circle, expectantly, 'who'd like to kick off?'

I stared at him in disbelief. *Family crisis.*

I shifted my weight, leaned forward, my body trembling. What was he talking about? What family? What the heck was going on? If I'd been calmer, I might have just got up and left, run down to the car park to call him. But I couldn't move. I just sat there, flushed, struggling to think.

Already someone was opening a notebook and heading to the front to perch on the corner of the desk, as Ralph always did, clearing their throat and preparing to perform.

I don't know how I got through it. I kept my eyes on my shoes, the new black shoes I'd chosen with such care that morning, wondering, as I picked them out of the wardrobe, if Ralph would like the spiked heels. That morning seemed a long time ago.

I tried to keep my face passive as they read, one after another. I had no idea what their work was about. All I could think about was Ralph. His eyes. His smile, so direct, so personal. The feel of his hands on my skin.

Calm. A family crisis could mean anything. A parent. A brother. A niece or nephew. So why did I feel such a sense of doom?

I think I knew, deep down. I just couldn't admit it, even to myself.

*

I hung around as the others gathered together their coats and bags and surged into the corridor. I positioned myself next to the science teacher who'd led the session.

'Sorry to hear about Ralph,' I said as evenly as I could. 'Hope it's nothing serious?'

He gave me a short, sideways glance. 'Anna's hurt her arm. They've taken her to hospital.'

He turned away from me to speak to someone else.

Olivia Fry, coming up behind me, added, 'She fell off the monkey bars, that's all. They just want to check it's not broken.'

'Anna?' My mind whirled.

Olivia nodded. 'Anna Wilson. Year two.' Her eyes were on my face. 'His daughter. Didn't you know? You must have come across his wife, Mrs Wilson. She comes in for reading.'

I gazed at her vacantly. *Mrs Wilson. His wife?*

I managed to stutter, 'That's dreadful.'

Olivia said, 'I'm sure she'll be fine. They just thought they'd get it X-rayed.'

She turned and disappeared with the others, off to the pub. Leaving me staring after her, feeling a fool, my heart cracking and breaking into bits.

Anna Wilson. His daughter.

Why hadn't he mentioned her? Why hadn't he told me he had a wife?

He called me late that evening.

'Did I wake you?' His voice was a whisper. I wondered where he was. Hiding somewhere in the house, away from his wife, calling me furtively. It made me sick to think of it.

'How's Anna?' My voice was strained.

He sighed. 'She's fine. Just a nasty sprain. Darling, I'm sorry. I need to explain.'

Darling? My heart twisted. I wanted to sob, to berate him. *Why, Ralph? Why didn't you tell me?* I wanted him to know how betrayed I felt, that I'd just been sitting here, crying, feeling my heart break. Instead, I said stiffly, 'Yes, Ralph. You do.'

A silence. 'I'm sorry. Really, Laura. I wasn't sure how much you knew about me.'

He sounded exhausted. I hesitated. Part of me didn't even want to listen. I wanted to tell him to leave me alone, to slam down the phone. But he sounded so desolate, so sad. I wanted to reach down the phone and brush the floppy hair from his forehead, to take him in my arms and comfort him. *Oh, Ralph.*

I waited, pressing the phone to my ear.

'It's complicated.' He sounded hesitant. 'Things with Helen…' He broke off. I hardly dared breathe. 'Things aren't so good. They haven't been for a long time. That's no excuse. I know that. But, oh, Laura…'

I strained to listen. That catch in his voice, *was he crying?* I bit my lip.

'You won't leave me, will you?' He sounded pitiful. 'I'll make it up to you, Laura. We're good together, we really are. We haven't known each other long. I don't want to make promises but—'

He broke off. I ran the back of my hand across my eyes.

'Why didn't you tell me? I'd no idea...'

His voice sounded so strangled, it hurt me to hear it. 'I meant to, Laura. I really did. It's just all happened so fast. And I wasn't sure. I thought maybe you'd heard that I... well, you know what school's like.'

I shook my head. I imagined Olivia whispering to Hilary about the two of us leaving the group together. The gossip in the staffroom, in the corridors. He was right. I knew exactly what school was like.

'I'm sorry. I've done this all wrong, haven't I?'

I couldn't answer.

'Laura. You still there?'

I swallowed. 'I'm still here.'

'It's different with you, Laura. It really is. You feel it too, don't you? Don't tell me you don't.'

I wiped my eyes with the back of my hand.

'We're good together. We belong together. Don't walk away from me.' He sounded so desperate. 'Don't do that, Laura. Please.'

I didn't know what to say. I couldn't do this on the phone. I needed him here. I needed to see his face.

'But you're married, Ralph.'

'I know. Just give me time. Please. I don't want to lose you.'

The room swam. I was so tired. I didn't want to hear any more. Not yet. I needed time too, to think. I listened to the silence, imagining life without him, going back to the emptiness.

'I don't know, Ralph.' I hesitated. 'Just try and be honest with me. Please.'

He let out a rush of breath. 'Oh, Laura. I just want to see you. When can I see you?'

I shook my head. 'Let's talk tomorrow.'

After we hung up, I sat very still, too sad even to cry. A text pinged through from *Number withheld*.

Love you, Laura Dixon.

I felt something twist and loosen inside me and all of a sudden I was smiling, despite everything. My fingers typed a reply before I could stop them.

Love you too.

CHAPTER 20

The memorial service stifled the endless chatter in the staffroom. The speculation about Ralph Wilson seemed exhausted, at last. Life moved on.

Gradually, I stopped looking up quickly, heart racing, every time the staffroom door opened, in case it was a summons. I stopped stammering when John Bickers paused to chat to me in the corridor, stopped wondering what his motive was, whether the police had asked him to watch me, whether I was on their list of suspects.

There were days, wonderfully ordinary days, when I realised I was once again utterly absorbed in teaching for whole stretches of time; writing up lists of ideas on the whiteboard or helping the class make 3-D maps of Peru or hearing their high, insistent voices debate the question of the week: *was it better to be rich or happy? If they could be an animal, which would they be?* On those days, I dared to think that perhaps it was okay, after all.

Perhaps we really had got away with it.

It hadn't entirely left me, though. Some nights, I still woke at 3 a.m., body sweating, and stared in panic at the dark ceiling. I still saw in the darkness, from time to time, Ralph's crumpled body at the bottom of the steps or the all-knowing, all-seeing eyes of Detective Inspector Johns, boring into mine and reading my guilt there. I drank whisky and warm milk to chase away the ghosts and practised deep breathing.

I wondered about Helen. I imagined her lying awake, red-eyed, as haunted as I was. I saw her kicking off the bedclothes, hollowed out with guilt, and pacing round the house. The shadowy sitting room. The deserted hall. Standing at the closed door to the cellar, remembering.

I wondered how often she thought of me and, when she did, what feelings took her. We were bound together by what we'd done. We were the keepers of a terrible, unspoken secret, a secret that could destroy us both.

I thought a lot about what she'd done. I understood it, I decided at last. She had been in shock and, if she had to lose her husband, her daughter's father, it was better to suffer a mysterious disappearance than to be the widow of an adulterer whose lover sent him tumbling down the cellar steps, naked, in a fight. She was right: the headlines, the trial, the endless gossip... it would be intolerable for her and for Anna too, as well as ruinous for me.

But I couldn't help feeling that the business between us had been left unresolved. I owed her. What I didn't know was what payment she might demand.

The more time passed, the more I wanted to know. The more I felt I had to know.

It was about that time that Sarah Baldini sent round a fresh memo about the annual whole school photograph. It had been postponed when Ralph went missing. It didn't take a genius to figure out that the school wouldn't be shown to its best advantage if we were all arranged in rows, scrubbed up, while a police investigation continued just out of shot.

Now all that was over and it was being revived.

Emails went out to parents with a few days' notice.

Freshly ironed uniform, please. No jewellery. Regulation hair accessories only. Clean, polished shoes.

The day of the photograph was blowy but dry. After morning assembly, Elaine took charge of organising the Lower School children to file up the hill, walking, one class after another, in an endless crocodile, to the Upper School. The photographic company had erected a tiered platform there, as they did every year. The Upper School, dominated by slouching, self-conscious adolescents, was already being ushered into place along the back section. The sixth formers, allowed to wear their own clothes at school, rather than school uniform which was mandatory for everyone else, painted a splash of colour down the last two rows, bounded only by the final row of teachers. Height wasn't the only reason the sixth formers were hidden away from view at the back.

We set about threading the line of younger children into the front rows. The year ones knelt up along the front, then the reception children sat right at the front, legs crossed. We teachers formed a frame, along the back and making two neat lines down either side, hemming the children into position. Only Sarah Baldini and John Bickers, the two heads, sat on actual chairs, right at the front, in the centre.

I was one of the last to take my place. I was helping Elaine to shoo the reception and year one children closer together so we had a chance of fitting them all in shot, scolding the children who thought it hilarious to ruffle up the neatly combed hair of the younger children in front of them and breaking up arguments before they had the chance to develop into fights.

I stood for a moment by the photographer's tripod, scanning the scene to catch any unruly behaviour. It was quite a sight. Nearly nine hundred pupils, from the smallest four-year-old to the coolest, lankiest eighteen-year-old, gathered together for the annual picture, all but the oldest dressed alike in white shirts and blouses, dark blue ties and pinafores, hair short or long, slicked back or tied back with blue and white scrunchies. To the left, the hill was thick with trees, marking the border between the Upper and Lower School. Behind the final row, the Upper School's main building – the oldest part of the campus – sat squat but imposing.

My mouth twisted as I took it all in. I'd stood in this same spot several times before, marshalling the ranks as the pupils got ready for the final inspection by Sarah Baldini before she took her seat, arranged her legs to one side, her hands in her lap, then signalled readiness to the photographer. There were children now in years four and five, standing with all the self-assurance of eight- and nine-year-olds who were starting to find their feet in life, whom I could remember in previous photographs as small, scared reception children, hunched cross-legged on the grass.

It had meant something to me, once, this mammoth display of the school's children. It had stirred me. But now, with all that had happened in the past year, without Ralph, I felt empty.

For the first time, it hit me. I'd have to leave. It was killing me, this pretending to the world that nothing had changed. Every day I was here, in these buildings where we'd met, I was weighed down by guilt and fear. More than that, I looked for him, longed for him, missed him. He was everywhere. In every classroom, every corridor, every corner.

How could I carry on here now, without him?

CHAPTER 21

One Thursday, I was setting up my year three class for a craft activity when I saw Anna race past the classroom windows, down the empty corridor. It was afternoon playtime and the children were supposed to be outside. I dropped my pots of wax crayons on the table and hurried after her.

I found her standing by one of the stacks in the Lower School library, her face blotchy and wet with tears. She turned her large, frightened eyes on me as I approached. Ralph's eyes.

'Anna! What's the matter?'

I pulled out a clean tissue and offered it to her.

She gulped, her breath snagged with crying and running, and blew her nose noisily.

'Sit down here.' I sat at one end of a reading settee and patted the empty place beside me. 'Let's have a chat.'

She hesitated. Her eyes stuck to her black school shoes, reluctant to meet mine. The leather shone with polish. Whatever Helen was going through inside, she was clearly managing her grief well enough to take care of her daughter.

'Come on. Tell me all about it.'

She turned and perched as far from me on the settee cushions as she could, twisting the tissue between her fingers.

'I'm not cross, Anna. I just want to help.'

Silence, broken only by her rough breathing.

'Anna?'

I was bracing myself for some upset in relation to Ralph's death. Distress, perhaps, sparked by another child saying something tactless in the playground about his disappearance, as young children did. Mean taunts or persistent questions about what had happened.

She gulped. The tissue was starting to shred now into wet strands.

'It's all right, Anna. You can tell me.' My tone was calm and friendly.

She tipped her head sideways and gave me a quick glance, reading my face. 'It's my bookbag.'

I leaned in, wondering if I'd misheard. 'Your bookbag? Have you lost it?'

She nodded miserably.

'Have you told Mrs Prior?'

She shook her head, her thin shoulders hunched. Even her plaits drooped.

'You're worried she'll be angry?'

A fresh tear gathered and splashed down her cheek and she swiped it with the back of her hand.

'Anna. Listen.' I lowered my head and inched closer to her. 'I want to be your friend. See? I want to help you. Whatever problems you have, I'm on your side. Okay?'

She didn't move. I wondered for a moment what she knew about me, then brushed away the thought. Whatever her mother felt, she'd never share it with her seven-year-old. Helen wasn't that kind.

I spoke softly. 'How are things, Anna? You had some time off, didn't you? Is everything okay, you know, at home?'

She nodded without looking at me. I let the silence expand, waiting for her to say more. She didn't.

Outside, in the playground, the five-minute bell rang. Very soon, hordes of children would come charging in through the double doors, hurtle up the stairs and hurry along the corridors to their classrooms, marshalled by shouting teachers: 'Don't run, children!' 'One at a time!' 'Edward, don't push!'

I didn't have long.

'Now, about this bookbag. Where did you last see it?'

She screwed up her face. 'Don't know.'

'Could you have left it at home?'

She shook her head.

'Did you do reading this morning?'

She nodded.

'Where? In here? In the year two corner?'

She mumbled, 'In here.'

'That's why you came back here, to look for it?'

She nodded.

'Well, you're not allowed in here at playtime, are you, Anna?'

Downstairs, the final bell rang. Any moment, they'd be upon us.

'Look. You run down and join your class, okay? If Mrs Prior asks where you were, just tell her you were having a chat with me. She won't mind. I'll have a good look round.'

She jumped to her feet.

I put a hand on her arm as she turned to race off.

'And remember, Anna, any time you want to talk, you can always come and find me. Okay? I won't tell anyone. I'm your friend, remember. Your secret friend.'

She fled without answering.

I made a hurried search of the library area and found her bookbag upside down, flattened by a floor cushion. Her daily reading diary was inside and the story she was reading, along with an empty snack box, covered with brightly coloured stickers, and a half-crayoned colouring sheet.

I hesitated. Judging from the stomping feet, my own class were already on their way up. I didn't have time to fight my way against the flow, take the bag along to Hilary Prior's classroom and be back before class started.

Of course, I should really have taken it down to Anna at the end of the school day. But by then, I had a much better idea.

CHAPTER 22

The Lower School car park was almost deserted by the time I headed out, Anna's bookbag on the passenger seat beside my work bag. Without thinking, I parked in the next street, out of sight of their house, as I always had in the past when I came to see Ralph. I only realised my mistake as I was walking down to their road. Hopefully, Helen wouldn't even notice.

I was almost at their gate, striding past the neighbours' house with the open curtains and large wall-mounted TV – switched on as usual – when I noticed him. He was sitting in a parked car, slightly further down the street from Ralph and Helen's house. He was in the driving seat but turned away, offering me a hunched shoulder. His head was bowed, his nose was deep in a newspaper. I stopped and looked. My heart raced.

Was it the same man? It couldn't be. The man I'd seen at a distance, disappearing into the cover of the trees as we walked away from the chapel after the memorial service. The man I'd seen sitting on a wall at the bus stop near my flat. I blinked. He was wearing an old-fashioned cap, hiding his hair. His jacket was different to the one I'd seen him wearing outside my house. I checked out the car. A crimson, four-door saloon. The paintwork along the passenger door was scraped and patched roughly with white.

He was too still. Unnatural. Too long on the same page of his newspaper. Almost as if he knew I was scrutinising him, as if he were waiting for me to lose interest and move on.

I tore myself away, opened the gate and went down the path to the gleaming, freshly painted front door. I pressed the front-door buzzer. It felt strange not to rap with bare knuckles, as Ralph had taught me.

As I stood there, waiting, looking into the streaks of reflected light across the glistening black, the time seemed suddenly to warp and I had an unnerving sense of flashback to my last visit to the house. When the door opened, I almost expected it to be Ralph who answered the door, furtive, barely revealing himself on the threshold, eager to usher me inside.

Helen. A small brown towel in her hands. A look crossed her face, fleeting and annoyed. After a pause, she smiled, feigning polite surprise.

'Miss Dixon!' Her voice was too loud, too cheery. 'This is very unexpected! Anna isn't in any trouble, I hope?'

'Not at all.' I held the bookbag high as if it were the chancellor's red box. 'Just returning this. She was quite upset at school that she'd lost it. I found it after class and wanted to get it back to her as quickly as possible.'

We stared at each other, both hesitant, as if we were waiting for someone offstage to give us a cue. She reached out to take it from me.

'Do you mind if I say hello to Anna, Mrs Wilson? I won't stay a moment.' I kept tight hold of the bag and made to step over the threshold. 'I just want to reassure her that she won't be told off tomorrow.'

She hesitated, then reluctantly opened the door wider to let me in. When she closed it behind me, I felt suddenly trapped. The hall was suffocating. This is where Helen had stood when she came home that evening and found us, one dead, one alive. My eyes strayed to the top of the stairs, where I had stood, then to the tiled space at the bottom.

Helen's eyes were on my face, taking it all in. When she spoke, there was an artificial brightness in her voice, as if she were auditioning for a part. Her body told a different story. Her eyes, when they met mine, were hard and vengeful. Her shoulders stooped prematurely, as if she were bowed by a great weight.

'Anna's watching something at the moment. In the sitting room. You won't get much out of her, I'm afraid.'

She led me dutifully through to the sitting room. Anna and Clara sat side by side on cushions on the carpet, legs crossed, their eyes focussed on the iPad which was propped up on the coffee table in front of them. Some cartoon was playing, I had no idea which.

'Hi, Anna!'

No response.

'I found your bookbag!'

Helen smiled. 'Sorry. No use trying to get their attention during screen-time. They look forward to it all day.'

She reached out and took the bag from me, opened it and checked through the contents.

'Well, we mustn't keep you.'

In the hall, as she tried to bustle me back out into the street, I leaned in and whispered, 'Someone's watching the house. A man.'

She glared.

'Crimson car with a scrape. Go and look.'

She hesitated, then went back into the sitting room. I stood in the doorway and saw her pass the girls, then stand to one side of the window, carefully peering out without being seen. She came back.

'You're seeing things.'

'I'm not!' I pushed past and crossed to the window myself, moved back the net curtain and scanned the road. He'd gone. I turned back to her. 'He was sitting right there, across the road.' I hesitated, wondering how much to tell her. 'And he was in the chapel grounds, watching everyone leave. At the memorial service.'

Her lips pursed. I remembered how battered she'd looked, struggling down the aisle to her seat in the chapel, leaning on her relative's arm for support. She hadn't realised. She hadn't known I was there too, paying my own respects to her husband. To my lover.

'Anyway, we mustn't keep you.' She held open the sitting-room door to usher me out again. She added with fake brightness as she propelled me towards the front door, 'So kind of you to pop round.'

Who was she really speaking to, in this strange, brittle tone? Not to me, clearly. Was it all for the benefit of the girls?

I didn't want to leave. I wanted to sit her down and ask her so much more. Ask her how she was, how she really was. If she could sleep at night. What the police had asked her. Were they suspicious? What had she told them about Ralph and the true state of her marriage? What did they know about me?

And what did we do next? What did we do when his body washed up, which it must, surely, eventually, whatever state it was in, what did we do then?

I leaned in close and whispered: 'I keep thinking, what about when they find him? What then? They'll know he didn't drown. They'll be able to tell. They'll know he was already dead when he hit the water. Then what do we do?'

Anger flared in her face. She didn't speak, just gripped my arm and pushed me towards the front door. Before she opened it, she hissed, 'Don't ever come here again. You hear?'

I nodded, dumbly.

'Keep your mouth shut. I'm warning you. Whatever happens. Keep away from me. And keep away from Anna.' Her eyes were sneering. 'You are not our "secret friend". Get it?'

She opened the door and pushed me past her onto the path.

'Miss Dixon? Hello!'

A woman in a belted mac, a battered leather messenger bag hanging from her shoulder, had her hand on the gate. She looked familiar. It took me a moment.

'Bea Higgins. Clara's mum.' She came striding up the path to join me at the front door. 'Hi, Helen. Girls okay?'

'Fine,' Helen, speaking from behind me, cut me off as I opened my mouth to explain. 'Miss Dixon brought Anna's bag round. She's just leaving.'

'That's kind.' Bea gave me a thoughtful look. 'Clara's always losing things. I'm short a cardigan at the moment. It's named.'

'I'll keep an eye out.' I tried to look concerned. 'Always worth asking Jayne in the office.'

Bea shook her head. 'I've emailed her but, you know, if you're not there in person…'

I remembered what Hilary Prior had said about Clara's mother being a single parent who worked full-time.

'You should've told me,' Helen said. 'I can ask Jayne for you.'

Bea smiled. 'Well, if you really don't mind. I don't want to be a bother.' She turned back to me. 'Thank God for Helen. Honestly, I don't know how I'd manage if it weren't for her. I know there's After School Club but it ends at five and then what are you supposed to do? Who's home from work by then?'

Helen said, 'Anyway, come on in, Bea. They're having screen-time.'

Helen bustled her friend inside before she could say anything else, frowning at me as she closed the door in my face.

On the drive home, my hands trembled as they gripped the steering wheel. Helen's anger clung to me. I don't know what I'd expected. Of course, we weren't friends, she was right about that. And I had no business turning up at their home and intruding on their family life. I just couldn't help myself.

She'd warned me right from the start, on the night we disposed of Ralph's body.

Don't get some idea we're bound together by this. I'll curse you till the day I die.

Even so, her vehemence frightened me. It felt as if she'd just punched me in the face.

I checked my mirrors nervously as I drove, the rear-view, the side, the far side, looking out for the crimson saloon car. I didn't see it, but I couldn't shake off the feeling that someone was following me. That unseen eyes were watching me. Maybe Helen was right. Maybe I was starting to imagine things.

At home, I waited at the communal front door before I put my key in the lock. I let my breathing settle and checked behind me, looking over my shoulder down the path and into the bushes, trying to reassure myself there was no one there. What was wrong with me? I remembered the tablets the doctor gave me after Ralph left me. I didn't want to run out. I'd have to go back to her, to ask for more. Something to quieten my nerves and help me sleep.

Inside the block, the ground-floor hallway was silent. I waited until the heavy communal door clicked shut behind me. I was in a safe space now. Alone.

I started up the carpeted stairs. The flat below mine, where the young man lived, was in darkness. I carried on to the top floor and my own front door and fitted my key in the lock.

I knew as soon as I opened the door that something was wrong. Very wrong.

It was the silence.

It took a second for me to register. No beeping security alarm. I always set it when I went out. My heart thudded. Surely I'd set it that morning, as I headed out to school? Hadn't I? It was instinctive.

So why wasn't it beeping now?

CHAPTER 23

I closed the door behind me with a bang. Unnecessarily loud. If someone was here, inside the flat, some burglar ransacking the place, this was their cue to run. To climb back out of whatever window they'd forced and shimmy off down a drainpipe.

Stillness. Nothing.

I dropped my bag on the carpet and started to walk through the rooms. There was no sign of a break-in. Nothing was disturbed.

Halfway down the hall passage, something reached out, caught at my heart and twisted it hard. That smell. *Ralph's smell.*

I opened the bathroom door. The shower mat was rumpled. The door to the bathroom cabinet was ajar. There was a faint, lingering smell of soap – different, surely, from the shower gel I'd used that morning?

'Ralph?'

My voice sounded thin, all alone in the emptiness. What was I thinking? Did I really expect him to answer, to appear in the doorway and say hi?

I stood on the threshold and strained to listen. Silence. My nerves strained.

I hurried into the kitchen. Everything was just as I'd left it. Toast crumbs on the bread board. Plate and knife in the sink. So why did I have the sense that someone else had been here?

I shouted, 'Is anyone here?'

I ran back through the flat, slamming open the doors and looking wildly round each room. Nothing. No one. I came to a halt in the middle of the sitting room, panting, staring round.

Nothing appeared altered and yet something was different. I didn't know why. I just knew. I couldn't shake off the feeling that someone had invaded my home.

My phone pinged. A message.

I looked down at my phone, lying there on the coffee table in its case. My hands hung stiffly by my sides. *I should look*. Something held me back. I thought of the strange message I'd received so recently. A wrong number, I'd decided. Sent to me by mistake.

My hands seemed to know better. They trembled, suddenly ice cold. They didn't want to pick up my phone and see.

I forced myself to open up the case and look, then, as soon as I'd read the words, let the phone drop to the carpet.

Like last time, the number was withheld and the message brief.

Did you really think I'd gone?

CHAPTER 24

Ralph had given me a smart speaker that Christmas, the must-have gift of the season. He came round on Christmas Eve to set it up for me, knowing how anxious I was about new technology. Matthew had loved gadgets. He used to keep me up-to-date. Since he'd left, I hadn't had the heart to bother.

Ralph found me amusing.

'My old-fashioned gal,' he'd say if we settled down in front of my TV, the old kind that sits in a corner on a stand with its DVD player on a shelf beneath. 'Let's select one of these – what do you call them, madam – DVDs, shall we?'

I didn't mind being teased by him. He and Helen streamed their films, of course. I understood the advantage, but I didn't see the point of committing to a monthly contract when I didn't really need it. I was trying to save from my salary, not pay out for things I could manage without. We had a perfectly decent local library. I could rent a DVD from there for a pound, if I fancied something different.

I already had a drawer filled with DVDs and I didn't want to buy those same films all over again. I never told him about the VHS tapes I still stored in another box under the bed.

I was careful with money. It was one of the issues Matthew and I argued about, towards the end. He was eager to be out every weekend, burning through cash. I didn't see the point of dining in a restaurant if you had a perfectly good kitchen at home. Or drinking in a bar when you could buy the same stuff from a supermarket for a fraction of the price.

Ralph and I had agreed to celebrate Christmas Eve together as if it were our Christmas Day. I understood why. He could get away on Christmas Eve. His wife wouldn't be too suspicious if he said he needed to dash to the shops. Christmas Day was important for his daughter, for Anna. I didn't like any of it, but I respected that. Even in the future, I thought, after he'd left Helen, he should make an effort to be with Anna for special holidays, at least while she was still a child. I'd always let him do that.

So that Christmas Eve, I cooked a small turkey and all the trimmings, chose a good wine and picked up a bottle of malt whisky. I set the table with a linen cloth and we pulled crackers and wore paper hats and ate and drank too much and, finally, made love on the sitting-room floor.

I thought of the Christmas I'd spent at my cousin's house the previous year, a mercy guest, the oddball at the table, a spare part in the midst of the happy chaos of their family, tolerated but not really wanted.

This year, I couldn't have felt more different. I felt loved. I felt special. I felt understood.

I gave him his presents. A grey cashmere scarf. An expensive silver pen, for writing his poetry.

As well as the smart speaker, he'd bought me a gold bracelet. He'd have it engraved, he said, he just hadn't had time yet. And a book of John Clare's poetry. No inscription. I lay in his arms on the carpet, cuddled under a wool blanket, and listened as he read to me.

'"I am" is one of the most profound poems in the English language,' he declared, and bent down and kissed the tip of my nose. 'Poor John Clare. He was locked up in the loony bin when he wrote that.'

I twisted in his arms and looked up at him, at his stubbly chin and long nose and soft brown eyes.

'Love you, Ralph Wilson.'

He kissed me on the lips. 'Happy?'

'Very.' I nodded. I was but, as always, it was bittersweet. I didn't want him to leave. I didn't want him to go home to Helen and Anna. I wanted him to stay here with me. Be mine, always. 'Don't go.'

He didn't answer.

As the afternoon wore on, darkness fell outside. There was a sense of Christmas drawing in. If we were a real couple, I thought, we'd put a film on now and stay snuggled up in front of it, only stirring for more drinks and snacks.

But we weren't. He lifted my arms from around him, got up, stretched and started to dress. I lay there, anguished, watching him hunt for his clothes, find his shoes, tie the laces.

I said again, 'Don't go.'

He acted as if he hadn't heard. I sat up, the blanket tucked around the naked lower half of my body, trying to hold him here with my eyes.

'Leave her. Please, Ralph.'

I'd had too much to drink. I'd thought it, of course, during all those heady, happy weeks. I'd always had more sense than to say it. Now, it seemed, I couldn't stop myself.

'Not today. Not at Christmas,' I went on. 'In the New Year. Make a clean break. Come and live here, with me.'

'Don't spoil it, Laura.' He fastened on his watch. 'Be satisfied.'

He went off to the bathroom. When he came back, he was buttoning up his coat, picking up the shopping bag that was one of his props. He knelt down and gave me a peck on the lips.

'Merry Christmas.'

It was childish, but I was so hurt that I turned away and wouldn't say it back.

It didn't make any difference. He still left.

The moment I heard the door close, I ran out into the hall, the blanket wrapped round my waist.

'Ralph!'

In a corner, folded back inside the wrapping paper were his new cashmere scarf and silver pen. For a second, I thought he'd forgotten them. Then I realised.

He couldn't take them home. He'd never be able to do that. Helen might see.

CHAPTER 25

The day after the strange incident at my flat, I had the locks changed, just to be sure.

I didn't tell the locksmith very much, just yes, it was absolutely an emergency job. I thought I'd had an intruder at the property. And yes, I'd pay the higher call-out charge to get it done straightaway.

The man they sent round was a young, thick-set lad, Eastern European probably. He was efficient as he worked, minding his own business, and silent.

I told him anyway – well, part of the truth. I told him I was worried because I'd given an old boyfriend a set of keys and things had ended badly between us and now I was frightened. I didn't mention that things had only ended for good because I'd killed him.

He didn't answer. He opened up his metal box of tools and rummaged through it, choosing what he needed. His hands were roughened along the backs of the knuckles. A wedding ring was embedded in the pouched skin of one finger.

He worked quickly. He detached the old locks with a flurry of cascading plaster, then tore glistening new ones out of their plastic wrappers and started to fit them with an electric screwdriver.

He looked like the sort of man who would never be afraid, who would get things done, however dirty the job. While he was standing there, sorting out my locks, I felt cared for. I felt safe again.

Afterwards, he handed me two sets of keys, then tore off a receipt from a pad of white and yellow pages. I paid with cash and rounded it up for a tip.

He started to pack away his tools.

I ran my fingers over the shiny locks.

'They're strong, are they?'

He gave me a sideways look. 'Of course.'

I realised I didn't want him to go and leave me on my own again.

'I mean, a burglar would struggle to get through these, wouldn't he?'

He closed up his toolbox and spoke without looking me in the face. 'You frightened of boyfriend, you tell police.'

I didn't answer.

His feet thumped off down the stairs, heavy and fast, off to change the locks of the next frightened woman.

*

I went inside and closed the front door behind me, then stood in the hall and spent time double-locking with each key in turn, practising being safe. The door still smelled faintly of the lock-smith, the dark grease on his fingers and stale coffee. I liked that.

I wondered why he'd told me to call the police. Did he have faith in our police force, in law and order? Or was he just trying to fob me off?

You're not my problem, lady. I just fit the locks. If you're being stalked by a crazy guy, call the authorities and report him. And good luck with that call, by the way.

I went through to the kitchen. Silence. Emptiness.

I made a cup of tea and sat for a long time at the kitchen table, considering the two sets of newly cut keys.

That was the trouble, I thought. *Whatever happened now, however frightened I felt, how could I ever call the police again?*

My ex-boyfriend might be stalking me, officer. The one I killed, then helped his wife to dump at sea.

From now on, whatever happened, I was utterly on my own.

When I entered the staffroom a few days later, Hilary and Elaine were discussing whether it was appropriate to buy a card. 'Appropriate' was one of Elaine's favourite words.

'I just feel we should say something. It's awkward.' Hilary was vigorously buttering cheese biscuits, one of her new ideas for a healthy lunch. 'Maybe it would be better coming from you, Elaine. Or from John.'

Elaine pulled a face. Her range of dismissive expressions was the nearest she ever came to criticising the Lower School headteacher.

'A card would be easier,' she said. 'I've got some blank ones in my desk.'

'But what do we put?' Hilary unwrapped a chunk of yellow cheese and started to cut it into pieces and then arranged the pieces on the biscuits. She seemed determined to leave no space without cheese. 'I mean, I don't want to be crass, but is he even officially dead yet?'

Elaine opened up her own sandwiches, ham and pickle. 'We don't need to be specific. We can just say "welcome back", can't we? No harm in that.'

Hilary bit into a biscuit, spraying crumbs. 'It's a bit, well, cheerful.'

'Not necessarily. Depends how you say it. It's all about tone.'

I settled beside them.

Elaine turned to include me. 'We're just talking about poor Mrs Wilson. Anna's mother. She's coming in again this afternoon to read with the children. First time back since…'

I knew perfectly well what it was since.

'I wonder how she'll feel,' I said. 'Being here again.'

Hilary said, 'Well, she comes to the school gates every day, anyway. And at least Anna's still in the Lower School. She doesn't need to venture to the Upper School just yet.'

In my mind, I walked down an Upper School corridor and into a classroom where Ralph was sitting, perched on the front corner of a desk, a book open in his hand, reading to the class. *That voice. Melted honey.*

'So maybe a blank card?' Elaine said. 'Something simple on the front, like flowers. I'm sure I've got one. I'll just write "best wishes" inside and get some people to sign it.'

Olivia joined us, stirring a cup of instant soup. The smell of spicy tomato engulfed us all.

Hilary looked up. 'Is there any news – you know, on what happened to him?'

'Nothing I've heard.' Olivia shrugged. 'They haven't replaced him yet. Not permanently.'

'That doesn't mean anything,' Hilary scoffed. 'You know what they're like. Sarah's probably trying to save money.'

'Anyway, we're going to give Mrs Wilson a nice card. She's coming in this afternoon. It's a gesture, isn't it?' Elaine said brightly.

It was a gesture, we all agreed.

CHAPTER 26

I saw Helen take up her place on one of the settees in the school library. She settled the basket of reading books and diaries on the table at the side, then rifled through with neat, precise movements and drew one out as the first child, a girl with floppy bunches, ran in from a classroom to join her.

I was standing at the photocopier, hidden away in an alcove at a distance from the library. I'd been in the middle of running off some worksheets and I paused when I realised it was her and stood there, peering round the wall.

Helen's head craned forward, her finger bobbing along the page, guiding the girl as she started, hesitantly, to read aloud. I watched for a while. She was calm and patient, murmuring now and then, offering encouragement. When the girl finished reading and closed her book, she looked up at Helen expectantly.

Helen handed her a sheet of stickers and the girl spent time choosing one, while Helen wrote a line or two in the reading diary, then folded the reading book inside and filed them back in the basket.

The girl, attaching the sticker with care to her school cardigan, jumped up and headed back to the classroom to fetch the next reader. And so it went on.

Helen sat, waiting. She shuffled a little on the cushioned seat and crossed her legs at the knee, tapped the free foot in the air. Her hair was sharply cut as if she'd been recently to the hairdresser's.

It was hard to believe that it was the same woman who'd zipped her husband's body into a surfboard cover nearly three months earlier and headed out onto a dark sea in a dinghy to tip it overboard.

The next child, a stout boy, came sauntering out to join her, one hand in his trouser pocket and the other clutching his reading diary and book. Helen greeted him by name – she seemed to know all the children – patted the empty stretch of settee beside her and he perched there, opened his book and, prompted by her finger, he began, haltingly, to read.

I turned back to the photocopier and focussed on my work. When I was finished, the papers stacked and clipped into bundles, I glanced over towards the library settee. The boy was leaving, pressing down the sticker on his school jumper as he ran off.

'Mummy!'

Anna came dashing out, hurtling towards her mother, all excitement. Helen smiled and opened her arms wide and Anna threw herself into them, bouncing beside her on the settee. I bit my lip. I had no business, looking. There was something so intense, so intimate in that fierce embrace. I blinked. Their arms were tight around each other, Helen slightly rocking the girl as she held her against her body. Helen's face was tilted into Anna's hair as if she were inhaling its smell. Her eyes closed. There was serenity, a softness in her face that I'd never seen before.

I felt as if a veil had been lifted back and I'd seen for the first time something precious, something which, until then, I hadn't wanted to admit, even to myself. Selflessness of a kind I would never know. I gathered up the papers and turned quickly away, the floor blurring. It had been there all this time, this love at the centre of their family, I saw that now. This family I'd been instrumental in breaking apart.

CHAPTER 27

I tried my best to keep an eye on Anna from afar. Ralph had adored her. I owed it to him to look out for her, at least at school, whatever her mother thought of me.

I wanted Anna to like me, to realise she was precious to me because she was my last link to him. Those gorgeous brown eyes. That defiant tilt of the chin. The passing dreaminess in her face that mirrored his.

I'd been disappointed that she'd clearly gone straight home after our little chat in the school library and repeated to her mother exactly what I'd said. That 'secret friend' jibe of Helen's told me everything. It was hurtful. My attempt to reach out to that girl had been kindly meant. It was for Ralph's sake, as much as anything.

Since that awkward visit to her home, I pretended not to notice each time I saw Anna looking in my direction. I didn't want to give her any reason to mention me to her mother. So I did what I could, covertly. I spoke well of Anna to other members of staff, I found her stray sports shirt in a corridor and returned it to her bag in the class cloakroom without even telling her, I pushed a chocolate once into her coat pocket before home-time and let her think it a present from Clara. They were anonymous kindnesses, carried out for Ralph.

It was only natural to see her often, even if I hadn't engineered it. The Lower School wasn't such a big place. I still had playground duty on a regular basis. I couldn't help but notice when she and Clara raced and chased round the kaleidoscope of the playground, often hand in hand. They had a close bond, those two. Everyone saw it. Inseparable.

Clara was the one I decided to speak to next, in my quest to find out how Anna was coping with the loss of her father, if she needed any extra support. Whatever question I needed to ask, she was just as likely to have the answer and maybe more likely to share it.

The opportunity came easily enough. I was on playground duty, as usual, when I saw Clara hanging around, sitting in a corner, on her haunches. It was something the two of them often did. But this time Clara was all alone. She had a bit of stick and was rubbing it back and forth on the tarmac.

I headed over and crouched down low at her side.

'Hey, Clara. How's things?'

She looked up to see who it was, then turned her eyes back to her stick. 'Hello, Miss Dixon.'

Her hair was shoulder-length and, although it was only morning break, her mother's attempt to harness it into a plait was already beginning to unravel. It made me want to grab a brush, undo it and start again. More evidence, perhaps, that Bea – was that her name? – was an overwhelmed parent.

'No Anna today?'

She shrugged. 'Off sick.'

'Oh dear. I'm sorry to hear that.'

No answer. Clara carried on drawing imaginary patterns with her stick. Without Anna, she seemed lost in the seething, bubbling mass of children.

'Poor Anna. I do worry about her.' I paused. Clara tilted her head to look up at me, listening. 'She must miss her daddy terribly, I'm sure. She loved him very much.'

She looked thoughtful, her eyes on my face.

I carried on, 'Does she talk to you about it?'

She sucked her bottom lip. 'Nope.'

'No?' I pulled a face. 'But you're such good friends, Clara! You and Anna.'

She muttered under her breath, 'Best friends.'

'Well, then. Imagine how much you'd need a friend if something happened to your mummy?'

She didn't answer but I sensed her muscles tense.

'You can tell me everything, Clara. I'm a teacher. What's she said about how her mummy's feeling? About missing her daddy?'

She shook her head. 'Nothing.'

I shuffled closer, sensing her awkwardness, sensing she had something to say and was struggling to keep it hidden from me.

'Sometimes, Clara, it's okay to share secrets.' I kept my voice low and friendly. 'Especially important ones. Sometimes, that's a really grown-up thing to do. A way of helping people we really care about.'

She didn't answer. Her cheeks flushed.

I said, 'I bet she tells you everything, doesn't she, Clara? You're such good friends. Does she tell you how sad she feels?'

Her eyes widened. 'She's not sad.'

I blinked. 'Why do you say that?'

She nodded. 'She says the grown-ups are wrong.'

She broke off and turned away, embarrassed by the scrutiny.

My pulse quickened. 'Why would she say that?'

She shrugged, her mouth rigidly closed.

'Clara! This is important. What do you think she means?'

Her mouth started to crumple under the strain. She shook her head and her eyes watered.

The five-minute bell rang out. Around us, a tidal wave of pounding children came shrieking across the playground towards the line-up doors, some gliding in with arms stiff as aeroplane wings, others flapping their sleeves and mittens like wild birds.

I reached out and grabbed hold of Clara's arm. She gazed at me with frightened eyes.

'Clara, tell me.'

She froze.

'Why would she say that?'

She gawped at me, then pulled away and ran off before I could stop her to join the cloud of children and find her place in the gathering lines.

I stared after her.

What was she talking about? Had Clara made it up, for something to say? Or was that how Anna was coping, missing her father so much that she was pretending with her best friend that everything was okay and he'd come home in the end, safe and well?

I swallowed and shook my head. Something else struck me, winding me as forcefully as a blow to the stomach.

I imagined Anna, not asleep after all, woken by the crash of her father's flailing body as it bounced heavily down the cellar steps. And creeping down the stairs in her pyjamas, peering out, still half in a dream, and seeing me, standing there by the cellar door, eyes wide, stiff with shock.

What if she knew that the story about her father simply going out one evening and never coming home couldn't be true, because she'd seen what had really happened? And if that were the case, what if she told?

CHAPTER 28

We never had many arguments, Ralph and I. I wasn't the sort of person who screamed and shouted if they were angry, not usually. I was a bottler. A sulker, at times, I had to admit, if something had really upset me.

As the New Year rolled round and a new school term started, he never referred to the way I'd begged him to leave his wife that Christmas. I never mentioned it either. I gave myself a good talking to. I had to be smart, if I really cared about him. That's what I told myself. I was in for the long haul.

I tried to see this as a waiting game. My job was to make him happy. When he thought about me, and I was sure he must, I wanted the thoughts to be positive. He should imagine, first and foremost, a fun, lively woman with a smile on her face, a sexy woman who was excited to see him. I wanted to shine in his life, making a brilliant contrast with his wife and whatever problems they clearly had in their marriage. I had to attract him, not risk pushing him away from me with demands and complaints. Ralph and I had something special. I didn't want to risk messing it up.

So the few times I let myself down and we did row, I remember clearly. They stood out for me like sores. I'd berate myself and send apologetic messages, full of love hearts and promises to behave if he'd just give me a second chance. I'd barely sleep until he'd finally reply and I knew he was still going to see me again, that I hadn't gone too far and been cast off, back into darkness.

One of the biggest arguments came in late January. I hated that month. Cold, grey and dark. Christmas was already a distant memory and Spring still felt out of reach. It was a month of colds and flu, of rain and gales, a time at school when the children seemed particularly crazy because they weren't spending enough hours outside in the fresh air, running off their energy.

Ralph and I were seeing each other once or twice a week, as often as he could manage without making his wife suspicious. I never asked him what lies he told her. I thought it best not to know. He was only doing it, I told myself, because he belonged with me. He'd realise that, in time.

Our dates were often at short notice. In the beginning, that had been part of the excitement. A delicious frisson when he suddenly messaged me without warning. *You free? Can I come over?*

A nervous thrill, even on the evenings I climbed into bed without hearing from him. The hope that, even now, he might still text me or the front-door buzzer might ring to say he was unexpectedly here.

But by late January, perhaps it was just me, but something between us seemed stale. The sudden appearances, the abrupt cancellations, were actually annoying, playing havoc with my nerves. I wanted him to myself. And I was also frightened in case, for him too, the initial excitement of our affair had worn off. I feared he was getting tired, even bored.

He was acting too much like a husband with me. Most of the time, he just came round to the flat to see me and I cooked for him, poured him a glass of wine and tried to cheer him up. We might cuddle up together on the settee, rain lashing the windows, and watch my old TV together. At least once, I tilted up my head to meet his gaze at a particularly moving programme and saw, with horror, that his eyes were closed, his mouth gaping. I had to shuffle against him, pretending I was moving to get comfortable, to nudge him awake again. It worried me, afterwards. There was feeling relaxed with someone and there was downright boredom. I was on thin ice. If his time with me stopped being special, why would he bother?

That evening, when we kissed a tired goodbye at the front door, I risked something I'd been building up to for a while.

'Let's go to the theatre next week.'

He blinked, taken aback. 'The theatre?'

I forced a smile. 'I'll surprise you. You tell me which day. I'll organise the tickets.'

He looked ambushed. 'Next week? Well…'

I kissed the tip of his chin. 'Come on, don't be boring. We can't stay in all the time.'

'It's just…' He looked embarrassed, his eyes darting away from mine.

'Just what?' My disappointment made me sound cross. He used to love the theatre. I knew he did. He talked about it, about the fact that he'd gone all the time before he was married. It was one of those things he'd given up since Anna came along, out of fatherly duty.

He took hold of my hands and lifted them gently off his shoulders. 'It's complicated. I'm sorry. I just can't, not right now.'

'Why not?' I'd already looked into it. I'd chosen a play; a new one I was sure he'd love. It could be a pre-Valentine's Day treat, I'd decided, because, of course, he'd spend the real Valentine's Day with his wife.

He didn't even seem sorry. 'Look, we'll talk about it another time.'

He twisted and reached his hand to the latch to open the door. I leaned against it, getting cross.

'Don't do that.'

'What?'

'Just walk out like that. Just brush me off as if my feelings don't even matter and go rushing back to—' I could bring myself to say it. I didn't need to. We both knew.

He looked impatient. 'Not now, all right? I'm tired. Another time.'

'Another time?' Something flared inside me, some part of the growing fear that I was starting to lose him and I didn't know how to stop that happening. I snapped, 'Tell me now. Right now, before you go anywhere. Why can't we go and see a play?'

His jaw set hard. 'You know why. Because someone might see us together. And anyway, money's tight. I can't afford it, *okay*? Can I leave now?'

He shoved me sideways and was thumping out and down the steps before I could answer.

I stood at the window and watched him stride away towards the labyrinth of nearby side roads where he usually parked. My hands shook. What had I done? I'd ruined things. I'd risked everything. Just because I couldn't learn to be quiet and stay patient.

Soon enough, I was sitting on the edge of my bed, phone in hand, texting apologies.

I'm so sorry. Really. Of course I understand. xxx

Silence. I paced round the flat, tidying away the dinner dishes and washing up our wine glasses. I couldn't believe how stupid I'd been. It was pride, that was all. Wanting to have too much of him for myself. Wanting to push for more, instead of appreciating what I had.

I shut the dishwasher and ran back to find my phone. No answer. He'd be driving now, heading home.

I texted again:

Text when ur home. So I know ur safe. Love u xxx

No reply.

*

I spent the night worrying. Why had I gone for him like that? What if he was angry, really angry? What if he was getting tired of me? I was stupid, stupid, stupid. I lay, staring at the ceiling, trying to read the shadows.

He had a lot of financial responsibility. I'd never thought about it before. But, of course, he was shouldering all the costs on his own. Helen didn't work. Food, household bills, clothes, petrol, everything Anna needed. It must be a worry. How could I have been so selfish, so insensitive?

The next day, I struggled to concentrate in the classroom, to keep my good humour with a restless gang of year threes. During breaks, I hurried to check my phone for messages. Nothing. At lunchtime, I considered making a dash up the hill to the Upper School to see if I could catch a word alone with him or even just give him a reassuring smile. There was simply no time.

It wasn't until the end of the Lower School day that a message finally came through.

luv u 2 xxx

Thank God. I could breathe again.

CHAPTER 29

It was a Friday. I'd already presided over a class assembly, taught fractions and then survived making a Viking long-boat.

Now, I was sitting on my own in a corner of the staffroom with a cup of tea, reading, when James Deacon, one of the young sports teachers, came over, a sheaf of papers in his hand. He stopped right in front of me.

I purposefully didn't look up at first. He was one of the so-called cool crowd – the young, recently qualified teachers who shouted across the staffroom to each other using silly nicknames and even played pranks when the rest of us were trying our best to have a break from childlike behaviour. They went out together socially at the weekends and made sure, from their loud conversations about it, that we all were aware of their antics. Olivia joined them on occasion.

'Laura?'

I let my eyes slide up from my page, hoping I didn't flush.

He was smiling at me, all politeness. 'I'm afraid I've stolen your mail again. So sorry.'

'That's okay.' I reached for the white envelope he was offering me. He'd started to tear open the corner by mistake, that was all. We were the only Lower School teachers with a surname beginning with 'D' and our post was often wrongly pushed into each other's pigeonholes, thanks to the fact that our school secretary, Jayne, wasn't as careful as she should be.

'Hope it hasn't been sitting there too long.' He grinned as he turned away with the rest of his envelopes. 'I'm a bit behind with all this paperwork. I'd rather be teaching.'

I nodded after him, then slid a fingertip under the seal, ripped open the envelope and drew out the papers inside. A printed form from the photographic company, inviting me to place orders for everything from large mounted prints to coasters and mugs. I shook my head. I didn't blame them for trying, but still.

I turned over the adverts and flyers and finally reached the sample copy of the full school photograph itself. I never ordered actual pictures, but the proofs were good to keep, just as a souvenir of the passing years. Especially now. Maybe this would be my last here.

I inclined it to catch the light and ran my eye along the glossy surface, covered with the word SAMPLE in giant lettering, just in case I was tempted to run off a few copies of my own and sell them on the side.

I found myself first, standing neatly to one side, close to the end of the year ones, my body angled towards the camera, my hands hidden by Hilary, standing just ahead and to one side of me. I liked the dress I'd chosen. It had a flattering neckline, good for photos, but even at this distance, I could see how tired I looked. There was something in the slump of my shoulders, the tightness of my face that suggested how haunted I was. I wondered if the police had a copy, if they'd be scanning it for signs of stress and guilt.

My eye ran across the very front row and the reception children sitting on the grass, some beaming, some shy, one or two pulling silly faces. Sarah Baldini wouldn't like that. There she was, sitting neatly in her starched blouse and calf-length skirt, her make-up immaculate, front and centre of it all, a queen ruling over her subjects.

I tipped the photo further into the light to have a better look at the other teachers who were arranged down the sides, rising with each tier of pupils until they formed their own line right along the very back. Then my eyes strayed, rising to the edge of the Upper School building in the background.

My hand shook. My breath stuck in my throat. I pulled the picture closer and stared, feeling my heart bang so hard in my chest that it hurt. My eyes strained. It wasn't possible. Was that what I thought it was? Were my eyes playing tricks on me?

I looked up sharply, my lips dry, expecting to see someone sniggering from across the staffroom, looking over at me. No one paid me the slightest attention. Fridays always brought a relaxed, anticipatory mood, even here in the staffroom. All I saw were other teachers standing idly around in small groups, chatting, their backs to me. Some sat at tables with cups of tea and coffee, sharing snacks. Others, here and there, had heads bent low as they tapped and swiped on their phones. No one seemed aware that I existed.

I hunched forward again over the photograph and stared. That shadowy figure standing by the window, looking down at the rest of the school below from a second-floor classroom. Wasn't that Ralph? His face was a darkened blur. Impossible to make out his features. But something struck me with force, something about the angle of his head, the haircut, his shape of his shoulders and upper body. Why did I think it was him? I blinked. It was impossible. What was wrong with me? Was I going mad?

The photograph swam and blurred and I wiped my eyes, struggling to focus again on the indistinct, shadowy figure hiding in the shadows, looking down on the assembled school.

How could I even imagine that? How could I think the man I'd killed had come back from the dead?

CHAPTER 30

I sat there for some time, struggling to steady myself. Finally, I opened my eyes and looked again at the photograph in my hand.

Could someone have doctored it, just this one copy? I looked again at the printed name label on the front of the large envelope. My name. My staff details. This was meant for me.

I examined with my fingertip the flap that I'd torn open. It was one of those commercial, self-sealing flaps. My brain whirred. Surely it was possible that someone had altered a copy of the photograph, then prised open the envelope in my pigeon-hole and swapped the faked image for the original one. Wasn't it? Someone who had access to school during the working day, who could pop along to the ranks of pigeon-holes outside the staffroom without attracting attention. Someone who knew too much about what happened and wanted to scare me witless.

I looked at my hands, still shaking. If that was the case, they were doing a pretty good job.

I pushed the picture and the other papers back into the envelope, shoved it all into the depths of my bag and fled for the door. I almost bumped into Hilary who was just coming in.

'Where's the fire?' Her teeth gleamed but her smile didn't reach her eyes. I hesitated, staring at her. What did she know? What did any of them know?

I pushed past, muttering an apology and took the stairs two at a time, then ran out of the side door of the building and down to the Lower School car park, fumbling for my car keys as

I went. I yanked open the driver's door of my car and fell inside, then pulled out my phone and the flyer with the photographer's details. I leaned forward against the hard rim of the steering wheel and stared wildly at the screen of my phone as I punched in the website address, then the code for the school's shoot and finally the staff password to give me access.

I sat, heart pounding, palms clammy, and stared at my phone, waiting an eternity for the photograph to load. *Go on, for heaven's sake. Please. Help me out, here.*

Finally, the pixels fell into place and the picture formed. I tapped on the screen and splayed my fingertips to zoom in as closely as I could on the Upper School building in the background. There he was. That shadow of a man, a step or two back from the window, concealing himself as he watched. I only realised how tightly I'd been holding my breath when it came rushing out again like air from a punctured balloon. He reminded me of Ralph. He really did.

The slightly turned head. That hairline I'd so often stroked, the soft skin along that neck. It was him. I couldn't prove it. It was too blurry, breaking up already into nothing but pixels. But I felt it.

I fumbled in my bag for tablets and swallowed a couple down. I didn't know quite how I was getting through them so fast, but I was running out. I'd need to go online for more.

I sat back and closed my eyes, seeing pulses of multi-coloured light floating across blackness. Chemicals coursed through my veins, calming my racing heart. What, then? It wasn't just my copy. It was on the original photograph.

But what did it mean? Had he been there? Of course not. It was nonsense. It was madness. I was starting to doubt my own senses, my own sanity. It was a coincidence. Just like the random text messages from that unknown number. Just like the strange feeling I'd had inside my flat.

*

That evening, I couldn't eat. I sat in silence in the sitting room with the school photograph propped up against an open book on the table in front of me and stared at the tiny, half-obscured figure. It burned into my eyes.

Suddenly, I felt a rush of hopelessness, of self-pity for the person I'd become. So shy and constrained, all the more so in the years since I moved to this city. My life had become so inward-looking. I'd been so focussed on Matthew and our life together, so determined to please him, to make it work, that I'd suffocated him. Then, when he tore a ragged, bleeding hole in my life, I'd withdrawn and focussed just on myself, nursing my own quietness and awkwardness.

Then Ralph came to rescue me from myself. And what had I done to him?

I thought again about the strange shadow in the photograph, the figure which looked so very like him that it tormented me, about the trace of his own, unique smell inside my flat. There was only one person I could imagine who would try so carefully to hurt me, to drive me to destruction.

Helen.

I grabbed my coat and car keys and drove, as fast as I could, to Ralph's house.

The light was mellow and starting to fade by the time I'd parked in my usual place and rounded the corner. Usually, I crept like a burglar along the pavement to their home. This time, I strode. I pushed open the gate and marched boldly to the front door, then pressed the buzzer. My heart was hard in my chest. I felt giddy, out of control, gripped by some determination that was strange to me. Silence. I rapped loudly on the shiny wood with tight knuckles. Waited. Listened for footsteps which didn't come.

The curtains hung open and I crossed to stand on the gravel, a low tangle of rose bushes grasping for my socks and trouser legs, and peered in. I pitched forward and put my hands on the white wood windowsill to steady myself. It was dingy inside, shadows creeping through the sitting room and slowly engulfing it. The television was dark. A streak of light gleamed on the large darkening mirror hanging over the fireplace.

I cupped my hands to my face, nose close to the glass, and strained to see further. The sitting room led through to the kitchen and the small downstairs toilet, I knew the layout only too well. But that too lay in darkness. I pulled back, leaving a wet smear on the window where my hot breath had condensed. I returned to the path and backed to the gate, then stared up at the windows on the first floor.

The curtains stood open. Ralph and Helen's bedroom lay over the sitting room, Anna's next to it on the same landing. No sign of life from either.

I frowned. It was too early for them to be asleep in bed but too late surely for them to be still out. I stood at the gate, thinking. The adrenalin rush which had propelled me to dash over here and confront Helen had ebbed away now into exhaustion. My legs felt suddenly a dead weight. All I wanted really was to feel peaceful, to go home and curl up in bed, take a couple more tablets to calm my nerves and sleep. But I couldn't go home, not yet. My mind was too agitated.

An engine throbbed into life, close by. I turned to look. A parked car, across the road from their house and further down the street, flashed its headlights. At me? I looked round, warily. The street was deserted.

I moved cautiously down towards it, watching. As I approached, the lights and engine clicked off and the car, a crimson saloon, sat again in darkness. I crept towards it.

He was sitting inside, in the driver's seat, looking right at me. It was the man I'd seen before, reading his newspaper at the bus stop near my flat and here in this road, parked watchfully in this same car. I stopped, pinned by his gaze. This was the nearest I'd been to him and, instinctively, I was afraid.

He was about fifty. His face was tight and weather-beaten as if he were used to an active, outdoor life. He looked almost entirely bald. Whatever hair still grew must be close-shaven. Without hair, his ears jutted out, one more than the other, which gave his head a lopsided look. His chin and upper lip were dark with stubble. But all this hit me as secondary. I was transfixed by his eyes, hooded and dark and regarding me with a calm, unflinching gaze. They were eyes which looked as if they'd seen sights he could never share.

I couldn't move. I didn't want to get any closer. I expected him to turn the key in the ignition at any moment and drive off, leaving me staring after him.

He didn't. Instead, he pressed a button to disarm the central locking system and gestured to me to come to the passenger door.

I hesitated. His eyes bore into mine.

A moment later, he lowered the electric window.

'You getting in, or what?' His voice was low and rasping.

I couldn't move. I was frightened now, wondering why I didn't turn and simply run back to the safety of my car in the next street.

'Offer's there.' He shrugged. 'Suit yourself.'

The window rose again and he shifted in his seat, turned his eyes down to the book which was open in his large, meaty hands, resting on the steering wheel. The moment his eyes left my face, I felt a sense of release. I breathed again, then looked round. No one.

I crept toward him, reached for the handle, opened the car door and climbed cautiously into the seat beside him, carefully leaving the door ajar, my hand now on the inside handle, so he couldn't lock it and seal off my escape.

He put down his book again and the eyes slid round to me. His tone was weary. 'Go on, then.'

The car smelled of old chip fat and stale, greasy meat. A dirty coffee cup sat in the cup holder. A nodding plastic unicorn was stuck to the dashboard, its flank decorated with a glittery rainbow.

A St Christopher hung from the rear-view mirror, dangling on a chain. I had the sense that I'd entered not just his car but his hideout, his world.

I moistened my lips and tried to decide how to start. I felt uneasy and far out of my depth. I didn't understand who he was, why he was here, why I needed to talk to him. There was a latent power in him that frightened and attracted me at the same time. This was a man I wanted on my side, whatever that meant. This was a man who would know the answers to the questions in my head. I sensed his impatience. He seemed to be making a supreme effort to restrain himself.

I took a deep breath. 'What are you doing here?'

He lifted his book. 'Reading.'

I narrowed my eyes. 'But why are you here? I keep seeing you. Hanging around. Waiting in the street. Spying.'

He pulled a face, as if to suggest that what I'd just said really wasn't very polite.

'Believe me,' he said, 'if I hadn't wanted you to see me, you wouldn't have.'

I frowned. 'What does that mean?'

'Just that.'

He looked at me levelly. His eyes were a cool grey with streaks of blue and green radiating from the pupils. This close, he looked older than I'd first thought. Sixty, maybe. His skin was heavily creased and although he was lean and muscular, the flesh under his eyes gathered in dark pouches.

'Why though?'

He pulled a face. 'It's my job. That's all.'

I blinked. 'Spying on me?'

He looked back, unruffled. 'On you. On her.'

I hesitated. Everything in his manner was direct. It was impossible not to believe him. But the car, the way he was sitting here all alone, hour after hour, it didn't make sense to me. 'Are you a detective?'

He raised an eyebrow. 'Not really. Put it this way. What they do is all about justice. I respect that. I used to do that once. But not now. Now I'm about cash. See?'

I said, 'A private detective?'

'If you like. Your words, not mine.'

I bit my lip. There was something about him. An edge. A darkness.

I nodded across towards the house. 'Where are they?'

'Not there.'

I narrowed my eyes, thinking about Anna. 'They're okay, though? Safe?'

He nodded. 'Safe enough. They won't be back tonight. Friday. Sleepover. With that little pal of hers.'

'Clara?'

'Pigtails. Thin kid. Comes home for tea after school every afternoon till her mum comes for her.'

'That's Clara. Clara Higgins.'

'Right.' He seemed to make a mental note, slotting away another fact. 'Well, Friday night, it's pay-back time. See? Once the mum's home from work, they troop round to her place. Free wine, free pizza, free film to soak up some of that free babysitting.'

I bristled. 'I'm sure they don't think of it like that.'

He said, 'Well, they ought to. Everything's got a price. Even friendship. Don't make that mistake.'

I blinked, considering. 'So why are you here, then? What're you waiting for?'

'You.'

CHAPTER 31

Silence.

His eyes seemed to take in my confusion. There was no movement there, just absorption. *How would he know I'd come here tonight? I hadn't known myself.* Was he making fun of me? I didn't know.

After a while, he adjusted his weight in his seat and said, 'So, are you done? Is it my turn to ask the questions now?'

I pushed the car door with my foot and it opened another few inches.

'What sort of questions?'

'What was the score? With you and Wilson?'

'Nothing.' I said it too forcefully. Too obvious. I felt myself flush. 'We were colleagues, that's all.'

'Just colleagues.' His manner was cool. *What did he know?* 'Right.'

I hesitated, stammered, 'Well, and friends, I suppose. I went to his writing group now and then. We'd go out for drinks occasionally.'

He shook his head and there was a sadness in his look, as if he were trying very hard to be nice to me and I was disappointing him.

'Miss Dixon.'

I started. I hadn't expected him to use my name.

'I'm not the morality police, here. You and Wilson fancying the pants off each other, the two of you having an affair, to be honest, I couldn't care less. Life is for living, okay? So let's get that out of the way. Adultery isn't a criminal offence, not the last time I looked. We're all grown-ups. Just don't tell the missus I said so, okay?' His lips twitched in the faintest suggestion of a smile.

I wondered if he really had a long-suffering wife or if it was just a mind game. I wondered what it would be like, being married to a man like him. *Safe. Always safe.* There was a roughness about him that made me certain he wouldn't think twice about doing what needed to be done to protect the people he loved, to protect his honour, within or outside the law. I looked at the rainbow-flanked unicorn. Maybe he was a family man, after all. Maybe he had grown-up children, even a granddaughter.

I wasn't going to admit to anything. I wasn't that stupid. But I had the sense, sitting with him, that I didn't really need to tell him very much. He seemed to have the answers already. 'I don't know what you mean,' I said.

'Of course you don't.' He sighed, slipped his paperback into the door's side pocket and turned more fully to face me. 'I wonder how well you knew Ralph Wilson, Miss Dixon? I mean, really knew him?'

I didn't answer.

'Did you trust him?' He shook his head, sadly. 'He was trouble, Miss Dixon. Some men just can't help themselves, it seems to me. One woman's never enough. They don't care who they hurt. And the riskier it gets, the more they like it.'

I stared at him. I wanted to say he was talking nonsense, that Ralph wasn't like that. I thought about the theatre and that stupid argument. The excuse which had pierced my heart, which had stayed with me. He didn't want to be seen in public with me. I was a dirty secret who might contaminate his family. *Someone might see us and tell my wife.*

Why hadn't I made more of a fuss? Demanded to know where I stood? I knew why. I had been afraid of losing him.

I imagined Ralph, my Ralph, with other women. Olivia, perhaps. I'd seen him looking, his eyes roving across those long legs. And with *her*, leading him on shamelessly after he'd broken it off with me.

'You deserved better, Miss Dixon.' His eyes were on my face, studying me. 'Really.'

I bent forwards, suddenly very dizzy. Had Ralph really been a *type*, a serial womaniser who couldn't help himself? It was hard to hear. Had he never truly loved me the way I'd loved him?

The man beside me pointed back along the pavement to an elderly man who was approaching us at a shuffle on a walking-frame.

'You might want to shut the door,' he said. 'That fella's going to struggle to get past.' He gave that thin half-smile again. 'Besides, there's an awful draught.'

I closed the door and sat very still in my seat, facing out through the windscreen, the unicorn square in my sights. I waited until the old man had dragged himself past us, then turned back to him. He was sitting quietly, watching me, watching the cogs inside my head turning, waiting to see what I was going to say next. I had the feeling that nothing and no one would ever catch him by surprise.

'Who do you work for?'

He nodded as if to say, *now, that's a sensible question.*

'Insurance people.' He kept his eyes on me. 'Life insurance. Like I said, I'm all about the cash. And I'll tell you something for nothing about insurance companies. First thing, they'll take a hit if they really have to but they'd rather not. Second thing, they don't play nice. They'll throw good money after bad, trying to avoid a pay-out. Go figure.'

'So that's what you're here for?' I hesitated. 'To stop Helen getting any money?'

He looked at me thoughtfully, as if I were turning into a promising pupil. 'Early days. I'm here to check it out. She's stopped the payments on his policy, see? Filed a missing person notice. That's stage one. So the company wants to know what's been going on, before they get any further. Next thing you know, she'll be trying to claim.' He shrugged, responding to the look on my face. 'It's a tough business, but a fella's gotta eat. Ask the missus.'

'But Helen will need money, don't you see? She doesn't work. And there's Anna.'

He nodded. 'Don't I know it.'

I bit my lip. 'Even if he did, you know… if he wasn't always faithful…'

'Go on.'

'What's that got to do with his life insurance? They'll still have to pay out, won't they? I mean, eventually?'

He widened his eyes. 'Oh, you'd be surprised. There's all sort of loopholes. I've just got to find one.'

My voice sharpened. 'You don't care what you do, do you? You don't care how you get your money. You'd stop a grieving widow and her little girl getting the money they need.'

'Like I said, a fella's gotta eat.' He didn't look offended, just thoughtful as if he were analysing my sudden flash of anger and considering what it meant. 'And, I wonder… grieving widow?' He raised a questioning eyebrow.

I hesitated, my pulse quickening.

'Something about all this missing person business,' he said with care. 'I don't know. Something just doesn't add up. Know what I mean?'

For a while, the silence hung heavily. He was motionless and, although I was so close to him, he made no noise at all. This was his skill. He seemed able to turn himself to stone for minutes, hours, days, if he needed to. I thought about how matter-of-fact he was, how knowing. Justice wasn't what mattered, he'd said. Only cash. Was he a man who'd do anything if the money was good enough and the risk low? I suspected so.

For my part, my pulse banged in my ears and my fingers twitched on the hard seats.

Finally he said, 'For one thing, there's the fact we don't have the body yet. Until we do, it's hard to know for sure what happened. And then, there's the wife. Mrs W.'

'What about her?'

'Her alibi.' He paused. 'It's a bit fishy, if you'll pardon the expression.'

I blinked and looked away. It was too much. I wanted to get out, to drive home, to pour myself a large glass of wine and get away from this man's all-knowing eyes. But I needed to know. I needed to understand how much he really knew. Or I'd never feel safe.

I thought about Helen, standing at the front door, staring at me in disbelief – about the way she'd prostrated herself over his body, wailing. About the way she'd forced herself to become calm, to make her mind work, as I vomited into the downstairs toilet. About the fact we'd driven Ralph's body down to the coast and sailed out to sea to dump it.

I said, 'What alibi?'

He sighed. 'She was at a parents' talk at school. No question about that. Dozens of people saw her there. Her husband was home with the little girl. Then she went home and took over from him. A school mum dropped her off. That friend's mum. Did you say Clara Higgins?'

I nodded.

'Well, Mrs W says her husband headed out as soon as she walked in the door. Must've been waiting for her to get back, ready for the off. She was a devoted mum, everyone says so. Meticulous. Low risk. Did everything by the book. Not the type to leave a seven-year-old on her own at night, right?'

I managed another nod. His eyes were sharp on my face. 'And then there's the texts.'

'The texts?'

'His missus sent a storm of texts to her husband, some barely ten minutes apart. They're all there. She starts off polite and a bit apologetic, asking where he's gone, whether he's okay. Typical wife stuff.' He pulled a knowing face. 'Then she starts to get worried. Frantic, even, by the end.'

I didn't move. My mouth was dry as stone.

He hesitated, his eyes on mine. 'Thing is, they were all sent from home from about twenty minutes after Mrs Higgins dropped her back. They ping off exactly the right mast. So she was there that whole night, all right, and the police have ruled her out. They'll lose interest soon. Mark it down as suicide or accidental, body or no body, and move on. Fella's a bit down, drinks too much, sets off on a long walk and does something daft. And you know what that means? Mrs W can start the clock, ticking down the years until the courts say he's dead. That's when she gets her hands on the insurance cash, see.'

I struggled to take all this in. How could Helen possibly have been sending all those texts from her house when she was at the coast with me? Even if Anna had been awake and willing to play a game like that, she was seven years old and a middling student. She could barely spell. And Bea Higgins must have been back at her own home by then, taking over from the babysitter who was looking after Clara.

'But you know what bothers me?'

I shake my head.

'Here's a man who's played around.' He lifted his hand as if to silence me. 'No offence. No judgement. Sorry to say, but seems to me, from all the gossip I've heard at school, that it's a fact. So why would his wife be so surprised if he disappeared for a few hours? Doesn't he do it all the time? He must do.'

He leaned forward to me, his grey eyes flashing in the low light.

'So why's she sending so many texts? Just feels a bit too neat, to me, you know? Almost as if someone's trying a bit too hard. See what I mean?'

Bile rose in my throat. I needed to get away, to be alone somewhere I could think through everything he'd said and work out how much he really knew. I twisted away from him and yanked open the car door.

'Before you go,' he reached out and put a warm, strong hand on my shoulder, 'you're quite sure there's nothing you'd like to tell me?'

I turned back to him, wide-eyed, and shook my head.

He nodded, slowly and deliberately, then lifted his hand from my shoulder. *Those eyes.*

'Did I tell you my name? Don't think I did. Mike. Mike Ridge.'

He held out a hand for me to shake. It was hard and strong, the kind of hand that could choke the life out of me, with little effort. I shuddered.

He reached inside his jacket and drew out a printed business card.

'If you find yourself in a mess, like poor old Ralph did – down some hole that's getting so deep, you know you'll never escape – you call me. I might be able to help.' He gave me a final, thin smile. 'Well, if the price is right.'

I snatched the card. My last sights, as I scrambled, flailing, out of the car, were of the St Christopher swinging on its chain and the unicorn steadily nodding its springy horned head.

CHAPTER 32

I was getting drunk. It was all I could do. I'd raced home and double-locked all the shiny new locks on the front door, then added the safety chain. Now I was slumped on the settee, under a blanket, drinking red wine.

Mike's card lay on the coffee table beside the emptying bottle and the school photograph. I'd turned it upside down now, hiding the picture from view. I couldn't bear to see it, couldn't stand to think about what it meant.

I thought about Helen and Bea, sharing dinner, maybe watching a film together. I'd thought Ralph's wife such a loser, such a control freak, with her neat home and all those bookshelves, so carefully arranged in sections, each section in alphabetical order.

Once a librarian, always a librarian, Ralph had said when I asked him about it. It was probably as much as he'd ever said about her. He made it clear, always, that she was off limits.

At the time, I was just glad that the two of them were so different. I never did understand how someone as bohemian and romantic as he was could ever have been attracted to an uptight woman with the mind of a railway clerk.

Now I wondered about her, all over again. All the times I'd seen her at school, the woman who clipped neatly down corridors with her hair clean and well-styled, always dressed in a way which was slightly old-fashioned but presentable, sitting, back straight, on the school library settee, listening to a procession of children come to her, one at a time, to read. Doling out her little stickers as rewards.

I'd dismissed her as nothing. A small-town librarian who'd become a house-proud stay-at-home mother with a failing marriage. I'd blamed her for Ralph's affair with me. It was her fault for failing to be enough for him.

I raised the glass to my lips and drank. The wine was rich and heady. My empty stomach gurgled and protested. How had she possibly covered her tracks, if Mike was right? And how, in heaven's name, had she organised all those texts?

When I stared across the dark room, I saw Mike's eyes, cold and grey and all-knowing. Could I trust him? No, trust wasn't the right word. Of course I didn't trust him. He was a force of darkness. A man who'd do anything for money. He'd said as much himself.

But I did believe him. He was terrifying because he was so direct, so real. He wasn't a man who wasted energy in deceptions. I don't know how I was so sure of that, I just knew.

Clearly, he suspected me. He already seemed to know far too much about me and my affair with Ralph. I just wondered how much more he knew. If he had any idea what else Ralph had done.

I've thought such a lot about how it ended. What he did before he died was wrong, terribly wrong. I'd never have thought him capable. But I'd have stood by him, if he'd only been honest with me. If he'd been repentant and asked for my forgiveness. I'd have tried to help him find a way out.

My first sense of the end came where it had all begun, at the writing group.

It was supposed to be a group just for members of staff. That was made crystal clear from the start. I remember reading Ralph's flyer on the Lower School noticeboard when it first went up at the start of the school year. It was eye-catching, with small photographs of famous writers forming a giant question mark after the words, *Interested in writing?* The pupils had their own clubs and classes and workshops. This was for us, for staff. It just happened to be held on school premises because that made practical sense.

Once I'd started seeing Ralph, I only went along to the group occasionally. It was partly because I felt so hopelessly focussed on Ralph, and he on me, that I thought our colleagues would guess our secret at once, especially when he started reading. He always made me feel as if his love poetry was written just for me. Then there was the awkward fact that I didn't write. It wasn't a requirement and I wasn't the only person who went along just to listen but once or twice, others had been called upon to overcome their anxiety and to share — and someone even suggested an impromptu session of flash fiction. Just the thought of that left me hot with embarrassment.

But by the end of January, I was frightened. Ralph had changed towards me. His text messages were far fewer and when I texted him, he sometimes took hours, even a day, to reply. When he came to see me, I tried to dote on him, buying him the best food and wine I could afford and, when he sat, dull-eyed, on the settee after eating, I'd try to give him scalp or shoulder massages to ease the tension. He seemed less interested in making love to me too. Clearly, something else was on his mind.

I agonised about it and decided in the end to start coming regularly to the writing group again, partly as a chance to spend time with him, and partly to show him how much I loved his poetry, one of his great passions. I didn't tell him beforehand. I wanted to see his face when he saw me walk in, to enjoy his surprise.

I dressed with particular care for school that first morning, picking out my best pencil skirt and a pink blouse. I had butterflies all day as I tried to keep my mind on teaching. Excited nerves, just as a woman should feel before a special date. Several times,

I reached for my phone, thinking I'd message him. Every time, I ended up pushing it back into my bag, laughing at myself. I was so bad at surprises, but I was determined to keep this one!

After the final bell, I hung behind in the deserted classroom, instead of heading to the staffroom. The class smelled of glue and disinfectant, of wax crayons and paint. I closed the door, then tidied up the book corner and washed down the arts and crafts tables. Afterwards, I hid myself away at the teacher's desk and tried to focus on marking a pile of year three's stories until the Upper School too finally ended its day and I could head up the hill to join the group there.

I forced myself to drag my feet and make sure I'd only arrived at the classroom after the start of the first reading, usually an honour given to Ralph because it was his group. All the way along the corridor, my heart thudded. It was a painful nervousness. The tension of looking for someone you know to be hiding, someone who might jump out at you at any moment. But there was excitement too. I thought about that first time I'd come looking for the group and the way he'd broken off his reading and come to the door, called to me, with such a look of delight as he ushered me inside. Then read to me, just to me.

Several things happened all at once as I arrived at the classroom. As I reached for the handle, I realised with a jump that it wasn't Ralph reading. It was a young woman, her blonde hair cut into a bob. She was sitting on the edge of the staff desk, wearing an absurdly short skirt, hitched up by her posture to reveal endlessly long legs dangling over the edge. Her feet, in low heels, rested jauntily on the seat of a wooden chair. Ralph, sitting right beside her, looked captivated. He was gazing at her with a rapt expression, akin to adoration.

As I entered, he turned to see but instead of delight, I saw a shadow of irritation cross his face. He gestured me to a seat impatiently, then turned back to pay homage to the young woman.

I slumped into a chair and scrutinised her. I hadn't seen her
before. A teaching assistant, perhaps, or a graduate student on
teaching placement? Her voice was strong and confident as she
read her poetry. Her skin was so clear that it looked translucent.
It seemed bare of make-up. Her hands, shaking where she held
her poem, showed long, slender fingers and neat nails. No nail
varnish. No rings.

When she reached the end, she lowered the paper and looked
round, half-smiling, her large blue eyes nervous.

Ralph lifted his hands at once and clapped. 'Bravo!'

The six or so others in the room joined in with half-hearted
applause. I shook my head, sickened and embarrassed for him.
We never clapped at this group. Never.

Ralph reached out a hand and helped her jump down off the
edge of the desk as if he were a knight guiding her down from
a horse.

'Amazing, Meg! Well done!'

Meg? My insides twisted.

He took care to settle her into a seat, close to Olivia, as if he
were handing over a treasure for safekeeping. *Why such a fuss?*

When he read his own work, he addressed some spot at the
back of the classroom, declaiming his unrequited love to somewhere north of year ten's map of the United States of America.
I sat, rigid, listening with misery, feeling utterly ignored. Even
Olivia, whispering now and then to the young woman at her
side, didn't deign to look in my direction.

At the end of the session, I stayed in my seat and waited to see
what would unfold. I wasn't willing to walk away without seeing
him and finding out who this young woman was.

Ralph was all attention, helping her on with her coat, asking
what she'd thought of the session.

I watched and didn't leave. As he ushered her towards the
door, I followed him.

'Ralph?'

He turned at last, forced to acknowledge me.

I put my hand out to the young woman. 'Hi. Laura Dixon. I don't think we've met?'

She had the grace to blush and hesitated, looking at my hand as if she didn't know what to do. Ralph stepped in. 'This is Megan. She's in my English set. She's just had an offer from Edinburgh. To read English. Obviously.' He smiled down at her. 'She's a very talented writer.'

She gazed at his face as he praised her as if he were a prince. *Her prince.* My fingers curled.

'Well, Megan.' I could hardly get out the words. 'Well done, you! You must have worked very hard.'

Ralph managed to tear himself away from her face for long enough to give me a parting glance.

'Look, sorry, I must go.' He pulled an apologetic face. 'I promised I'd give Meg a lift home.'

*

I stared after them as they hurried away together to the Upper School car park where Ralph's car was waiting. I thought of those long, elegant legs sliding into the passenger seat beside him, the short skirt riding up even higher, his hand reaching over to caress them. *Ah, she has legs!*

I put my phone on the seat beside me as I drove home, waiting for a message. Nothing. At home, I paced up and down the flat, opened a bottle of wine and began to drink. My body was tight with fury. How dare he humiliate me like that. With a schoolgirl. A girl in his own class. Had he gone mad? What was he thinking? They'd fire him on the spot, if anyone found out.

Gradually, as the wine took hold of my senses, my anger melted away to misery. I sprawled on the settee, on my bed, on the floor, tearful and despairing. *Ralph, was this it? Have you really moved on?*

At two in the morning, unable to sleep, I broke down and sent him a series of rambling texts.

I love you. Don't do this.
She's so young, too young for you.
Can't you see? They'll finish you if they find out. You'll never teach again.
Don't do this, please.
I love you so much.

Silence and again silence.

CHAPTER 33

I was always a fool for love. Perhaps I should have been more like Helen and bided my time. Perhaps if I hadn't said anything, if I hadn't done anything, the infatuation would simply have passed. Megan would be off to start a new life in Edinburgh soon enough.

But I couldn't. Besides, it was simply wrong. She was a child, a schoolgirl. He was her teacher. It was abuse, plain and simple. It would ruin him.

I didn't hear from him after that evening, not for days. Every minute hurt. I couldn't sleep. I could barely eat. The face in the mirror each morning was haggard.

At work, Elaine and Hilary whispered together when they saw me sitting alone in the staffroom, pretending to read a book. Elaine took me aside at one point and said she was worried about me, was everything all right?

I went to the doctor. Just to appease Elaine and stop them talking.

'I can't sleep,' I told the doctor. 'I feel panicky. I need something to calm my nerves.'

She gave me a cursory examination, then sat down heavily and turned to me, sober-faced, all white coat and stethoscope, trying her best to bond with me in the remaining two minutes of our ten-minute slot.

'I can offer some medication that might help,' she said. 'But it's only a temporary fix. If there are underlying causes...'

The word 'depression' hung heavily in the air between us, unvoiced.

I left with a repeat prescription, a promise to go back in three months' time for a review and a bunch of printed leaflets about healthy eating, managing stress and counselling services. I dropped the leaflets in the bin on the way out.

I fell to messaging him every evening. After a glass of wine or two, the pain became unbearable. My texts grew incoherent. Begging. I was humiliating myself. I knew it and I hated him for it. I hated her. My imagination drew pictures of the two of them together, his broad, middle-aged body, her immature one, the fresh white skin, the firm breasts, the legs. It was obscene.

I tortured myself. He couldn't do this. To leave me for another woman, another adult, that would be painful enough. But this, this madness, it wasn't love, it was criminal.

I sent him all manner of texts. Angry. Threatening. Pleading. Most of all, late at night, desperate and full of loving forgiveness.

Please. I love you. I'll do anything. Answer me. Come and see me. We need to talk about this. Please.

An endless cycle of scolding and cajoling. Message after message, spent on empty air. I wondered if he even still used his Romeo phone or if he'd thrown it away. If he'd bought a new burner phone for her. For Megan. I wondered what name he used with her.

His silence tormented me.

The only thing that kept me functioning were the doctor's tablets. I stocked up, asking for repeat prescriptions before I really needed them, and stashed them everywhere, within easy reach, in my handbag, in the car, in the bathroom cabinet, in my bedside table.

I wasn't a fool. I never took more than two at a time. I'd read the dire warnings inside the packet. But I needed them. It was my only chance of getting any sleep at night.

CHAPTER 34

The middle of February. Half-term. A week away from school.

I already knew that Ralph and his family were going on holiday to Portugal. Helen, with her librarian's efficiency, booked everything at least a year in advance. Since the autumn, when Ralph and I first got together, I'd dreaded it, thinking how forsaken I'd feel while they were away together, imagining them having candlelit dinners, sharing a bottle of wine, playing happy families with Anna. Even though I knew their marriage was a sham, it would hurt.

Now I was almost glad. If he was away from me for a week, at least he was away from her too, from Megan. At least I had that.

I spent the week at home, reading in my flat, taking long walks along the river and through the park, trying not to dwell on everything that had happened, trying not to think about Ralph.

The daffodils were out, sudden spikes of yellow along the tree-lined paths through the park. The bushes would soon come into sticky bud. The sunshine, still weak, was tempting people out into the open again after the long, cold hibernation. Elderly couples, well-wrapped in coats and scarves, rested on benches, gloved hand in hand, and watched the river slide by. Young women with pushchairs encouraged their toddlers to climb out and run across the grass, smell the earth, make round, wet stains on the knees of their trousers when they fell.

I was heading back to the flat, tired after a bracing walk but wondering what else I could do to fill these final few days before the return to school, when I saw her. Megan. I stopped, still a distance away, moving to the side of the path so I could observe her stealthily from the cover of a large leafy bush.

She was sitting on the grass with a group of other young people of similar age. They'd spread out a waterproof sheet and, on top of it, a patchwork of jackets and sweatshirts. There must have been half a dozen of them, a mix of boys and girls, lounging there, encircled by bags. They were cradling cans. Soft drinks, perhaps, or alcohol – I didn't recognise the brands. Chatting and laughing.

There were schoolbooks open on the clothes around them as if they were kidding themselves that they were there to study. Clearly, they were doing very little work.

Megan sat cross-legged, her long limbs folded with ease, her shoes kicked off. Her blonde bob swung as she turned from one friend to another, her face filled with laughter, with life. She wore a strappy top, too skimpy for the season, and frayed jeans. Already, she looked not a schoolgirl but a young woman, ready for university, for independence, for the world.

I hesitated, shaking with emotion at the sight of her, so young, so carefree, so confident. I couldn't tear myself away. It wasn't just her youthfulness. I'd been that young once. But I'd never been like her. So easy with the people around her, so natural and, I had to admit it, so very lovely. I couldn't walk right past them, I simply couldn't, but I wasn't ready yet to pull back and find a different path to bring me out higher up the road.

I was still there, shrinking back into the trees and bushes, when she jumped up, pushed her feet into her shoes, grabbed her bag and came bounding down the path towards me, followed by another young woman. I couldn't move. Whatever I did, she'd see me. If I emerged from the branches and tried to walk away, in whichever direction, she'd know I'd been hiding here. I froze.

She was almost upon me when I stepped abruptly out of the sparse foliage. I hadn't planned to confront her. I could only think later, when I reflected, that it was fate that brought us together that afternoon. It was meant to be.

She started when she saw me and put a hand to her mouth. Her friend, running, almost collided with her. The two of them stared at me.

'Miss Dixon?' Her eyes were large and blue, shining with sunshine.

'Megan.' It was my stern, school teacher's voice. I couldn't help it. She was a pupil, not my friend.

The other girl, sharp-featured with short-cropped, spiky hair, said, 'You all right, Miss Dixon?'

I flushed. 'Could I have a word, Megan? Alone.'

The friend pulled an amused face at Megan. 'Shall I see you there?'

Megan nodded and watched as the friend sauntered off in the direction of the park café.

She turned back to me. 'Is something the matter?'

I bit my lip. 'I'm concerned about you, Megan. Very concerned.'

Her eyebrows lifted a fraction. *I must seem impossibly old to her. Past it. Sad old spinster.* I imagined her mimicking me to her friends, there on the grass, after I'd gone. Maybe even to Ralph. My insides tightened.

'What exactly is your relationship with Mr Wilson?'

She cocked her head. 'He's my English teacher, Miss Dixon.'

'I'm aware of that.' I knew how absurd I sounded, how uptight. I couldn't help myself. My hands, at my sides, clenched into fists. 'He seems very... fond of you.'

She shrugged and looked away. I didn't know what I'd expected. That she might seem embarrassed, perhaps, or even contrite. That she might burst into tears, realising I was onto her, and beg me not to tell anyone. Her eyes swung back to meet mine. They were cold.

I swallowed. 'You should watch yourself. You're a schoolgirl. A child. You don't know what you're doing.'

Her expression hardened. 'Actually, I'm nearly seventeen years old.' She hesitated. 'And anyway, it's none of your business.'

My legs trembled. I could just see her with him, naked, bold and alluring, entwining herself round his body. I wanted to slap her self-satisfied face.

'Don't you see? He's your teacher. It's abuse. He could go to prison. You'd ruin him, if this got out.'

'If what got out? What are you even talking about?' She turned back and looked, checking out the distance from her friends. 'What're you doing here, anyway?'

'Taking a walk. I live near here.'

'What a coincidence.' She tightened her lips. 'Looks to me as if you're spying on me.'

I tutted, flustered. 'Don't be absurd.'

She tossed her hair, sprayed with sunlight. 'It's true then, that you had a thing for him? He's so over you. If you don't believe me, ask him yourself.'

She flounced off, leaving me standing still, too shocked even to cry, staring after her.

CHAPTER 35

I barely remember the following weeks. I drank, mostly. It was too painful to be sober.

If I closed my eyes, I saw Megan. She was a siren, luring him to destruction. It had to end.

I messaged him even more. Begging him to see me, just to talk to me.

I need to see you, I typed. *Don't shut me out. I love you.*

Even once he was back from holiday, my messages went not just unanswered but unread.

I tried everything to see him. When I wasn't actually teaching, I raced up the hill and haunted the Upper School corridors, trying to catch a glimpse of him. I hung around the Upper School car park at the end of the school day, trying to intercept him. Somehow, he managed always to evade me.

I wrote to his home address. What option did I have? I threatened to inform Sarah Baldini. Then, I'd write to the school governors and tell them everything. I'd expose him. He was under a lot of personal stress, I understood that, but what he'd done was still wrong. He was a teacher, with young people in his care. He had to uphold moral standards. Didn't he see?

Eventually, after a few weeks, I received a text from him. Brief but exactly what I'd longed for. A summons. To his home.

My hands shook as I got ready.

I didn't turn up uninvited. He summoned me, with a text. The last thing on my mind was killing him.

Well, you know what happened after that.

CHAPTER 36

My encounter with Mike Ridge that Friday evening shook me to the core.

He knew the truth. I sensed it. I didn't know how, but he knew. He was biding his time, studying us both, Helen and me, wearing us down, waiting for us to crack.

The next day, I didn't leave the flat. I hid myself to one side of the sitting-room window and kept watch, a glass of wine or whisky constantly to hand.

By evening, as darkness fell, my head swam. I didn't bother eating, just refilled my glass and staggered back to my vantage point. So far, there'd been no sign of him.

I checked again. I couldn't see his car. I ran my eye along the wall to the bus stop. It was deserted.

I closed my eyes and buried my head in my hands. I felt exhausted, dizzy and very sick.

Don't do this, I'd written to Ralph, time after time. *Stop it. I love you. Don't destroy yourself!*

I'd thought I could save him. How wrong I'd been. I'd been the one to kill him, in the end.

I held out a hand, trying to steady it, watching it shake. Who was destroying herself now?

I was getting drunk. It was late. I should go to bed. But I was afraid to. The nights were so dark, so long, so bleak, even with a tablet or two.

How had I ever thought I could kill someone and get away with it? They were coming for me. Tonight or tomorrow or another day, who knew when. They'd find out, sooner or later.

I started to cry. Alcoholic sobbing, slobbery and pathetic. *Oh, Ralph, I'm sorry. I'm so sorry. I never meant to—*

My phone pinged. I sat up. Listened. It pinged a second time. I wiped my eyes on the sleeve of my jumper and shook myself, then crawled, hands and knees, across the carpet to see.

Miss me? Come to the boathouse. I'm here. Waiting.

*

My hands shook as I opened the car door, slid into the seat and turned the key in the ignition. I adjusted the rear-view mirror and blinked at myself, ran a hand down my flushed face and tucked stray, damp hair behind my ears.

I'd had too much to drink. I knew that. I wasn't safe. But what else could I do? This was it. After all this waiting, all this pain, this was a chance to find out the truth, to see at last who was tormenting me. My stomach knotted.

I lowered the windows and swung out into the road, drinking in the warm evening air. The streets were quiet. I hummed to myself as I drove, trying to stay calm. My mind was racing.

By the time I reached the car park at the back of the line of boathouses, I was close to tears. I was befuddled and drowsy with wine but spiked too with adrenalin. *I had to do this. I had to know who had summoned me here and why.*

I was also frightened to move. I switched off the engine and sat in the car, thinking about Ralph, feeling the cool, salty breeze blow into the car from the sea, listening to the steady rhythm of waves bursting onto the shingle, then rattling loose stones as they drew them back into the water.

My phone rang. I pulled it out of my pocket and stared, stupid with tiredness.

Number withheld.

I hesitated, heart thumping, then pressed to answer.

For a moment, silence. Breathing.

'Hello?'

'I can see you.' The voice was so low, it was almost a whisper. A man's voice.

'Who is this?'

He spoke so softly, I could barely hear. 'So soon forgotten? Oh, Laura.'

My heart seemed to stop. *Who was this? It sounded like him, like Ralph, but how could it be?* I clutched the phone, pressing it closer to my ear, shaking.

The voice whispered, 'You look lovely, Laura.'

I twisted round in my seat, trying to see if anyone was watching me. Nothing but shadows, silvery with streaks of moonlight across the shingle, thickening to utter blackness along the side of each boathouse.

'Where are you?' I pulled open the car door and spilled out. The earth was soft under my rubber-soled shoes. I stood, lost, turning and looking round for him. 'Is it you? Ralph?'

He sighed. In the background, the sound of the waves shaking handfuls of dry bones. *Was he here then? Was he really here? It was impossible.*

'I'm waiting. Come to me. Come to the boathouse.'

I stuttered: 'Are you there?' Silence. I ached to see him, to touch him. 'Ralph? Don't go!'

The line went dead. I let out a cry of frustration, then fumbled to switch on my phone's torch and picked my way, stumbling, onto the grassy verge, over a lip of rocks and down between two buildings onto the open shingle. Away from the shelter of the row of boathouses, the wind caught me, chilling my cheeks. I blinked and struggled on to their friend's boathouse, further along, crunching over the shifting stones.

'Ralph? Is it you?' My voice was thin and weak, snatched away at once by the breeze.

I struggled on. Damp seeped into my shoes through the sides, the toes, chilling my feet.

My ears raged with the sound of the waves. I hurried on, panting now, battling the shingle and the wind. The door of the boathouse stood ajar. Weak light spilled out, drawing a thin arc in the blackness. Ghostly. Otherworldly.

I broke into a run, my arms outstretched.

'Ralph?'

I pushed through the doorway and stood there, blinking in the light, trying to focus.

The smell of the boathouse hit me in the stomach. Petrol and the sharp chemical scent of wood varnish. It brought back instant memories of Ralph, of making love here, after we'd brought the boat back in and were finally getting warm again, sharing each other's body heat.

The dinghy, on its frame, sat in the shadows, pressed against the back wall. In front, a row of thick candles, each one shielded by a glass chimney, burned side by side along a narrow wooden table. I shuddered. Ralph loved candles. I stepped closer, looking around, shaking.

I steeled myself and peered into the far corners, cluttered with picnic and beach equipment, an abandoned child's bike, fishing tackle, all obscured by darkness which the weak candlelight couldn't penetrate.

I went back to the wooden table and looked over it. A bottle of wine and two glasses stood together. The bottle, Shiraz, of course, was already opened. One glass was used but drained. The other held a couple of inches of wine.

Beside it, a note.

Drink a toast. To us. Then come and find me. I'm waiting, my love.

I ran my fingertips over the writing. It was Ralph's untidy scrawl. I'd know it anywhere. My spirits lifted. A surge of hope. Could this be real? I laughed, looking at the way he'd so carefully set the scene.

Typical Ralph. *A toast, to us.* That flair for the theatrical was so very him.

I lifted my glass, wondering if he could somehow see me, and raised it to the silence.

'To us, Ralph, my love. To happiness.'

The wine was bitter on my tongue but I drank it down, then headed back to the door. I pushed it properly open and strode out into the wind.

'Ralph? Are you there?'

Behind me, the door loosened, blew shut, extinguishing the little light from the boathouse. The darkness of the beach deepened. The sea beyond, endlessly noisy, was barely visible, its undulating surface gleaming here and there with watery moonlight.

I stumbled forward, not sure which direction to take, my breath short and sharp. The alcohol was hot in my stomach, fire running down my arms and into my fingertips. I tried to imagine Ralph's warmth, the strength of his arms as they wrapped themselves around me, the relief of coming home to him.

'Ralph?' My voice sounded shrill with nerves. The sound of it frightened me. *Where was he? Why was he playing such games?*

I was getting close to the sea now. I stopped, struggling to get my breath back, buffeted by the strengthening wind. My limbs were heavy, my feet numb. I stood there, a tiny, lone figure on the shore, dwarfed by the scale of the sea. I shivered and twisted round, narrowing my eyes against the gloom, searching for a glimpse of him.

Memories crowded in. Helen, her face resolute, dragging the boat out across the shingle on its wheeled stand. The two police officers, huddled together, sipping coffee and looking out to sea. Ralph, always Ralph. I shook my head. I was going mad. What was I doing, standing here in the darkness? He was dead. I knew he was. His body would have rotted by now, swollen and broken into pieces by the salt water.

Something moved. There, further along, close to the narrow breakwater. A figure, crouching low.

'Ralph!' Could it be? I lifted my arm to wave but already the figure had disappeared from view, merging into the blackness of the rocky breakwater, a sleeping dragon with its head stretched into the waves.

But I'd seen him. I had. I forced myself to run, stumbling and slipping, towards the breakwater – my hair, caught by the wind, flying in all directions.

The distance seemed endless. My legs, suddenly dead weights, struggled to move. It took all the strength I could muster to keep in motion, to hold my head erect, to keep my eyes from closing.

Ahead, the darkness shifted again.

'Ralph. Is it you?' My voice was desperate now.

A figure, still there, silhouetted against the stones.

Why won't he come to me? My legs were so leaden, I could barely throw myself forward anymore. Every step was such an effort. My feet seemed disconnected from the rest of my body, thickened and numb.

The figure stepped forward. I started to scream, my hands lifted now not to embrace him but to ward him off, to protect myself.

Whoever it was, he wasn't alive. A man stood before me, soaking wet, his arms limp at his sides. His ragged clothes, streaming seawater into pools at his feet, hung from his body. His saturated hair was plastered to his head, dripping tendrils of seawater across his face. His skin gleamed deathly white.

I blinked, struggling to focus, and my vision blurred. *Ralph...* Could those blue lips be the same ones I'd once kissed, once parted with the tip of my tongue? The eyes, wide and staring, fixed on mine, rimmed with blood.

I staggered, losing strength in my legs and crashed onto the stones before I could reach him. I writhed there, almost paralysed. The beach spun. The scream stuck in my throat.

It was over. My eyes closed. Blackness.

PART TWO

HELEN

CHAPTER 37

I thought the teachers would assume that, this year, after all that had happened, I wouldn't have the gall to go along. That was all the more reason I was determined to be there.

I knew what they were like, those end-of-year Lower School socials. They thrived on gossip. And this year, I knew the gossip would be about Miss Dixon and what happened to Ralph and, indirectly, that meant it was also about me.

Besides, it was a matter of pride. I always turned up at school events. I was an involved parent, someone who could be relied on. A volunteer reader.

Bea, who usually hated these things, agreed to come too, just for an hour. Moral support. We'd agreed a strategy: go late, leave early.

We met up in the car park and pushed open the door of the pub together, Bea sticking close by my side as we made our way past the bar, through the crowd of regular drinkers to the long, narrow function room at the back.

'You okay?' Bea asked, for about the hundredth time.

I managed a smile. 'Fine.'

'One drink,' she whispered, steeling herself. 'And we're done.'

I hesitated on the threshold, reading the room. Already, it had divided into groups. I recognised several knots of year two parents who'd congregated at the far end, close to the tables where trays of cheap sandwiches, crisps and sausage rolls had been set out. I could guess the conversation. Job chit-chat. Summer holiday plans.

The teachers, having done their duty and endured small talk with the parents, had settled together at the other end, closer to the bar.

I patted Bea's arm as she headed off to join the parents, waved in by a mum she seemed to know, then I turned to join the nearest teachers. I made a point of socialising with them, when I could, for Anna's sake. That was why I'd started volunteering in the first place. And I suppose I was feeling bloody-minded. If anyone thought I was embarrassed about being there, humiliated by the unspoken connections between Miss Dixon and my husband, I was determined to show them I was not.

They smiled and made space for me as I picked up a glass of orange juice from the bar and joined a few of the teachers I knew.

'I still can't believe it,' Mrs Prior was saying. Her face was flushed. 'She'd been acting strangely for a while, though, hadn't she? On edge. I said so, didn't I?' She turned to Miss Abbott. 'Didn't you go and have a word with her?'

I sighed to myself. They were talking about Miss Dixon, already. I wondered how much I could stand.

Miss Abbott nodded. 'She was a very private person.' She stared into her glass of white wine. 'I did try to ask her once, well, ask if everything was okay. I got the sense she didn't want to talk about it.'

'Apparently, she'd been taking sleeping pills for weeks,' Miss Fry put in. 'You'd think she'd know to keep off alcohol. That's what did the real damage, apparently. Mixing them.'

'She was lucky to survive.' Miss Abbott shook her head, doleful. 'I heard it was touch and go.'

Mrs Prior lowered her voice. 'Jayne said they had to pump her stomach. Not nice.'

I said, 'How is she doing? Any news?'

They turned to me as if they'd already forgotten I was there, putting on their public faces once more.

'Out of hospital,' Miss Abbott said. 'That's something. It's early days, but they don't think there's any permanent damage.' She looked embarrassed. 'You know, physically.'

Miss Fry said, 'I can't imagine she'll be coming back to school though, will she?'

Mrs Prior said, 'Definitely not before the end of term. As for next year…?' She gave an exaggerated shrug.

Miss Abbott said to me, 'They think she'll need a bit of support for a while. You know. Counselling.' She hesitated, with the air of someone searching for something more cheerful to add. 'Jayne sent flowers from us all,' she said at last, 'when she was discharged from hospital.'

Miss Fry pulled a face. 'I suppose someone ought to go and see her.'

They looked round at each other, doubtfully. No one, it seemed, wanted to volunteer.

'I always wondered if she had, you know, a bit of a drink problem?' said Mrs Prior. 'I mean, we all like a drink now and then, don't we? To unwind. But I do remember one time in particular when she came in late and said she'd overslept. Which wasn't like her. She looked so pale and her hands were –' she held out a hand to demonstrate trembling – 'like this. She said it was flu. But I did wonder.'

'Well, it takes all sorts,' Miss Abbott said, more kindly.

Mrs Prior turned to Miss Fry. 'You said how weird she was with the police, after Mr Wilson disappeared.'

Miss Fry gave her a warning look, reminding her not to say too much. I shifted my weight to steady myself. It was my husband she was talking about.

Mrs Prior said quickly, 'Oh, I didn't mean… it's just so awful, isn't it? One thing after another.' She paused, trying to read my silence. 'You must think we're dreadful.'

'Not at all,' I lied.

I'd heard them in action plenty of times before. Miss Fry and Mrs Prior had been giving me sidelong glances for weeks, every time I saw them in school.

Miss Fry said, 'Laura always was a bit of a dark horse, but it does make you think. The fact you can work alongside someone every day and have no idea what's really going on with them.'

Miss Abbott turned away to speak to a mother who'd crossed the room to catch her for a word.

As soon as Miss Abbott had gone, Mrs Prior lowered her voice. 'It can't have been an accident. Surely. That many pills? And all that wine.'

Miss Fry said, 'She left her car door open, apparently. Did you hear? Jayne told me. In the car park. Windows down and everything. That tells you something about her state of mind, doesn't it?'

'It doesn't mean she intended to... you know, take her own life. She clearly wasn't herself,' I said.

'Cry for help?' Mrs Prior hesitated, her eyes on Miss Fry. 'Maybe. But you've got to ask, haven't you, if you *want* to be found, why drive all that way, and to a beach?'

Miss Fry gave Mrs Prior a meaningful look and then turned brightly to me. 'Anyway, Mrs Wilson, how are you? Anna's such a lovely girl! And doing so well.'

I forced myself to look her in the eye and nodded. 'Thank you. I'm very proud of her. Ralph was too.'

Mrs Prior took the chance to leave us, heading back towards the bar.

Miss Fry said, in honeyed tones, 'We're all so sorry. About what happened.'

'That's kind.' I nodded, considering. *Knowing how much these women gossiped, a few careful words now might prove useful.* 'Anna's loved school. She'll really miss it next year.'

Miss Fry pricked up her ears. 'You're leaving?'

I gave a rueful smile. 'It's a big decision. But yes, I feel we should. I'm still exploring options. It's just… we've both got too many memories here. I'm sure you understand.'

She nodded. 'Well, we'd certainly miss Anna. And you, Mrs Wilson. But of course, whatever you think is best.' She peered across to the bar where Mrs Prior was chatting to some young male teachers. She looked as if she couldn't wait to dash across to join her and share the news.

She looked down at my almost empty glass. 'Another drink?'

'Thank you.' I gave her a tight smile. 'But I think I've had enough.'

Bea had been right. We shouldn't have come, not this year. It was too much.

I went to find Bea to tell her I was leaving and say a quick goodbye.

CHAPTER 38

I was just opening my car door to leave when a rasping male voice called, 'How are you, Mrs Wilson?'

I jumped and turned. The man in the next car had wound down his window and was looking directly at me. He was sitting in the passenger seat, a book open in his hands, as if he'd been killing time, waiting for someone. His car was a battered old saloon, scraped along the side.

'Sorry, do I know you?' I peered at him more closely.

Someone from school, perhaps? A janitor?

His bent elbow rested on the car window. A bulge of muscle along his upper arms and chest filled the contours of the tattered fleece he was wearing. His body looked well cared for, younger than his face which was lean but weathered.

He smiled, a playful smile as if to say, *of course you know me, why do you ask?*

I blinked. His eyes bored into mine. They were a muddy mixture of grey, blue and green and gleamed like a cat's in the low light. I hesitated. I had a sudden urge to climb into my car and drive away at speed, to escape him while I could, but something – uncertainty perhaps – held me back.

'Were you at the drinks?'

He considered this. 'In a manner of speaking.'

I pursed my lips. 'Are you a parent?'

He inclined his head. 'I am, but not here.' He sighed as if the effort of establishing his credentials was wearisome to him. 'You went in with Mrs Higgins. Clara's mother. You had an orange juice. You talked to the teachers for a while, not for long. Listened, I should say.' He paused, watching me. 'Your mind was elsewhere, wasn't it, Mrs Wilson?'

I considered him. 'You seem to know a lot about me, Mr...?'

He stuck a meaty hand out of the window towards me. 'Ridge. Mike Ridge.' His grip was crushing. 'It's my job, Mrs Wilson. Knowing about people.'

Panic fluttered in my stomach. It struck me that he had been sitting there, just waiting for someone. Waiting for me.

He opened his door and climbed out. He was shorter than I expected, but solidly built. Powerful.

'I wondered if we could have a little chat. In your car, if you like?' he said, calmly.

I hesitated. We were right outside the pub. The car park was busy with people, coming and going. Soon, the crowd from the school drinks would start drifting out too. I could scream for help if I needed to.

My fingers tightened around my car keys. 'What exactly do you do, Mr Ridge?'

He was already walking around my car to the passenger side and climbing in. I got in too and sat behind the steering wheel, doing my best to twist to face him. His bulk dominated the space. He smelled of body wash and fried food. He leaned in close, coffee on his breath.

'I'm an investigator, Mrs W.'

I tried not to react. My insides contracted. I thought about Ralph. The sight of him, lying there, still and silent, at the bottom of the cellar steps. The look of horror on that woman's face. I took a deep breath and fumbled with my car keys, ducking my head to fit them in the ignition, playing for time.

When I'd straightened up again, I said, 'Are you with the police?'

He shook his head. 'Not anymore. I'm private now. Case-by-case basis. You know, gun for hire.'

My eyes flicked at once to the fleece, imagining a weapon concealed there. I looked quickly away.

'So, Mr Ridge, what can I do for you?'

'I'm interested in what happened to your husband.' His eyes burned into mine, as if he were trying to read my mind. 'Terrible, losing a loved one like that. Not knowing what happened to him.'

I nodded. My mouth was dry. *He knew*. I didn't know how nor how much but, somehow, he knew. I wrenched my eyes from his and sat stiffly, staring forward through the windscreen. A young couple was getting out of the car parked just in front of mine, talking and laughing.

We sat in silence for a while. I struggled to breathe normally, to swallow. The young couple locked the car and set off towards the pub, hand in hand.

Finally, he said, 'It was the life insurance company. They sent me. Always worth a closer look when they don't find a body. Loose ends, you see. Sorry to say, but they just don't like them.'

I didn't speak. *What could I say?*

'The police have to move on, after a while. Sooner than I do. Can't blame them. Plenty more cases waiting. Been there myself.'

I managed to say, 'The police have been very thorough but, so far...' I swallowed, 'they've failed to find any trace of my husband. I'm sorry but I don't quite see—'

He nodded. His hand moved to his chin and gently rubbed it, as if he were thinking this over.

'I know where you're coming from, Mrs W. I really do. And you might be right to draw a line, holding that memorial service and everything. Very classy service, by the way.'

I blinked, registering what he was telling me. That he'd been there too.

He went on. 'So, you bide your time. Apply for a death certificate eventually. Then, bingo! You're home and dry. There's every chance the insurance people will pay out, after all. How much is the policy worth?'

I couldn't look at him. 'My husband dealt with all that.'

'Often the way. My old lady's the same. Trust. It's at the heart of every good marriage, isn't it?' He hesitated. 'We're talking several hundred thousand, though, in your husband's case. That's worth having, isn't it? Even if it can't bring him back again.'

I steadied myself and turned again to look him in the eye. 'Mr Ridge, I'm afraid I need to—'

He nodded. 'Relieve the babysitter. Course you do. Time's money. Ten quid an hour, you pay, don't you? Top whack.'

I stared, struggling not to show my shock. 'Was there something you wanted to ask me?'

'Ah.' He reached into his fleece. I tensed, imagining a gun. Instead, he rummaged in an inside pocket, brought out a business card and handed it to me. 'I wanted to give you this. Just in case.'

He climbed out of the car and closed the passenger door with care. My body deflated with relief as soon as he'd withdrawn, as if I'd been punctured.

I leaned forward and rested my arms on the steering wheel. In a moment, I'd switch on the engine and head home to pay off the babysitter, just as he'd said. First, I needed to sit still and calm the shaking in my hands.

When he appeared suddenly at my window, I started. He rapped on the glass and I lowered it.

He was smiling as he leaned in, his tone full of admiration, as if he'd just lost a tough bout, fair and square.

'Gotta hand it to you, Mrs W,' he said in his low, rasping voice. 'However you did it, you did a good job.'

CHAPTER 39

I'd had a lot of time, recently, to think about Ralph.

About the way we met. About the way we came to marry, in such a headlong rush. About our life together.

I loved him to distraction. That's the truth of it. He brought me to life, touched my black-and-white world and turned it rainbow-coloured. He made me dizzy with his energy, his light. Blinding light. I just wished he'd been as true to me as I was to him.

I'd met him because of Mimi, my crazy boss.

We were running the main section of the local public library together, taking up the whole of the ground floor. She'd hired me, I discovered, as part of a drive to bring in new blood and shake up the staff culture there. Mimi, with her spiky hair, streaked blue and pink, and flowing vintage clothing, was leading a fight against the threat of closure with the only weapons we had: passion, energy and ideas.

First, she rattled cages by getting local businesses to foot the bill for new chairs, tables and shelving for the children's section. A computer repair shop agreed to give us some second-hand computers – and maintain them for us.

Then she announced that she wanted to launch a programme of evening events, on days we already stayed open until late. Before I knew it, I found myself in charge.

I did my best. I started a monthly book group, although only three people turned up for the first meeting and only one of those had actually read the book. I arranged a film screening and found money for cheap wine and snacks. The average age was about seventy but even so, it was a start. A local artist staged an exhibition on the library walls for a week, then came to give a talk about her technique. So far, so dull.

Then, one day, Mimi called me over from the stacks where I was shelving returns.

'You've got an event query.' She had a teasing look in her eye. 'You're gonna like this one.'

A young man stood at the desk, steadying himself against it with three fingers of one hand as he gazed up at the ceiling. The library wasn't a grand building, but it was Victorian with some of the follies of the time – from faux wooden panelling in the study room upstairs to the mock-Tudor beams and rafters on our floor. Normal people never even noticed them.

He seemed lost in thought, a tall man with floppy hair and even floppier clothes. I could see why he'd excited Mimi. A rebel. A romantic. Rather her type.

He turned as I approached and smiled, holding out his hand.

'Ralph Wilson.' That voice. Rich and mellow. His hand was warm with delicate fingers. An artist's hands. 'Poetry.'

I gawped at him, wrong-footed. I was twenty-six, but I hadn't had a steady boyfriend for several years and frankly I was rather getting used to the idea of staying single. Suddenly I wasn't so sure.

'Poetry evenings.' His eyes were deep brown, his smile broadening as he looked at me. 'Mimi here says you're the woman to ask. Helen, wasn't it?'

I managed to lead him off into a quieter area of the library where we could talk without disturbing readers. Mimi pretended to be busy sorting through reservations, close enough to keep an eye on the two of us. Every time I glanced up, she was watching, an infuriating grin on her face.

As soon as he left, carrying a bundle of papers about library policy and applications to stage an event, she dashed across.

'So?'

'Don't get so excited.' I packed away the information folders, ready to put them back. 'He wants to use us for poetry readings, but he looked horrified when I told him how much we charge.'

She waved away my words. 'So? We can make an exception. Poetry! Exactly the sort of thing a library should be hosting.'

I narrowed my eyes. 'Really? *No exceptions.* Isn't that what you said to that man from St John's Ambulance?'

'That was different.' She winked at me. 'Ralph Wilson. Great name. Wedding ring?'

'Didn't notice,' I lied.

'You are hopeless.' She tutted. 'Is he a professional poet?'

'English teacher. At secondary school.'

'Perfect!' Mimi beamed. 'Partnership with education. One of our objectives. Here's what you do. Give him a call. Tell him if he can guarantee, let's say, twenty people, he can have the space. Free of charge. Say it's a trial.'

I picked up the folders and started to head to the back office.

After a moment, Mimi came bustling through to find me.

'Just thinking,' she said. 'If there's anything of mine you want to wear, for poetry night, just ask. Okay?'

I looked down at my black jeans and dark blue sweater, a variation on the work uniform I wore every day, then at Mimi's multi-coloured outfit.

'Thanks, Mimi,' I said. 'Really. But I'll be fine.'

That first poetry night, Ralph seemed nervous. Those long fingers raked through his hair. His lips were dry. I didn't make a fuss, just noticed and did what I could to help.

A small table by the lectern for a jug of water and glasses. Making small talk with the first arrivals to give him time on his own. Telling him, just before it all began, how great he looked.

He was the last to read. I sat there, the plain, twenty-something librarian in the back row, spellbound. When he stepped up to the lectern and shuffled his papers, cleared his throat, nervously stooped for a sip of water, then finally began to read, it was like a conductor taking control of an orchestra. The room fell silent. His voice, first, was a delight in itself. But his words too. His language rolled from him, rich and resonant, and stirred emotions I'd almost forgotten in my contented little life. *Passion. Regret. Longing.*

When he finished reading, there was quiet. Someone coughed. A woman shuffled in her seat. I started to clap, a slow, theatrical slapping of palms that I instantly regretted. *What was I thinking?* People in the row in front twisted round to look.

Then someone near the front joined in and suddenly everyone was clapping and the relief was exhausting. I'd happily disappeared again, back into anonymity, into the gathering.

He took some of us out for drinks in the wine bar around the corner.

Ralph was as effusive as he'd earlier been afraid. He ordered champagne and declared the evening a marvellous new beginning. He raised a toast, dubbing me an 'angel of mercy!' One of his teaching friends whooped.

I remember looking round the table, at the clatter and chat, a wild gang of teachers and writers and friends – most of whom I'd never met before this evening. I felt swept up by their camaraderie, their enthusiasm for life.

Later on, Ralph, whose eyes had seldom strayed from mine, came to sit beside me. His thigh pressed, warm and solid, against mine.

'So, madam,' he said, in that rich, sexy voice, 'it seems to me, I have a lot to thank you for.' When he looked at me, the rest of the room seemed to blur and fall away. 'I wonder how long it will take me to show my appreciation? Hours? Days? Years? If, that is, you're willing to let me try?'

My cheeks flushed, my body felt electric.

It was the champagne, of course. It was the novelty. But most of all, it was simply Ralph.

CHAPTER 40

He never stopped. That was the thing about Ralph. Being with him was like being lifted by a tidal wave, tossed and tumbled and terribly out of my depth. There were days when I was so tired, I longed for him not to call, to leave me alone to crawl home and have a quiet evening in, an early night. Even then, he almost always did call, sometimes very late.

'Don't be boring!' he'd say if I protested that it was after midnight, I'd already gone to bed. 'Live a little!'

Other nights, I was woken by a rap at the door and he'd be standing there, slightly drunk, declaring his love for me.

'You're not cross, are you, angel?' He'd play the little boy, frightened of being in trouble. 'I just had to see you. I just had to hold you. Or I might have died.' He paused, dramatically, ready to make me laugh. 'Literally.'

It was impossible to be angry with him for long. It was so flattering, for one thing, to feel so adored. And life was so exciting, even if I did sometimes struggle to stay awake at work.

We'd been together for four mad months when he surprised me at one of his library readings, a regular fixture now.

He'd been working on some new poems, he said. I've no idea where he found the time. Hours stolen from the night, perhaps. They were the start of a new sonnet series, about love and time.

Sometimes he read his poetry to me at home, before the event, just to practise before an audience, his adoring audience of one. Not this time. These came out of the blue.

I sat in my usual place in the back row, watching and listening, drinking in the rhythms, the sounds. Proud too, now, of his talent and charisma.

I didn't realise at first what he was doing. I was drowsy and already wondering how I might engineer a way of getting an early night. Just this once. Maybe I could persuade Ralph to skip drinks this evening and come back with me? So, I only half-caught the meaning of his words.

Then I realised he'd come to the end and was smiling out at me, finding me hidden away at the back; then, starting to feel hot with awkwardness now, I realised that the couple in front of me was twisting round to look; finally, that his bearded friend, the science teacher, was clapping. The atmosphere in the room had become newly charged.

A middle-aged woman two seats away from me in the back row, a complete stranger, leaned across the chair between us, eyes shining, and whispered, 'What a proposal!'

Ralph paused dramatically, making the most of this grand moment of theatre, then came out from behind the lectern and started a purposeful walk towards me, his right hand dipping into his pocket.

I remember thinking, *Oh no, please, no. How embarrassing. Don't do this.*

But of course, there was no stopping Ralph, there never was, whatever the look on my face.

He had to push chairs out of the way to make enough room to get down on one knee.

'Helen, my muse, my angel, will you do me the honour of marrying me?'

He'd flipped open a jeweller's box and there it was, a large ruby set in a silver ring. Unusual. Artistic. Showy. Not me at all.

I wanted to run away and hide. He looked faintly ridiculous, wobbling there. I sensed people crowding round us, pressing in, whispering, smiling. *I hardly know you*, I thought, taking in the floppy hair, falling forward now over one eye, the self-conscious nervousness of his smile.

The thought flitted through my mind, *maybe once we're married, I'll get a bit more sleep.*

I couldn't move. I couldn't speak. The weight of expectation was suffocating.

Behind me, someone said, 'Well, go on!'

Did I even have a choice?

I leaned forward and murmured, 'I don't know what to say. Why now?'

He plucked the ring out of the box, took my hand and forced it onto my finger. Someone whistled. Someone cheered. Chairs were scraped back, arms pushed into the sleeves of coats.

The tension dissipated as quickly as it had grown. *That was settled then. Time for a drink. Time to go home.*

Ralph, holding me now, laughed. 'Why now?' He drew me closer and whispered into my ear. 'Why not? What are we waiting for? Come on, Miss Librarian, just for once, do something crazy.'

Reader, I married him.

And he was right. It was the craziest thing I've ever done.

CHAPTER 41

'Stop it!'

Anna was slighter than Clara and had to fight hard to tug her jacket free of Clara's fist. Anna set off at a run, with Clara in pursuit.

I charged after them both, the rucksack bouncing on my back.

'Anna! Wait!'

I caught up with them on the corner, just as we turned left into a smaller, narrower street.

'Calm down, both of you.' I turned on Anna, scolding. Her face was sullen with fury. 'What's the matter with you? Don't run off down a main road. It's dangerous.'

She shot Clara a look of pure hatred and stomped off, a few paces ahead. Clara allowed me to grab her by the hand and we followed.

'So,' I asked Clara, trying to restore order. 'How was school?'

'Good.'

'What did you get up to?'

'Nothing.'

'What did you have for lunch?'

'Can't remember.'

Anna, scuffing her shoes against a wall, waited for us to reach her.

'Smell this!' She opened her fist to show Clara the remains of a rotting flower. 'Dare you.'

'Eugh! That's disgusting.'

'Come on, girls. Let's go. Nearly home.'

It wasn't far but, on bad days, this walk from the school gates to our front door was the most stressful part of my day. They both came out of school tired and manic and their friendship flashed back and forth between hatred and love.

Other children looked easier. I caught glimpses of girls from their class walking home sedately, one hand dutifully holding their mother's, the other swinging their bookbag. Only these two seemed to act like the crazy gang. I hated that madness, especially in Anna. It reminded me too much of Ralph.

*

By the time we arrived home, they were fast friends again. They tumbled into the hall, pushing and shoving, kicking off shoes and shedding their jackets like second skins.

'Any homework?'

No answer. They charged into the kitchen. 'Can we have a snack?'

'You've got spellings tonight, haven't you? I'll test you on them.'

I chopped up apples and a banana and warmed some milk in the microwave, then, while they were eating, set out slips of paper and pencils.

'We'll practise spellings first, okay? Come on, it won't take long. Then you can play while I get tea ready.'

Anna groaned. 'Mum-my!'

Clara, more subdued, muttered, 'Smelly spellings.'

That set them both giggling. Anna started using her straw to blow bubbles in her milk and Clara copied her and by the time we started the spelling test, the plastic tablecloth was splattered and I was stern again.

Afterwards, I sent them off to play in the sitting room, then boiled the kettle and started cooking pasta and heating up some Bolognese sauce.

They left the connecting door ajar and their voices drifted through to the kitchen. They were playing vets with Anna's old doctor's set, taking it in turns to be the vet or the worried owner, coming along with ailing soft toys. I half-listened as they started to disagree about the rules of the game, their voices rising, then found a compromise and quietened again.

Once the girls had eaten, I put children's television on for them and they sprawled on their stomachs on the carpet, legs kicked up behind, heels waving in the air, chins resting on their hands.

When the doorbell rang, Clara looked round at me and declared, 'Mummy!'

Then her eyes flicked back to the screen.

Bea looked flustered. She was late. She never quite believed me when I said it didn't matter. I knew how lucky I was to be a stay-at-home parent, rather than juggling a full-time job and childcare. I was happy to cut her a bit of slack. Heaven knows, she'd more than paid me back.

I opened the door wide. 'Come on in! Don't look so worried! Cup of tea?'

She kissed me on the cheek with cold, dry lips. She smelled of the outside world, of petrol and work.

'Everything okay?' She paused in the kitchen to peer through the connecting door to the sitting room, taking in the sight of Anna and her daughter. They lay motionless, totally absorbed in their cartoon.

'All good.' I put the kettle on and bustled round the kitchen.

Bea sank into a chair. She looked exhausted.

'How was work?'

She pulled a face and didn't catch my eye.

'One of those days, eh?'

She nodded. ''Fraid so.'

I put a mug of tea in front of her and slid into a chair with my own. I waited. From the sitting room, the strains of cartoon music drifted through, punctuated now and then by the girls giggling together. Their laughter was high-pitched and uninhibited.

'What's on your mind?'

'I don't know.' Bea shook her head. Her face was weary. 'Last time, it was Clara, wasn't it? Not coping with her maths. Now it's Megan I'm worried about. Always one or the other. Welcome to motherhood!' She tried to laugh but it wasn't convincing.

'What's up with Megan? I thought she was all fired up about Edinburgh.'

'She was.' Bea hesitated. 'But she's started on about taking a year off first. I just really don't think it's a good idea. She already knows that – we'd talked it all through before she applied. Then she brought it up again last night. There's some girl at school who's planning to go travelling round South-East Asia. So, of course, now she wants to go too.'

I sipped my tea. 'She might enjoy university more if she's had some fun first.'

'What if she does something stupid, though?' She looked up, her eyes full of anxiety.

'Like what?'

'I don't know – like gets herself killed. There was that girl in the papers last week. Raped and murdered when she was hitchhiking. And that boy who fell off a cliff and died.'

'That can happen anywhere.'

'I know. But they take more risks when they're overseas. They do stupid things. Things they wouldn't do in their own country.'

I tried to imagine Anna at that age, striking off on her own. I supposed I'd be worried.

'Megan is nearly seventeen…'

'Exactly. A whole year younger than most of her friends.' Bea rolled her eyes. 'She's always been brainy, that's why they put her up a year. But she's not as worldly-wise as she likes to think.'

'I know I can't stop you worrying,' I said at last. 'But she's going to leave home anyway, one way or the other. A year abroad might help her mature.'

Bea blew out her cheeks. 'I don't know what she's planning to use for money. She hasn't saved enough for the airfare, let alone all the rest. And I haven't got it.'

I nodded. 'She'll manage, somehow. They all do.'

'Maybe.'

We sat in silence for a while, drinking our tea, listening to the musical bleed from the cartoons.

Suddenly, Bea said, 'It's not just that. She's been very odd, recently. Short-tempered. Bursting into tears for no reason. I know she's a teenager – I get it. And exams and everything. But even so… I think she's got something on her mind. Something she's not telling me.'

I considered. 'You've tried talking to her?'

'Of course. She just fobs me off.' Bea stretched a hand along the top of the table towards me. 'You wouldn't have a chat to her, would you? You're so good with her. And, I don't know, it might be better coming from you. She's very fond of you.'

I was fond of her. Ralph had been, too – impressed by her writing. Bea never talked about Megan's father, or Clara's. We were good friends – mum friends – but some things were still off-limits. All I knew was that the girls were half-sisters, spawned by two fathers who'd both been very absent from the scene.

I shrugged and reached out, gave Bea's hand a squeeze. 'I can try. No promises.'

'Thank you. Let's find an excuse to get her over here one evening, when Anna's asleep. I'll think of something.'

'I'd be glad to see her. She's always welcome, you know that.'

Bea pushed back her chair as if she were getting ready to head home with Clara to start the bedtime routine.

'Bea? Don't go yet.'

She let her weight settle again and looked at me sharply. 'That sounds ominous.'

'Well, it's sort of good news. For me, anyway.' I hesitated, watching her face. 'But maybe not what you want to hear.'

She frowned. 'Go on. Get it over with.'

I took a deep breath. 'You know how, since, you know… Ralph went missing, I've been talking about a fresh start? Well, I think I'm ready.'

'You're really leaving?' She gaped.

I nodded, lowered my eyes to the table.

'But… why so soon?' She looked as if she were struggling to understand the enormity of what I'd just said. 'What's the rush? Why not give it another six months, Helen, and then see how you feel?'

I shook my head. 'I've found a couple of places near Bristol that might work. Renting, to start off with. Until I get to know the area.' I paused. 'I've got to get a move on if I'm going to get Anna into a new school for September.'

'I see.' Her voice was tight.

Snorts of laughter erupted from the sitting room. We both turned to look. The girls' heads were almost touching, side by side in front of the television.

'Does Anna know?'

I shook my head. 'Not yet.'

'I don't know what to say.'

I took a deep breath. 'I know it'll be a pain, finding childcare and everything. Especially with Megan leaving home too. But you could ask around. There might be another mum—'

She lifted a hand and interrupted me. 'It's not that. Well, it is. But we'll miss you. Clara adores Anna, you know that.'

'I know.' I slid my eyes away from hers.

'Are you sure, Helen? It's a big decision.'

I focussed on my hands, folded neatly on the top of the kitchen table. 'I know. But I can't stand it here. Not now. I can't stand all the sideways looks. The gossip.'

'Right,' she said. 'Sounds as if you've made up your mind.'

'Don't be like that.'

'I'm not being like anything.'

I shook my head. 'I want a clean sheet. New school. New place.'

The tinny cartoon voices filled the silence between us.

'So, you've put the house on the market.' Her voice was cool.

'It's on a few websites, yes.'

She nodded, taking this in. 'It might take a while, even so.'

'I know.' I paused. 'That's another reason we'll just rent to start with.'

She raised her eyebrows at me. 'With what?'

'We'll get by. I've got savings. And there's Ralph's life insurance. Not just yet but, you know, eventually.'

'Well!' She got to her feet abruptly and turned her back to me, washing up her mug in the sink.

'I know it's a shock, Bea. I'm sorry.'

Her shoulders were hard. She didn't answer.

'I'm just sorry for the girls,' she said finally as she gathered up her things to go. 'Clara will be so upset.'

'I know.' I put a hand on her arm. 'Anna, too.'

She didn't answer but her jaw was set as she headed through to the sitting room to prise Clara away and take her home.

Anna and I stood at the window and waved as they set off down the path and headed towards Bea's car. Clara and Anna blew each other kisses and mouthed some silly joke of their own.

Bea didn't look back. I didn't blame her. As we turned back into the house, I felt suddenly wracked with guilt.

Bea was my best friend here. I hated having to lie.

CHAPTER 42

The house was different without Ralph. It sounded different, especially once Anna fell asleep. A new silence pressed down on me, wherever I sat, in the kitchen, in the sitting room. The fabric of the house, the furniture, emitted creaks and groans I'd never heard before. Sighs.

I had too much time to sit alone in the stillness and worry. Mostly, I worried about Anna.

I thought about the way she and Clara had played vets, taking it in turns to wear the white coat and place the stethoscope on a soft toy's fluffy stomach. On the surface, she seemed fine. Almost too fine.

I didn't want to distress her by making her talk about her father all the time, but it felt strange for us to be carrying on together as if nothing had happened, as if he'd just stepped out one day and we'd barely noticed that he'd never come home again.

In the first days after the accident, I told Anna a half-truth. I sat her on my knee and threaded my arms around her and told her that Daddy had gone away for a while.

She frowned. 'Where?'

'We're not sure. Everyone's looking for him. Looking really hard.'

'Did he go in an aeroplane?'

I swallowed. 'He went for a walk, I think, sweetheart.'

She put her head on one side and considered this. 'When he comes back, will he bring me a present?'

I blinked, trying to think what to say.

'I'd like a puppy.'

I reached for my difficult conversation voice, slow and careful.

'If you miss Daddy, it's all right to tell me. Okay? It's okay to talk about it.'

Anna said, 'I ate and ate and was sick on the floor.'

I frowned. 'Pardon?'

'Miss Fry taught me that.'

'When? You were sick at school?'

Anna laughed, delighted at having tricked me. '*I ate and ate and was sick on the floor*. Eight eights are sixty-four. Get it? It's maths.'

I had the sense I'd just lost the chance to make progress with that difficult conversation, to talk with her about Ralph. Her mind was already elsewhere.

She squirmed out of my arms and ran off to play and, for a while, that was that.

The second time, she raised it herself, out of the blue, one evening, about a week later.

I'd just read her two chapters at bedtime from a story about mice detectives and she'd laughed and bounced on her bed and generally seemed her normal boisterous self.

Then she asked, as I bent to kiss her goodnight, 'Is Daddy back tomorrow?'

I stopped and stared at her, the mood suddenly changed. She was looking at me with such hope, such innocence, it broke my heart. 'No, sweetheart. I'm sorry. They're still looking for him, remember?' What else could I say? I wanted to tell her more. Desperately. But she was too young to understand.

'In the water?'

That was new. Someone at school must have said something about them dragging the reservoir. I perched on the edge of the bed and opened my arms to her.

'Everywhere. They're looking really hard, but they haven't found him yet.' I held her close, steadying my breathing, avoiding looking her in the eye.

'But why did he go out?' She pulled away, cross. 'Without me?'

'He went for a walk, petal. It was very late. Past your bedtime. You were asleep in bed.'

'Wait a minute! He went for a big walk – in the *dark*?' She laughed softly. 'Daddy, that is *so* not a good idea!'

I kissed her forehead and she wrapped her arms round my neck and pulled me lower.

'Silly Daddy.'

I sat in the quietness, thinking about her, wondering at what point she might grieve. I wondered if I ought to launch a new conversation with her about her feelings. Or if, at seven years old, she was better off handling it all just the way she was doing, on her own terms, in her own time.

I picked up a book and tried to read but I couldn't concentrate. I read the same few paragraphs repeatedly, realising each time that I hadn't taken them in. I went through to the kitchen and put the kettle on, then sat on a chair and waited for it to boil, wondering what I was doing.

Was this how Miss Dixon had felt, when she realised Ralph was losing interest? This sense of vacancy, of meaninglessness? Is that what drove her to see the doctor and start amassing pills?

I tried to remember how I'd lived before Ralph. I'd been content, hadn't I, in my small flat, neat and ordered, busy with books and films and meeting up with friends from university? Their lives had changed too. Everyone had married, one by one, then started families. My closest friends had moved away. That life wasn't still there for me to step back into. It was history.

And the person I'd been then was nothing more than history too. I thought back to her. A more naïve person, a more optimistic one. What had happened to me, since I married?

I hadn't stopped loving him, never. But I'd stopped trusting him. I'd stopped believing.

He made elaborate excuses, at first, about where he went. He made a fuss about attending a weekly poetry group which, I was sure, only met once a month.

He'd always fancied himself a bit of an actor and started a drama group for the sixth form, putting on a production each year. Not even the Royal Shakespeare Company could need as many read-throughs and rehearsals as he claimed to attend. It gave him an alibi that stretched over months.

I heard rumours, sometimes, about his affairs. Did he really think I didn't know? The woman who shared his bed, his home – who was the mother of his daughter?

It wasn't easy.

I remembered lying in bed, muscles taut, listening to Ralph as he rattled his key in the front door lock and banged about downstairs, clearly the worse for the drinks. His footsteps mounted the stairs. When he drew back the duvet and crawled into bed beside me, his breath fell in low, warm puffs against my shoulder.

I kept my eyes closed, my body still, trying not to tremble as he fell quickly into sleep.

There were days I thought about confronting him and then, inevitably, of leaving him. He couldn't change. I saw that now. He thrived on drama. He needed intrigue and risk. It was so much part of who he was.

But, whatever else he'd done, he'd given me Anna. The other love of my life. I wouldn't alter anything, however hard our marriage had been at times, if changing the past meant missing out on her. And they were short-lived, these other women. Fireworks that flared and sparked across the sky, then burned out. He always came back to us, Anna and me. In the end.

I couldn't leave him. It wasn't only for Anna's sake. And it wasn't because he paid the bills – although I was grateful he did. It was because, despite everything, I cared about him. And I couldn't extinguish the hope that eventually, one day, when he finally grew tired of the chase, he'd change. He'd turn those deep brown eyes on me and see me afresh, as if for the first time, and realise just how precious our life together was, right here, at home.

I made a cup of tea and went through to the hall, on my way upstairs, to lock up.

Ralph's coat hung there on the rack. Watching me. His old shoes sat underneath, worn to the shape of his feet, alongside a pair of ancient wellies he'd rarely worn.

I swept them all up and bundled everything into a plastic bag, then opened the front door and stuffed the lot in the outside bin, replacing the lid with a clatter. I felt better when I turned the lock and put on the chain. Cleaner.

After that start, I took my tea upstairs to his study and closed the door behind me. My heart quickened. I was trespassing. I felt as if I might, at any moment, hear Ralph's heavy tread on the stairs and see the door-handle turn. That he might catch me standing here, in his space, and say with false jollity, with suspicion in his eyes, 'What're you up to in here?'

He never liked me being in here. It was a tacit agreement, formed early in our marriage, about his and hers territory. I'd respected it partly in the hope that, if he had his own space in our home, he mightn't feel the need to escape it so often in the evening. To grab his jacket and car keys and head out, with some mumbled excuse, leaving me alone.

Now, I looked around. His desk was a mess of poetry books and novels, scraps of paper, scrawled with half-written poems, fragments of ideas. I'd bought him a wooden desk tidy once, for pens and pencils, but he never used it. Pens, missing lids and pencils were strewn everywhere.

A jacket, creased and in need of a wash, hung on the back of the chair. On the mantelpiece, his hairbrush, still holding strands of dark hair.

I stood in the silence, my pulse racing. *Ralph*. I could almost feel him here. Resisting me. Mocking my love of neatness, of systems, of order.

But he wasn't here. And for the first time in a long time, I could do as I pleased.

I rolled up my sleeves and set to work.

It took me all evening, working methodically, without pause, until late into the night.

*

By the time I'd finished, all I wanted to do was have a shower and crawl into bed to sleep alone.

But I'd done it.

I'd gathered together all his poetry, sheets and sheets of sprawling handwriting, and shoved it into the recycling.

I'd taken all his books off the shelves and set them out on the floor, sorted them out and divided them into categories: poetry collections (individual), poetry collections (anthologies), poetry criticism, novels, biographies, humour (mostly presents from friends) and miscellaneous.

I'd picked out a small number of expensive hardbacks – plush anthologies, mostly, and complete works – and set them to one side.

I'd arranged the rest by category and then in alphabetical order, by author or editor, and stowed them all away into boxes, each box carefully labelled. Ready for the charity shop to collect.

I sat back on my heels and looked at the empty shelves, wiped clean now of all trace of Ralph. The boxes were neatly arranged along the wall.

My back and arms ached. My blouse was grimy with dust. But I felt strangely satisfied. Happy. It was a start. I was imposing order, in my own way. I would take back control.

CHAPTER 43

I used the books as an excuse to get Megan to come round to see me, one evening the following week.

She appeared on the doorstep, soon after eight, her face drawn, peering at me through a bunch of sweetheart roses – a swarm of yellow, pink and red.

'For me?' I took them and kissed her on the cheek, ushered her indoors. 'You shouldn't have.'

It had been a while since I'd seen her. She hadn't been over to visit us since the night Ralph disappeared. Fear of my grief kept her away, I'd decided. The embarrassment of knowing the right thing to say when in fact there was nothing to say, nothing at all.

She was still only sixteen, but she seemed older, standing here in the hall. A young woman almost ready to leave home. She was wearing a light cotton jacket over low-slung jeans and a cropped top that lifted when she moved to expose a flat, tight stomach.

She'd changed in other ways too. Her hair, always so neatly bobbed, looked straggly and ready for a good wash. Her cheeks were hollowed and there were dark circles under her eyes.

I led her through and busied myself with the flowers, finding a vase, cutting the stems and arranging them, then poured us both a glass of water. I didn't say anything about it, not yet, but I could see exactly why Bea was worried. Megan had a nervy jumpiness to her that I'd never seen before. Something was clearly on her mind.

She always used to seem very much at home here. Last year, before her schoolwork picked up, she used to babysit for us about once a month, if I had a school meeting or a talk to attend. Ralph could never be trusted not to let me down. The previous year, when she was only fourteen and the girls had just started in reception, Megan came by with them sometimes after school, spreading out her books on the kitchen table and munching biscuits while she tackled her homework, as Clara and Anna played in the sitting room. She liked to chat to me – liked the idea that we were two adults, able to see eye to eye, while the little ones played.

Now, she perched on the edge of a kitchen chair, her body listless.

I sat down too, my hands nursing my warm cup.

'So, getting excited about Edinburgh? It must take the pressure off, knowing you've already got an offer.'

She nodded, her eyes pinned to a spot on the kitchen floor. 'I still need to pass.'

I smiled to myself. She'd been predicted stellar results. It was hard to see how she'd fail to get the grades she needed.

'You sound a bit worried.'

She lifted a hand and scratched behind her ear. 'I am. Exams start next week.'

I nodded. 'But you've worked hard, Megan. You'll be fine. Don't you think?'

She pulled a face and squirmed on her chair. 'I don't know what's wrong with me. Mum doesn't get it. She keeps saying, *what are you worrying about? You know your stuff.* But that's not it. I just can't concentrate.'

'When's your first exam?'

'Tuesday.' She sounded panicked. 'English lit. It should be a doddle. It's all in there' – she tapped her head – 'or at least it was… but when I try to focus, to go through quotes and essay stuff, I can't remember. It's all blank.' Her hands plucked at each other in her lap. 'What if I'm like that in the exam? What if I fail?'

I sat, watching her. 'Maybe you need some rest? I know it's easy to say, but maybe you need to relax a bit.'

She sat very still, her eyes downcast. The house was oppressive with silence. We might be the only people left in the world. I looked at her nails, chewed at the corners, at the tension in her face.

I smiled. 'I've got something for you. Did your mum say?'

For the first time, her eyes lifted and flicked across to look at me. 'Not exactly…'

I got to my feet. 'Well, don't get your hopes up, but I've been doing some clearing out. There were a few things I thought you might like.'

I led her up the stairs to Ralph's study. She hesitated in the doorway, looking round, taking it all in. The boxes, neatly labelled, along the wall. The pile of books on his desk. His chair. She bit her lip.

'Is this where he worked?'

I nodded. 'He used to read in here. And do his marking.' I turned to her, smiling. 'He probably marked some of your essays in here, over the years.'

'And his poetry? Did he write that here too?' Her voice was tight.

'Sometimes. More often, sitting on the floor over there.' I pointed to the radiator in the corner and pictured him there, his back against it, his knees drawn up, hunched over a pad of paper, his hair falling forward. A glass of wine by his elbow. In the zone.

I was so proud of his writing, when we had first met. When he first wrote about me, about his love for me, his poetry seemed such a precious gift.

Things changed, first between us, then in the poetry too. The writing became restless, as he did. Poems about unfulfilled longing, about escape. And then, finally, about his passion, thinly disguised, for other women. He seemed to think he had the right to betray me publicly in poetry. An artist's right. It was about him, after all, this poetry. About his ego, his needs. There was no loyalty in it. That was when I stopped going to his events to hear him read.

I picked up the pile of books I'd set aside for Megan.

'I'm giving away most of his things, but I just wondered... these seemed worth keeping.' I handed them to her. 'If you wanted them? I'm sure Ralph would be pleased for you to have them.'

She looked over them, one book at a time, going through the motions of opening each volume and scanning the contents, flicking through the pages, stopping here and there to run her eye down a particular poem or quotation. One or two still bore Ralph's flamboyant signature on the flyleaf and I saw her pause and stare at it, as if she were spooked by the idea of taking a dead man's possessions.

I put my hand on her arm. She was trembling.

'Don't take them if you don't really want them. It's fine. Honestly.'

We left the books where they were and trooped back to the kitchen to sit again at the table. Again, she focussed on the floor, avoiding my eye. This silence was so unlike her. I watched, trying to understand.

It was all wrong between us and I didn't know why. She was so withdrawn, just as Bea had described. I'd always been her friend. We'd got along easily. I'd always kept her confidences when she'd confided in me — worries about boyfriends, best friends, schoolwork. I'd never betray her, and she knew it. Her secrets were safe with me.

'Is it the books? Have I upset you?' I spoke quietly. 'I'm sorry.'

'It's not that.' Her voice was hard with emotion, as if it hurt her to get out the words.

The kitchen clock ticked down the silence.

Finally, I said, 'What is it, Megan?'

A shadow passed over her face. 'I don't want to talk about it, okay? Just stop asking! You're as bad as Mum.'

I reached out a hand to her, soothing. 'It's fine. Look, forget it.'

I opened my arms to her and she pressed herself into them and clung to me. Soon, her body started to heave with hard, dry sobs, her face against my neck. I put my arms around her and held her tightly, as I might hold Anna, stroking her hair with one hand and pressing her to me with the other.

'Sssh, Megan. I'm sorry,' I whispered into her hair, trying to calm her. 'I didn't mean to pry. You just seem upset.'

She pulled away. 'How can I tell you? I can't tell anyone.'

I shook my head, looking at the distress in her eyes.

'Why not? What is it, Megan?'

She withdrew from me altogether, leaving me with empty arms. 'You'll blame me.'

I blinked. 'For what?'

She looked so guilty.

'Oh, Megan.' My heart stopped. 'You're not – you're not pregnant, are you?'

'Pregnant?' She looked horrified. 'No! Why would you even think that?'

I blew out my cheeks. 'I don't know. I just thought, maybe, a new boyfriend…'

She glared at me.

I hesitated, feeling my way. 'Is that it? You're seeing someone?'

'I'm not seeing him.' She retreated again, perching on a chair, her legs pulled up. She looked so young, hugging her knees. 'I thought he was on my side, but he started saying stupid things. That he loved me. Needed me.' She banged her hand on the table as if she couldn't bear it, as if she couldn't hold it in any longer. 'He said it was all my fault – that I'd led him on. But I didn't! I just… I never thought he'd get so weird.'

I tried to piece all this together. 'Can you tell me who he is?'
'No.'

I took a deep breath. 'Okay. Can you tell me what happened?
How far did it go?'

She flushed. 'We didn't...' Her shock made her seem terribly
young. Terribly innocent, after all. 'He just, you know, he tried.'

'Tried?'

She shuddered and fixed her eyes on the tabletop and the
fingers picking at each other there. Her voice became mechanical.
'He took me for a drink one evening. Mum doesn't know.'

I didn't move, frightened of breaking her flow.

'It was a while ago. I'd just got my offer from Edinburgh.' Her
face contorted with shame. 'He didn't force me to have a drink.
I wanted to. I was happy.'

I kept my voice even. 'So, you went for a drink?'

'He drove me to a pub, miles away. It was really quiet. I'd
never been there before.'

I bit my lip. 'Then what happened?'

She swallowed hard. 'He went to the bar and came back with
a whole bottle of wine but he only had one glass because he was
driving.' She paused. 'I couldn't manage the rest, not all of it, but
it didn't feel polite...'

She trailed off. I tried not to show how angry I was, not with
her but with him, for being so manipulative.

'So, you were pretty light-headed by the time he took you
home?'

She nodded miserably.

'And then what?'

She grimaced. 'He parked in the next street from ours and I
said goodbye and tried to get out but the doors were locked and
then he leaned over and—'

She broke off.

I closed my eyes, picturing it even as I struggled not to. 'And what?'

'He held me down and kissed me. It was gross.' She shuddered. 'He stuck his tongue down my throat. I couldn't breathe. Then he put his hand on my leg and he tried to slide it further up and I grabbed it to stop him. He only stopped when I got hold of his hair and yanked it. I kept telling him to stop. He looked so surprised and sort of hurt. He said how much he liked me and he thought I felt the same way and why didn't we go out again, he'd take me somewhere special next time.'

Silence. I thought about Anna, asleep upstairs, and what I'd do if some boy tried the same moves on her when she was older.

Megan's lip puckered as she started to cry again. 'I felt so stupid! He must have thought I was such a baby... I didn't mean to make him angry, I really didn't. I always liked him. I just didn't like him like that.'

'And was that it? That one time?'

I opened my eyes to watch her. She was rummaging in her sleeve for a tissue to wipe off her face and runny nose.

'Kind of. He kept texting. Saying he was sorry and, like, *please can I see you? Just once. Just to explain.* I didn't know what to do.'

'So what did you do?'

'Nothing. I didn't answer. I deleted them and pretended it hadn't happened. I kept out of his way.'

I thought, *it could have been worse. Thank goodness she had such good sense. Thank goodness she'd pushed him off.*

'Is he still pestering you?'

Her eyes were fixed again on the floor.

'Is this why you can't concentrate?'

'I can't stop thinking about it.' Her hands trembled. 'Maybe I really hurt him. What if he meant all the things he said, that he couldn't bear to live without me?'

'Oh, Megan.' I reached forward and clasped her hot hands in mine. 'From what you've said, he sounds like a nasty piece of work. You did nothing wrong. In fact, you did exactly the right thing.'

She lifted her red-rimmed eyes to mine. 'Really?'

'Really.' I looked into her eyes and spoke clearly and calmly. 'Megan, you've done nothing to feel bad about. Absolutely nothing.'

She looked beseeching. 'I never meant—'

'I know. I can see that.'

Something relaxed in her face as relief hit home. *Poor Megan. Had she carried this guilt for months, since her offer from Edinburgh came through?* I felt badly. I'd been so caught up with my own problems, maybe I hadn't noticed hers.

I forced myself to smile. 'Here's what you're going to do. You're going to let go of all this now. Right? For me. All you need to think about is your exams. And afterwards, you're going to go out into the world and have an amazing year away before university. I'll help you persuade your mum. She'll come round. But in the meantime, clear all this from your mind and focus on your work. Can you do that?'

She blew her nose and managed a weak smile. 'I'll try.'

'That reminds me. Sit there a moment. I've got something for you.'

I hurried up to my bedroom, found my chequebook and wrote her the biggest cheque I could afford.

Downstairs, I hid it behind my back.

'Put your hands out. Go on. Eyes closed.'

She stuck out her hands, too tired to be excited. I laid the folded cheque across her palms and folded her fingers round it.

'Okay. You can look now.'

Her eyes popped when she read the amount.

I said, 'This is between us. Put it in the bank and don't tell your mum. Promise?'

She tore her eyes away from the cheque and looked at me. 'I can't… I mean, it's too much.'

'You absolutely can. It's for your year out, once we've persuaded your mum to let you go. She said you were a bit short.' I smiled. 'Think of it as an extra thank you for all the babysitting you've done.'

She tipped her head to look at me again, more hesitant now. 'But you don't have to—'

I shook my head. 'You don't know how much you've helped me, Megan. Now, we both need to get to bed. Shall I call you a cab?'

'That's okay. I'll walk, thanks.'

She tucked the cheque into the inside pocket of her jacket and zipped it closed.

On the doorstep, she looked up the street, then hesitated. Her face clouded.

'You okay, Megan?'

She stepped back into the hall. 'That man. In the car.'

I peered past her at the saloon car further down the road, scraped along the side. Mike Ridge.

'What about him?'

'I don't like him. He came to our house, asking questions. Mum said she'd already told the police everything and sent him packing.'

I nodded. I wondered why Bea hadn't mentioned it.

'And he came up to me in the street the other day. In town.' She looked wary. 'I wondered afterwards if, maybe, well… if he'd followed me.'

I looked up sharply. 'What did he say?'

She squirmed. 'He wanted to know if I'd been babysitting for you recently.'

'What did you say?'

'That I'd been over sometimes, for a bit of extra cash.'

My heart hammered. 'And?'

'He asked if I had a key to your place. A spare key. I said no.'

'Well, you haven't.' I considered. 'It's your mum's key, isn't it? You just borrow it. So you didn't lie.'

'That's what I thought.' She went on. 'He asked if you'd ever leave Anna on her own. I said no way, you'd never do that. Not even to pop to the shops like Mum might, if she's desperate. You're strict about safety.'

I nodded. 'Good girl.' She was bang on script, just as we'd discussed. 'And?'

She steadied herself. 'He asked if I knew anything at all about that night. You know. When Mr Wilson…'

I stiffened. 'What did you say?'

'I said no, of course.' Her lip trembled. 'But he seemed to know I was lying. What if he tells the police?'

She sagged forward and sank her face into cupped hands, close to tears again.

'He won't.' I put my hand on her shoulder. 'He's just trying to rattle you.' I lowered my voice to a whisper. 'If you hadn't come over that night, after I'd dashed out, how could I have kept looking for Ralph? I couldn't have left Anna on her own all that time.' I sighed. 'I know I didn't find him. But at least I tried.'

I took a deep breath. 'And the texts you sent him, from my phone. If just one of them had reached him in time, it might have changed everything. I really believe that. We might have saved him, Megan. And it would have been thanks to you.'

She leaned into me and I stroked her hair and soothed her as if she were a much younger child. Her skin was warm and firm through her flimsy clothes, trembling as she pressed against me.

When she seemed calmer, I patted her back and drew away. 'Better?'

She nodded. 'I can't thank you enough, Mrs Wilson. Honestly. For—'

I interrupted, pushing her out into the night, smiling as I spoke. 'Enough. We're even. And good luck in your exams. I'll keep everything crossed.'

*

On my way upstairs, I went to check on Anna. She was splayed across her bed, one leg sticking at an odd angle out of the pink duvet, her arm wrapped around her pillow, her hair scattered. I lifted the stray leg and placed it gently back under the covers, then tucked it around her. She stirred and muttered.

'It's all right, sweetheart. Only Mummy. Off to sleep now.'

My own bed was cold. I curled in a ball, hunched on my side of the mattress as if Ralph were still there beside me, filling the rest.

I closed my eyes, but I couldn't sleep, thinking about Megan and the man who'd preyed on her. She'd clearly been through Hell, weighed down by guilt for something that wasn't her fault.

I got out of bed, padded to the window and drew back a curtain just enough to peer out at the street. The saloon car had disappeared again. I frowned, uneasy.

Why had Mike Ridge made a point of following Megan? Why had he asked her so many questions about the night Ralph disappeared?

CHAPTER 44

Miss Abbott was the one who asked me to go.

I'd been in the school library, listening to children read, and had just reached the end of my session. I packed up, put the remaining reading diaries into alphabetical order, as I always did before I handed them back, and put on my coat.

Miss Abbott must have been waiting for me. 'Could I have a word, Mrs Wilson?'

My insides contracted as if I were a naughty schoolgirl being called to the teacher's office. I followed her back along the corridor, carrying the tray of diaries with me, and to her tiny office. She reached past me and managed to close the door.

'Is Anna okay?'

She waved away my anxiety. 'She's fine. It's not about Anna, it's about Miss Dixon.'

I narrowed my eyes. 'Miss Dixon?'

Miss Abbott looked past me at some meaningless spot on the closed door. 'I'm sorry to bother you, really I am, but I went to see her at the weekend and she was in a poor way. She made me promise to pass on a message to you and I said I would. She was very insistent. I hope you understand.'

My arms, supporting the plastic tray, stiffened. I couldn't imagine any message from Miss Dixon that I'd be pleased to receive.

Miss Abbott carried on addressing the door. 'She wants you to visit her. At home.'

My face must have betrayed me. 'I'm afraid I'm terribly busy, Miss Abbott. You can imagine. I'm on my own now and—'

She raised a hand to arrest me in mid-flow. 'Of course. I quite understand. I did say as much to Miss Dixon. And believe me, I wouldn't be passing on her request at all if I weren't so concerned about her.'

Miss Abbott gestured to the chair which was crammed into the narrow space on my side of the room and edged around her desk to reach her own chair on the far side.

I hesitated. I didn't want to sit down. I wanted to get away from school and head to the supermarket before I was due back at the school gates to collect Anna and Clara. It was absurd, this game of sardines in Miss Abbott's cupboard of an office but the sooner it was over, the better. I sighed, set the reading diaries down on the top of her desk and manoeuvred myself into the chair.

'She's very unwell, Mrs Wilson.' Miss Abbott leaned forward and lowered her voice. 'I know I can tell you this in strictest confidence. They're trying various medications to work out what's right for her but she's so agitated. She seems to have suffered some sort of breakdown.'

She hesitated, as if deciding how much more to tell me.

I said, 'I'm sorry to hear that, Miss Abbott, but I really can't see why—'

'Let me explain. I don't know how best to say this… I know it's painful.' She took a deep breath. 'While I was there, she kept talking about Mr Wilson. She seemed obsessed by something she saw. She says she can't rest unless she talks to you about it.'

I rolled my eyes. 'It sounds as if she needs professional—'

'I know! I know exactly what you mean. I agree. She seems very unwell. Mentally. And of course, you're under no obligation. None at all. But she made me promise to pass on her message and I have. That's all.'

I shook my head. 'It's very sad.'

'Extremely.'

We both got to our feet.

Miss Abbott drew a slip of paper from the pile on her desk and handed it to me.

'This is her address and phone number. Just in case. She rarely leaves home at the moment. And I didn't get the impression she had many visitors.' She hesitated, her eyes on mine. 'She always struck me as rather solitary, here at school.'

You mean she didn't have a friend to her name, I thought, taking the paper and pushing it into my pocket.

Miss Abbott managed a smile. 'Thank you, Mrs Wilson. I know it's a lot to ask.'

I opened my mouth to say, *you're wrong. I'm not going to see that woman, however desperate she is. Let her rot.*

I found my mouth closing again. Miss Abbott knew as well as I did that, however much I resented the cry for help, I would do the decent thing. I would respond to it.

CHAPTER 45

I went round to her flat the following morning. She buzzed me in downstairs without speaking. When I reached her landing, two floors up, her front door was ajar. The paintwork was chipped where shiny new locks had been fitted.

'Hello? Miss Dixon?' I pushed the door open and went through into a narrow hall. 'You there? It's Mrs Wilson.'

I hesitated. The flat had a stale, musty smell as if she had sealed herself off from the sunshine outside. I called again, 'Miss Dixon?'

A weak voice called from towards the front of the building. 'Come in.'

I closed the door behind me and headed through. The hallway gave onto a sitting room, bright with sunlight. She was sitting in an armchair with her back to the door, positioned in front of the window. She had the vacant air of someone who sat alone all day, looking out for someone or something to arrive.

A small table sat by her side, cluttered with used glasses and mugs, an empty plate, soiled with crumbs, a pile of closed books.

I sighed to myself. It was sad. She was in a sorry state, clearly. But I wouldn't be drawn into it. I'd stay for a brief chat, then make my excuses and leave. That would be it. Whatever state she was in, I'd never come back.

I crept round to the side of the chair to see her properly. She was dressed, but her shirt looked crumpled and her feet were bare, pushed into faded slippers. Her hands rested on the yellowed pages of a book which lay open in her lap. I blinked, feeling a memory stir as I looked and struggling to place it. A leather-bound book. Poetry, judging by the layout.

She turned her head very slowly to meet my eye, as if movement were difficult for her. Her hair looked unkempt, sticking together in clumps. Her face was bare of make-up, the lips chapped as if she'd fallen into the habit of licking them.

'I didn't think you'd come.' Her eyes looked rheumy. 'Thank you.'

I considered. 'Shall I make us both a cup of tea?'

She didn't answer. I gathered up the dirty things on her table and bustled through to the kitchen. It was small but bright and could have been pretty if it had been clean. In fact, dirty plates and bowls were stacked haphazardly in the sink and on the nearby counter, giving off the sour stink of rancid milk.

I did my best to clean out two mugs with washing-up liquid and a scrubber, found teabags and kettle and made us both tea. I'd only pretend to sip mine, I decided. I didn't want to swallow anything that came out of this kitchen.

By the time I came back, she'd moved from the armchair to the settee down one side of the room. I set her tea on the coffee table, drew up a straight-backed chair and sat across from her with my own mug.

'So,' I said. 'You wanted to see me?'

She didn't answer. We sat there, suspended. Distant sounds drifted up from the street, muffled. A bus or lorry beeped as it reversed. A man's voice shouted instructions.

Finally, she lifted her eyes and looked directly at me.

'He came for me. Ralph.' Her voice was calm. 'He's been sending me messages. I know it's him. He summoned me to the beach where, you know. Where we took him.'

I swallowed, then shook my head. 'I'm sorry. I don't know what you mean.'

She frowned. 'I'm not mad. My memory isn't clear, but I remember that night.'

I shook my head. 'I'm afraid you've lost me. Are you talking about my husband?'

She gave me a canny look. 'Your husband. Oh yes, that's right. As if I could ever forget that.'

I felt myself flush. It had been a mistake, coming here. I was a fool to think I was obliged, to show that I was a better human being than she was, that I was at least kind.

'I'm afraid I can't stay long.' I put the mug to my lips and pretended to drink. 'Was there something else?'

'He came out of the sea. Dripping. Undead. I saw him.'

I took a deep breath. 'Miss Dixon, the pills—'

'Laura! Call me Laura. No one does, anymore.'

I sat a little straighter in my chair. 'Miss *Dixon*,' I said firmly, 'the pills may have caused you to imagine things. Things that weren't actually there. My husband has not been found. I can assure you that, whatever you think you saw, he did not rise from the waves and come back to haunt you.'

Her tongue snaked out and ran round her chapped lips.

There was a hardness in her face. 'I remember some things. He left me a glass of red wine – Shiraz. It was bitter. But I drank it for him, I toasted him, as he asked. Then I went out onto the beach and saw him there. Calling me. Waiting for me.'

I stared at her. 'I don't know what you want from me, Miss Dixon. I'm sorry for you, I really am. But you're not well. You need to rest and get properly better.'

Her lips buckled. For a moment, she seemed to be sneering at me. Then I realised she was crying, quietly and messily. I stiffened. I wanted to get away.

'Come on, have some tea.' I jumped up and picked up her mug, tried to place it into her hands and help her fingers grasp it. They trembled so much that hot tea sloshed over the sides and dripped down onto the carpet.

She scrambled to get a better hold and I helped her lift it to her lips and held it while she drank, as I used to do for Anna when she was younger. It seemed to calm her down. I set the mug back on the table where the drips made an instant circular puddle.

'It's the medication,' she said. 'It gives me the shakes.' She paused, then looked up at me, uncertainly. 'Apparently, I tried to kill myself. Maybe I did… I don't remember. They had to pump my stomach. I remember that.' She scrutinised my face as she spoke as if she wanted some sort of confirmation of what had happened to her. 'I don't remember taking the pills, but they found the empty pack in my coat pocket. How could I have been so stupid?'

I said, 'You haven't been well. But you'll get better. It takes time, but you'll put this behind you and move on.'

'Do you really think so?'

I tried to smile. 'I'm sure you will.'

'I nearly died. I keep thinking about it. About my life. My sins.' She paused. 'About Hell. What it must be like.'

I hesitated. 'I doubt you'll go to Hell…'

She looked up with such hope in her face that I pitied her. 'You really think I won't? After what I did, after what we both did?'

I shook my head. 'I don't know what you're talking about, Miss Dixon. But I think everyone deserves a second chance.' I paused, thinking. 'Even you.'

One of her hands clutched at the other. 'Thank you. That's more than I deserve. Thank you.'

I picked up my mug and got to my feet. 'Was there anything else you wanted to say?'

She looked me over. 'When I went down to the shore, when he summoned me, the boathouse was open. He had set out a row of candles, protected from the wind by glass covers. The bottle of wine and two glasses, one for him and one for me.'

I didn't move.

'But the man who found me, that jogger, he said the boathouse was all closed up. So did the paramedics. They said I'd been hallucinating. And when the police had a look, later, there was no trace of any of those things inside. That's why I'm on such heavy medication. To help me forget. The scene inside the boathouse. The wine. Ralph, rising from the sea. Apparently, I imagined it all.'

I turned to leave. 'Well, maybe that's right, Miss Dixon. Maybe it was the pills playing—'

She cut through me, her voice suddenly sharp. 'I know what I saw. Some parts are hazy but those things, I remember clear as day. So it doesn't make sense. Doesn't make sense at all.' She leaned forward, her hand a shaky claw on the arm of the settee and whispered, 'What do you think?'

CHAPTER 46

After school, Anna and Clara were full of a new game they'd invented.

'Mummy, what's this?'

I was trying to persuade them to sit properly at the table and eat their fish fingers and beans.

'What?'

'Listen – *mish-mash giggiwok cam-bam looloo.*'

She and Clara burst out laughing. Clara managed to get out, '*May-may ding-dong schammer-dammer.*'

They turned flushed faces to me.

I made a show of considering. 'Are you speaking Spanish?'

They giggled, pleased to be outsmarting me. 'No, Mummy. Listen!'

More nonsense. I leaned forward and speared a piece of fish finger with Anna's fork, then put the fork into her hand. 'I'll have another guess once you've both finished two bites of fish fingers.'

'Mum-my!'

I waited while they laboriously chewed, eating as painfully as if the food were cardboard.

Finally, two bites later, they set off again.

Clara said, '*Dibber-dabber-dishcloth!*'

Anna nearly fell off her chair laughing.

'*Tarty-starty-barty,*' she answered.

They rounded on me again.

'Go on! Guess.'

'That is tricky.' I tried to look thoughtful. 'Icelandic?'

They looked at each other and frowned.

Anna said, 'Wait. Is that even a real thing?'

'It is indeed. It's what they speak in Iceland.' I took the peas out of the microwave and added them to the girls' plates. 'You know Iceland? It's a country. Right at the top. Very cold.'

'Have you been?'

'No.'

'Has Daddy?'

'No.' I tried to distract her from thinking about Ralph. 'So, can I have one more guess?'

'One more. And that's it.'

'Hmm.' I screwed up my face. 'I know!' I held up a finger in triumph. 'Mer-language.'

'No!' Clara roared, delighted.

Anna said, 'Mer-language? That's just silly.'

'I don't see why. How can mermen and mermaids talk to each other if they haven't got their own language? *Sblib-sblob-nooney-noo?*'

'That's not even it,' Anna said. 'Anyway, you're wrong. It's alien language and Clara and I are the only people who know it.'

'Well done. If any aliens come to the door, I'll ask you to come and talk to them.'

Anna gave me a scornful look. 'Aliens aren't real, Mummy. How are they going to come to the door?'

The only person who came to the door was Bea, about an hour later.

We headed for the kitchen for our usual quick handover chat before she took Clara home.

'Have you done something to your hair?' Bea followed me down the hall. 'You look different.'

'Do I?' I waited until she caught me up, not sure what to say.

Bea paused, looking me over. 'You look great, Helen. It's not your hair, is it? It's you. You're all sort of sparkly.'

I laughed. 'Oh, come on. If you need a favour, just come right out and ask me. You don't need to butter me up.'

'I mean it. You looked so tired before, after...' She looked embarrassed.

I knew exactly what she meant. After Ralph disappeared.

She carried on, quickly. 'But now, you look fab. Better than ever.' She gave me a closer look. 'You're not seeing someone, are you?'

'As if.' I went back to washing up the girls' dishes and pans. I thought about Ralph and all the dramas, all the disappointments. 'Anyway, I've got one special person in my life. Anna. That'll do me.'

Bea picked up a tea towel and started to dry. 'How's Anna doing?'

I hesitated. 'She doesn't talk about him much, but she's having nightmares. She had one last night.'

Bea pulled a sympathetic face. 'Poor thing.'

I nodded. It had taken Anna a long time to calm down last night, even after I'd woken her. I'd ended up taking her into my bed with me and cuddling her to sleep. At least there was plenty of room, now, without Ralph.

I hadn't slept much, after that. Anna's distress wasn't my only worry.

I took a deep breath. 'I've got news.'

She raised an eyebrow. 'Good news?'

'I hope so.' I took a deep breath. 'You know I said I was looking for a new place? I think I've found one. I put an offer in yesterday and I just heard. It's been accepted.'

'Yesterday?' She looked taken aback. 'Why didn't you tell me you had found somewhere?'

I shrugged. 'I didn't think it'd really happen. I didn't want to jinx it.'

Bea blew out her cheeks. 'That's great news.' She was straining to look pleased. 'Well, tell me all about it. Where? What? Have you got photos to show me? Is it online?'

I looked away, through to the sitting room where the girls were practising their forward rolls down the length of the settee, giggling and giving each other exaggerated high-fives.

'Let's not do that now. Anyway, it's nothing special. A two-bed on the outskirts of Bristol. There's a decent school nearby.'

She stared. 'Why Bristol, anyway?'

I shrugged and focussed on the grill-pan which I was scrubbing with unnecessary force.

Bea stopped drying. She stood next to me, the tea towel limp in her hands. 'When did you get to see it? At the weekend?'

I hesitated. 'I haven't seen it, exactly. Just photos.'

Bea blinked. 'You're telling me you've put in an offer on a property you haven't seen? In a place you don't know? Sorry, but am I missing something here?'

I didn't answer.

Clara came belting through from the sitting room to hug her mother. 'Is it time to go?'

'Just about.'

Anna trailed behind, hanging round the doorframe. 'Can't she stay a bit longer, Mum? Please.'

I looked at Bea. 'If you want. Another five minutes. Okay with you, Clara?'

'Yaaaaay!' They turned round and went tearing back to the sitting room together.

Bea waited until they'd gone, then turned back to me. 'You don't seem very excited.'

I put the grill pan upside down on the drainer and reached for a greasy oven tray.

'I am.' I couldn't look at her. 'It's just, you know, a big change. For both of us.'

'You can always come back, if it doesn't work out. You know that, right? You've always got a place with us, if you need it.'

I thought of Bea's cramped flat, already overcrowded with three of them.

'That's kind.' *It was too late for regrets. Too late for second thoughts. This was it.*

Something in my tone must have alerted her. She took hold of my arm and pulled me round.

'Hey, what is it?' She looked me hard in the eye. 'Don't go all sad on me. It's not the big goodbye. We'll still be friends, right? Wherever you are. Even Bristol.' She smiled. 'You can't get rid of us that easily. We'll come and visit whenever we can.'

I smiled but my heart wasn't in it. All I could think was how very wrong she was.

Where Anna and I were going, she'd never find us again.

CHAPTER 47

Six weeks later

For weeks, I'd worked flat out, emptying drawers and cupboards, filling sack after sack for the charity shop, then driving just as many more to the dump.

I got rid of all Ralph's clothes, the bohemian jackets and trousers, the suits, the Noël Coward dressing-gown, his shoes, his books, his old bags and suitcases and the sports equipment in the loft.

Even without him, Anna and I had so much stuff of our own. I filled a whole room with boxes of old toys and almost all our clothes, pre-school children's books and my recipe books, towels and bed linen. I sent it all to the charity shop. Once we were on the brink of leaving, a team of men came round with a truck and cleared first the kitchen, then the furniture from the rest of the house. What they couldn't sell or donate, they'd send for disposal, they said.

It was the start of August, and our street – dusty and sticky underfoot with melting tarmac – seemed unnaturally quiet. Everyone was away on holiday. Even Clara was going away, staying with her grandma, Bea's mum, in Wales for two weeks.

Bea was at work. I wondered how long it would take her to realise that the Bristol address I'd dutifully written out for her was a false one. That my usual mobile number would soon no longer be in service.

Anna, restless and bereft, had hung around as the adults cleared the house. She'd watched the activity with a gloomy expression and tearful eyes.

The previous night, our very last in the house, she'd screamed herself to sleep, her angular body curled into a ball, tight and resolute, even as I lay beside her and tried to relax her with rhythmical strokes and soothing words.

'It'll be okay, Anna. It will. It's always hard leaving a home. I know that. But wait till you see the new one. You'll love it!'

'I won't!' Her face was swollen with crying. 'I'm not going. I'm not, Mummy. You can't make me!'

Now, the charity team had closed up the truck and left and everything was suddenly quiet again. Anna looked exhausted, her small frame hunched as we held hands and walked together on a final tour through the empty rooms to say goodbye.

The house looked alien, the rooms shrunken and without personality now the furniture had gone. Without carpet, our feet echoed on the wooden floors.

I remembered the first time we'd viewed the house, Ralph and I. I was so in love with him and full of optimism about the future. Upstairs, we'd walked into the spare bedroom and he'd snaked his arm round me to give my waist a squeeze.

'Children's bedroom,' he'd said in a low voice. 'The twins can share this one. Bunk beds, maybe. And the triplets can go in the big bedroom at the top.'

I'd laughed, sharing the joke, hopeful that bearing five children fathered by Ralph was a happy possibility. I always knew he was a charmer, of course I did. I just thought the charm was reserved for me.

Now, clunking across the bare boards, conscious of the dirty streaks across the painted walls, the cracks in the brickwork, life seemed impossibly different. Without us, the terraced house seemed narrow and poky.

'Have you left him a note?' Anna turned large, anxious eyes on me as we headed back to the hall. 'How will he find us?'

'Oh, Anna!' I crouched down and kissed the tip of her nose, then took her in my arms and held her close. 'Is that why you're so sad about leaving? In case Daddy comes back and can't find us? Oh, sweetheart!'

Outside, I settled her in the back seat of the hire car, hemmed in beside the bags of possessions we were keeping, including her soft toys, then went to lock the front door for the last time and post the key through the letterbox for the estate agent to find.

As we pulled out, I glimpsed a movement in the rear-view mirror, from a car which was parked a little further down the street.

I turned to look more closely. A battered saloon car with scraped paintwork. Its driver, Mike Ridge, was leaning out of the window, his hand raised in salute, his eyes on mine and a knowing smile on his lips.

CHAPTER 48

Deep in the country, the roads narrowed and I scanned the horizon for oncoming traffic, hoping to catch sight of cars before they disappeared into hollows and behind tight corners, then appeared in front of me too late, forcing me hard against the verge.

The visibility wasn't helped by the drystone walls which edged the road. They bordered undulating fields dotted with sheep and, above, rising fells, richly coloured in the dying light by bracken and heather, nippled with stone cairns.

Anna, exhausted after the emotions of the last few days and lulled by the drive, was asleep in the back. Her head drooped sideways, bouncing lightly against the hard shell of her child seat. Her lips were parted. Her hair, newly short and spiky – like mine – still surprised me.

I whispered, 'Nearly there,' into the empty hum of the car.

A lay-by loomed ahead, an entrance to a farmer's field. If I'd been alone, I might have pulled in, just for the chance of surveying the valley. The hump-back bridge over the river which was streaked gold, touched with pink, in the gathering sunset. The clusters of stone cottages set along the main street. They climbed the opposite hill and forked, here and there, into more modern housing, grouped into crescents.

The long, lean pub and hotel on the riverbank with its stone arch, offering an entrance to the hidden car park behind. The church with its reaching spire, also made from the same grey

Yorkshire stone as the pub, the bridge, the older houses. There were visitors too, for August. One of the farmer's fields, close to the riverbank, had been turned over to a row of caravans and tents. Barbecues and camping stoves sent up wisps of smoke which dispersed rapidly in the light breeze from the river.

I smiled to myself. *Space. Clean air.* I'd been a child, not much older than Anna, when I first came to this village for a one-week holiday. We'd stayed in a bed and breakfast on the main street, with cold, dingy bedrooms and heavy quilts. Most days, I'd taken a fishing net and splashed at the edges of the river, my trousers rolled up to my knees, heaving rocks to build dams and fishing for tiddlers. There'd been picnics – wads of ham sandwiches and crisps and pop – on Dad's tartan blanket which, however long it lay stretched in the sun, never lost the smell of his car. In the evenings, fish and chips and pies in the pub garden.

As I manoeuvred the car over the hump-back bridge and through the arch to the pub hotel car park, the sun gleamed round and red as it sank from view, as if it had seen us safely home and considered its work done. At once, as I switched off the engine and sat, rubbing my neck, rolling the knots out of my shoulders, the landscape became dark and brooding, the wind chill.

I turned to the back seat. 'Anna! We're here!'

She stirred, heavy with sleep, and groaned. She struggled to see out of narrowed eyes into the darkness.

'I'm cold, Mummy.'

'That's okay. We'll soon get cosy in bed.' I climbed out and went around the back of the car to help her. She was slow to move. I had to reach in to unbuckle her, then prise her from the seat.

In the car park, she stood uncertainly, lost. She looked at the hotel. 'Is this our house?'

'We're just staying here tonight. We'll explore the house tomorrow, as soon as it's light.'

I grabbed our overnight bag, then took her hand and led her across the cobbles to the main entrance. A lion was carved in the stone above the door. The air was fresh and sharp and carried the smell of sheep, of peat, of the moors.

I rang the bell on the deserted reception desk until a young man came running through from the bar. His hair stood up in clumps, raked through by his fingers.

'Mrs Mack,' I said. 'I've booked a room for tonight. Twin beds.'

I winked at Anna. She stared at me, still unsure. We were starting a wonderful game, I'd told her when we'd stopped at the motorway service station on the way up the M1. Like pretending to be foxes or puppies or princesses or any of the other games we played together.

'We're new people now,' I told her. 'With new names. Anna Mack. What do you think of that?'

She'd hesitated, her lip wobbling. 'I want to be Anna Wilson,' she said. 'Or Princess Celestia.'

I'd considered. 'We'll call you Anna Celestia Mack, then.'

Now, the young man opened up a ledger and ran his finger down the columns, then plucked a printed form from a drawer and handed me a pen. I filled in the details I'd learned. The new address, here in the village. The new name. The phone number of the cheap pay-as-you-go mobile I'd swapped for my old, easily traceable one.

I left the credit card details blank. 'Okay if I pay cash?'

'Sure.' He peered at the form. 'I'd need you to pay now though, for tonight.'

'No problem.' I rummaged in my handbag and counted off notes from the large wad there.

He handed over the room key, attached to a heavy leather fob.

'I see you're not going far. Craven Barn. You booked in there for the week, Mrs Mack?'

'Longer than that.' I tried not to let Anna see how anxious I felt. 'It's our new home.'

*

Once the pub closed, the hotel fell silent.

Anna was curled tightly in her bed, duvet and spare blankets piled on top of her. The thick iron radiator was dusty. The room carried the dank chill of old stone walls.

I sat on the window seat in the darkness, with my coat wrapped around my knees and the curtain drawn back, keeping watch. The trees along the riverbank shuffled their branches in the wind. When I pressed my face against the window, the glass was cold and solid. I breathed a circle of condensation and wrote 'Anna', then enclosed her with a heart. The night outside was intense. The only relief were the microscopic threads of moonlight that flashed on the fast-moving surface of the river.

The smells here stirred memories for me. I thought back to the sense of strangeness I'd felt on holiday here as a young child. The small differences. The soggy cornflakes at breakfast, in a shallow china bowl. The thick creaminess of the milk. Farm eggs and greasy sausages. Being urged to try black pudding and feeling revolted by it. *It's blood*, I'd remembered. *Pig's blood.*

A crunch of gravel, down in the car park. Someone was there. I stiffened and drew back a little from the window, still looking but better concealed. I waited, straining to see and hear.

Silence. Then it came again. Not animal but human. Footsteps. Stealthy and slow.

I narrowed my eyes in the gloom, trying to see. A dark figure eased its way around the car park, keeping to the shadows. It crept along the ragged row of vehicles as if it were sniffing them out, then stopped at mine. I held my breath.

A man. Crouching to look at my car. His shape shifted and I had the sense that he'd turned to look up, his eyes scanning the darkened windows of the hotel, searching for someone. Searching for me.

I shrank further back and closed my eyes, blood pounding in my ears.

When I looked again, he'd gone, slipping as quickly and stealthily out of the car park as he had come.

CHAPTER 49

Anna woke early the next morning and padded across the cold floor to join me in bed. She seemed lost and a little frightened. She put icy feet on my warm legs and I wrapped my arms around her.

'Are you okay?'

She didn't answer, just pressed her forehead into the soft flesh of my arm.

'Does it feel very strange, waking up here?'

She gave a jerky nod.

I kissed the top of her head. 'I know, sweetheart. It's different, isn't it? We'll get used to it.'

I thought of all the times in the last two months that I'd woken in the night to the sound of her screaming. The nightmares spoke for themselves. She'd suffered, without really understanding why, as she struggled to come to terms with losing Ralph. It wasn't something she knew how to talk about.

I held her safe in the circle of my arms.

'Listen. What can you hear?'

We lay very still and listened.

'Clanging,' she said. 'A man talking in a funny voice. Footsteps.'

Downstairs, doors slammed as people moved to and fro. Someone was preparing breakfast.

'What else?'

She shrugged.

'Listen harder. What do they have here, in the countryside, that we don't have at home?'

She frowned with concentration, then broke into a smile as she fixed on the distant sounds of animals in the farms around us. 'Cows! Doggies!'

'Dogs,' I corrected. 'Farm dogs, probably. Working dogs. And did you hear that rooster?'

She jumped out of bed and we hurried to get dressed.

'What animal do you want to be?' I asked. 'A sheepdog?'

'Yes!' She considered. 'No! Pretend you're a farmer and I'm a little lamb and you've just found me, asleep on your bed and you're going to take me home. Say, *what's this? A lamb! How cute!* And pretend I could talk.'

After breakfast, Anna played in the hotel garden until the estate agent opened and I could take possession of the keys. More thick wads of cash. We took the car the short distance up the hill, turned off at the top of the high street and bounced down a rutted farm track. It skirted the hillside, fringed by dry stone walls and fields, then dipped and brought us down to the barn itself, set in a natural hollow.

Anna strained forward, peering out. 'Is that it?'

'Looks like it.'

I skidded to a halt on the rough ground in front of the barn, scattering loose stones, then we headed inside.

The photographs online had exaggerated the size, but the style was exactly what I'd expected. The barn was basic but cleverly converted, making the most of its thick stone walls, its position and its cavernous scale. The vast interior was divided into two levels with a wooden spiral staircase joining the upper and lower floors.

Apart from a cloakroom with a toilet, near the front door, the downstairs area was open plan. The designer had created a dining area with table and chairs and a low pendulum light. I walked past to the kitchenette, set across from the spiral staircase. It was modern, with slate worktops and a ceiling crossed by salvaged wooden beams.

Anna clattered upstairs to explore. I opened kitchen cupboards and drawers. They were well-stocked with cutlery and crockery, mixing bowls and electronic scales. It was like moving into the home of a complete stranger and taking on their identity. We could simply unpack the few clothes and toys we'd brought and become new people.

Beyond the kitchen, the downstairs floor opened into a sitting room, with vast windows which looked out across the valley on the far side of the property. It didn't yet have curtains and the sunlight streamed in, setting the house alight.

'Mummy! Come and look!' Anna, halfway down the stairs, hung over the bannister to call me.

I headed up the wooden stairs to join her, taking note of the open slats.

'You need to be careful on these stairs, Anna. Okay? Mind you don't fall.'

She wasn't listening. She grabbed my hand and pulled me after her into a small bedroom across the upstairs landing. There was no doubting it was meant for her. The white walls were decorated with colourful animal stencils, brand new children's paperbacks sat on the shelves. On the bed, where the pillow might be, sat a large, furry sheepdog, its pink tongue lolling.

'Look, Mummy! A doggie!' She bounced onto the mattress and pulled the stuffed dog onto her lap, buried her face in its fur. 'Can I keep her?'

I hesitated, taken aback. 'I suppose so.'

'I'm going to call her Buddy.' She looked up at me, expectantly. 'Good idea?'

'Great idea…'

I left her there, whispering to Buddy, and crossed the landing to find the master bedroom at the front of the house. Like the sitting room directly below, it was well-proportioned and sunny. The same broad picture windows, arched here, looked out across the valley. Another, more modest window was set in a side wall, giving onto a copse of trees.

A king-sized bed dominated the space, with narrow bedside tables on each side. Fitted wardrobes ran along the length of one wall. I opened a wardrobe door to find drawers hidden inside as well. Plenty of storage. An armchair, a little fussy for my taste, had been placed near the picture windows, looking out, as if it were inviting me to sit and admire the view. I thought of Miss Dixon, slumped in her armchair, day after day, looking out at the streets below, waiting for someone who never came.

I crossed the room to the low door at the far end. It creaked open to reveal a narrow en-suite bathroom with a slanting ceiling. It was fitted into the space under the eaves, white and freshly painted, the suite modern.

As I turned away, my eye caught my flushed face in the mirrored front of the bathroom cabinet, reflected back to me at an angle as the loosened door swung. I opened it to see how it fastened.

I'd expected it to be empty. It wasn't. I stared, my breathing hard.

An upturned shot glass sat on the middle shelf and, beside it, a miniature bottle of red wine.

I didn't need to peer more closely to see what it was. Shiraz. Left there for me to find.

I stood, trembling, thinking hard. About Miss Dixon and the bottle of bitter wine she'd said was waiting for her in the boathouse, a glass already poured for her to drink.

I thought about the bathroom cabinet and the way its front swung open, inviting me to look inside. Why, of all places, there?

CHAPTER 50

Anna agreed to go to bed early that evening. She looked worn out, her cheeks pale and hollowed.

I sat on the edge of the bed with her as she drifted into sleep, stroking her soft, spiky hair away from her forehead and studying her features. My stomach twisted as I looked at her, so vulnerable, so unaware. The fair skin, her long, dark eyelashes, fluttering now as she tipped backwards into oblivion, her bow-shaped upper lip, the deepening puff of her breath. Buddy the sheepdog was tucked in beside her, his head on the fleshy cushion of her upper arm, as if he could protect her from what lay ahead. I waited, keeping watch over her as she slept, frightened to leave her alone in this house. She stirred but didn't wake when I kissed her on the forehead.

Downstairs, I heated a ready meal in the microwave and poured myself some orange juice.

I settled in the sitting room, glass in hand, gazing out over the valley. There was no TV, no WiFi, not even a telephone. I'd lost my mobile signal as soon as we'd come over the ridge and dipped down into the hollow. It was hard to imagine being more isolated.

I sat very still, listening to the silence. Ahead of me, the valley steadily darkened, the black tinged with pink as the sun set. I wondered what Bea was doing. If she and Clara missed us. I thought of our old terraced house and the neighbours on either side, audible every time they plugged an appliance into a socket or turned up the volume on a film.

I imagined this place in winter. The caravans and tents and bed and breakfast trade would pack up and leave. It would be desolate here. Barely a soul. I thought of Mike Ridge, quietly watching from his car as we packed up and drove away.

The darkness, thick now, pressed down. All I saw, as I looked at the windows, was the reflection of the room, hanging there in the blackness. The settee, the coffee table, the lamps and in the midst of it all, a woman I didn't yet know, Helen Mack, silent and still, glass in hand, looking back at herself.

Crack. I started. Stiffened as I listened. *Could it be a large animal which had strayed too close?* I reached for the lamp and switched it off, hiding myself in sudden blackness. The only light now spilled weakly from the other end of the barn, from the overhead lights left on in the kitchen.

I sat, rigid, waiting. For a moment, nothing. I started to breathe again. Then another crack. I jumped. The sharp retort of a dry stick breaking. A person. I was sure of it. Creeping down the side of the building.

I moved as quietly as I could, dropping low and clinging to the deeper shadows along the lines of the furniture. I reached up to switch off the lights in the kitchen, grabbed a kitchen knife from the block and ducked low again. I crawled under the dining-room table and crouched there, my knees drawn up to my body, my arms wrapped around them, trembling.

A footstep, quiet and careful, crunched across the loose stones near the front door. I held my breath. Silence. A sigh. A scuffle of soft shoes against the wooden door. I shrank back further into the darkness, thinking of Anna asleep upstairs, tightening my grip on the handle of the knife.

A key scraped in the lock and the door opened. A man stood there, silhouetted against the night sky.

'Helen?' A throaty whisper.

I sat up abruptly, cracking my head on the underside of the table.

'Helen, it's me.' His tone was theatrical, savouring the drama.

I scrambled out and switched on a light. Ralph. He was standing there, just inside the front door, blinking in the flood of light. He looked different. His face was leaner. The floppy hair had been cut away, replaced by a military-style razor cut. He was wearing a waxed green jacket and black jeans, already dressing for his new part.

'Ralph!' For a moment, I just stared, then my mouth crumpled.

He opened his arms and I ran straight into them, pressed my face into his chest. His smell, sudden and familiar. The feel of his body, broad and muscular firm. His warm skin.

He lifted my hand and looked with amusement at the knife I was still clutching.

'That's not a very nice welcome.' He laughed. 'And after I came all the way back from the dead, too.'

'Oh, please.' I twisted to drop the knife on the counter, then wiped my eyes and hugged him again. 'You scared the life out of me.'

He kissed the top of my head, then loosened my arms, unzipped his jacket and hung it on the back of a dining chair.

I watched him, still dazed. 'I thought you weren't coming for another week or two.'

He shrugged. 'It's boring, being dead. How's Anna? Is she okay?'

I glanced at once towards the spiral staircase. 'She mustn't know, Ralph. Not yet. I need to prepare her.'

'That'll be interesting. What're you going to say? That I'm an angel?'

'Hardly.' I smiled. 'Anna will be fine. I never told her you were dead. I kept saying missing. But I need a bit longer, Ralph. She's been through a lot.'

He gestured round the barn, at the furniture, the lights, the scenes he'd set as if he were dressing a stage for one of his grand school productions. 'Like it?'

I nodded. 'Very much. You've always had great taste.'

He looked satisfied. 'Did Anna like her dog?'

'Loves it. She's called it Buddy.'

He lifted my top and ran cold hands over my skin. I shivered. 'She didn't ask who'd bought it. But it was a bit risky, Ralph.'

'I love risks,' he murmured into my ear, tightening his hold of me. 'I thought you knew that by now.'

CHAPTER 51

I searched the fridge for food and started to cook him what I could find, sausages and eggs. Already, the kitchen was absorbing the smell of his body. He changed the air in a room, just by being there.

I set the sausages sizzling and spitting, feeling his eyes on me, watching my movements. I dropped a fork to the floor with a clatter, banged dishes, clumsy with nerves.

Once he'd eaten, we sat on the settee, side by side, Ralph's arm tight around my shoulders, and looked out into the darkness that veiled the Yorkshire landscape.

Ralph, heavy now with food, said, 'I don't want to say I told you so. But I was right, wasn't I? We did it.'

I didn't answer. I thought about the life ahead, a life in hiding, pretending to be people we were not. It wouldn't be easy, but he'd promised me it would all be worth it. This was our chance of a fresh start. There would only be one woman in his life from now on. Two, if you counted Anna.

I said, 'I've been paying cash for everything, like you said. I've brought a few thousand.'

'Good. I'm nearly out.' He nodded. 'We won't need a lot. It's pretty cheap, round here.'

I tried to smile back. I imagined walking down the High Street with Anna, constantly checking shop windows to see if anyone was following us. Jumping every time I heard footsteps. Being constantly afraid of a knock at the door in case someone had traced us. I still wasn't sure I could do this. Live a lie.

'I was good, wasn't I?' He chuckled to himself. 'I nearly did break my bloody neck, hurtling down those steps in the dark. Gotta hand it to me. The sound effects were awesome. I deserve an Oscar.'

'I had my heart in my mouth on the sail back,' I said. 'You grabbed hold of the rope okay?'

'That water was freezing.' He grimaced.

I thought back. There'd been no moving him, once he'd come up with his crazy plan. *Don't you see?* he kept saying. *It's perfect. We get that mad bitch off our backs and, once the insurers pay out, we'll be rich. We can start again. Clean sheet.*

He said, 'And we were right about Laura Dixon. She bought everything. She really thought she'd killed me.'

Poor, weak Miss Dixon. I'd sensed how unstable she was. I'd felt her anxious eyes seek me out, all those times I'd been sitting in the school library while children stumbled through their reading.

Ralph went on, 'It's shut her up, anyway. Served her right. I never thought she'd be such a mad bitch. '

I cleared my throat. 'How was the cottage?'

We'd chosen one of the derelict cottages along the coast, its windows boarded up, the flooring dank with mildew. It stank of foxes, rising damp and wood rot. I'd done my best to clean it up and Ralph fixed the door and padlocked it, then stored his things there, a supply of dried and tinned food, spare clothes and his camping gear. That's where he'd headed once he'd swum the final stretch to the shore that night.

He shrugged. 'I survived. Can't say I was sorry to leave.'

I considered the vacancy in our own house, after he'd gone. The air had seemed empty without him. I'd missed him terribly. But, over time, I'd sensed something else too. The cautious fluttering of my old self. My more assertive, more independent self.

I remembered the evening I'd entered his study and cleared it, the satisfaction I'd felt when I'd categorised and ordered his books and packed them neatly into boxes. I remembered the things Bea had said about me, once I'd finally started to adjust to living without him. *You look fab. Better than ever. All sort of sparkly.*

'How was my memorial service?'

'Not a dry eye.' I pulled a face. 'You'd be amazed what lovely things people found to say about you. Even Miss Baldini.'

'Shame I wasn't there.' He looked amused.

I considered him. *Ralph. My husband. The father of my child. The man I'd stood by. The man I'd carried on loving, no matter how many times he disappointed me.*

I said, 'I went to see her. Laura Dixon.'

He stared out towards the darkened windows, his jaw set.

'What were you thinking?' I went on. 'Why did you send her texts? She might've gone to the police. And why did she change the locks? That was you, wasn't it, letting yourself into her flat?'

He shrugged, splaying the fingers of his free hand. 'Harmless enough. Anyway, she had it coming.'

'Harmless?' I sat up and twisted to face him.

'What?'

I took a deep breath. 'You tried to kill her, didn't you?'

'Kill her?' He laughed. 'Come on.'

I persisted. 'You drugged her with her own pills. Was that why you went round to her flat – to get them?'

He looked taken aback. 'What're you talking about?'

'You crushed them into the wine you left her in the boathouse.' *It was bitter, she had said. But I drank it for him.*

He lifted his arm from the back of the settee and made circles with his stiff wrist.

I said, 'She knew something was wrong. She was just in too much of a state to think it through.'

'You know what? I'm sorry they found her.' He was still flexing his fingers, bringing his wrist back to life. 'A couple more hours and it would have been too late. Honestly? Far better if she'd just died.'

I looked away. I thought again about Miss Dixon, hunched in her armchair, gazing out vacantly at the passing world.

Ralph said, 'She was trouble. You know she was. If she'd gone bleating to Sarah Baldini about all her crazy theories, they'd have come after me. They'd have to make a show of taking it seriously. Suspending me. Launching an investigation. Who knows? I might've ended up behind bars.'

'In prison?' I stared at him, suddenly chilled. *What was he talking about?* He'd been a fool to pursue Laura Dixon and if she'd carried out her threat and told the governors about their affair, maybe they'd have disciplined him. But prison? 'What crazy theories?'

'She's delusional. That's all.' He got to his feet and strode over to the windows, suddenly hiding his face. 'Anyway, we're shot of her now. Thank God.'

I scrutinised him as he stood, hands on hips, looking out towards the valley.

'What crazy theories, Ralph? What do you mean?'

He didn't answer. I sat in silence, my eyes on his back. Something was bothering me. This wasn't just about his fling with Laura Dixon. There was something else.

'Can I really not stay the night?' he said, turning suddenly to face me. 'I'm sick of camping.'

'I know. You must be.' I managed to smile. 'But we said we'd wait one more week. Let's not blow it now.'

He sighed. 'Tell Anna tomorrow. Get it over with.'

I shook my head. 'She's only just got here. Give her a chance to settle in.'

He took a deep breath and blew out his cheeks, deciding whether to make a fuss.

I looked at my watch. 'It's getting late. I should get to bed.'

He said, 'Maybe I could come up too? Just for a while. I'll make sure I'm gone before Anna's up.'

'It's too risky. What if she wakes up in the night and comes looking for me?'

'Spoilsport.' He knelt down in front of me and kissed my hands, lying there in my lap, then worked his way up my blouse to my lips. I shivered.

He pulled away and kissed me lightly on the tip of my nose.

'You're right.' He got to his feet. 'One more week.' He ducked to me again and whispered, 'You know what's keeping me strong? The thought of all that lovely money. Ours for the taking.'

He chuckled to himself as he headed to the downstairs cloakroom.

I listened to the door click shut behind him, then jumped up and went to his jacket. I rifled through the pockets until I found his new phone, bought with cash. Pay-as-you-go, clean and untraceable.

I slipped it into my pocket just as the toilet flushed.

When he emerged, his stubbly hair looked raked through, as if he'd been examining it in the mirror, admiring himself.

He stepped forward and put his hands on my waist. 'So, Mrs Mack, can I come calling again tomorrow? After dark, of course.'

I kissed him. 'I'll cook properly, if you like. Steak? You bring the wine.'

He winked. 'It's a date.'

He pulled his jacket on and turned to open the front door. I saw his hand go into his pocket, feel around the emptiness. He stopped, turned suddenly back to me.

I froze, trying to think of an excuse, a plausible reason why his phone was suddenly in my pocket instead of his.

'I can't get used to walking everywhere,' he said. 'I keep searching for car keys.' He laughed at himself. 'Soon as this is over, I'm getting a four-wheel drive. Don't argue. We can afford it, now.'

He set off on foot, crunching and cracking his way to the footpath down the side of the house. I stood at the picture windows, watching. When he rounded the house, he paused and twisted to peer back at me through the darkness. It was the same searching look I'd seen last night when he came snooping round the hotel car park in the darkness, checking for the hire car to make sure we'd really arrived.

Then he turned again to the track and was gone, heading down towards the neighbouring valley and the sleepy campsite waiting for him there.

I stood for some moments, looking after him, thinking. Something wasn't right. I couldn't shake the feeling. There was something important that he still wasn't telling me.

I swallowed. What did Laura Dixon know that frightened him so much? *Something that could put him in prison.*

I felt a wave of nausea and my legs trembled. He'd promised me there'd be no more secrets from now on. We were supposed to start again with a clean sheet. That was how he'd persuaded me to go along with his fraud. So we could emerge afterwards as Mr and Mrs Mack. A happy couple.

It was all I'd ever wanted. To give our marriage a second chance. I wasn't like him. I never cared about the insurance money. He could keep it. It could pay for him to write poetry all day, if that was what he wanted. All I needed was already right here.

I pulled his new phone from my pocket and considered it. It lay hard and solid in my hand. He used the same number code for everything. If there were secrets stored inside, they were mine for the taking.

I hesitated. I'd learned not to spy on Ralph. Never to read late-night texts that popped up on his phone. Not to look at emails if he left them open. I'd schooled myself to look the other way. It wasn't worth the hurt.

Now, if I was going to give up my old friends, my old life for him and become Mrs Mack, if I was going to force Anna to do the same, I needed to know the truth. I needed to know if he was finally being honest with me.

I was just afraid of what I might find.

CHAPTER 52

It didn't take me long to find the messages.

He hadn't made any effort to delete them. It was almost as if he enjoyed the danger. As if the risk of being caught was part of the thrill.

The texts had been sent in the last few weeks. After Laura Dixon's overdose. After he'd moved up here to start preparing our new home together. After he'd promised on his life never to betray me again.

Run as far as you like, princess. You'll never escape me.

Then, a few days later:

Can you feel me? I'm right here. Waiting. We're not done yet. Not until I say so.

Just two days ago:

Still here. Miss me?

There were no replies.

I shook my head, imagining their impact on Laura Dixon. She'd know it was him, of course she would, even if she didn't recognise his new number. What was he playing at? She was damaged enough. She didn't need this.

I read them again. The tone was menacing. The words of a man threatening revenge because his pride had been hurt. I didn't understand. Why was he doing this, trying to needle her? He'd tried to kill her. Now he wanted her back?

I thought about the slip of paper Miss Abbott had given me with Laura Dixon's address and phone number. I put Ralph's phone aside and went in search of my old smartphone, hidden in the pocket of a bag, then pulled up the scan I'd taken of her details.

I frowned, confused, then looked again at Ralph's menacing messages. It wasn't her number. Unless she had a second, secret phone? I shrugged. *It was possible but…*

Run as far as you like, princess.

I stared again at the number on Ralph's phone. There was something about it that felt familiar, but I couldn't place it. I felt suddenly hot, my hairline prickling. I moved to my contacts list and started to trawl through it, looking for a match.

The screen blurred. I sat, struggling to understand. I could barely focus. My mind whirled as I stared, in disbelief, at the number.

Oh, Ralph.

Megan, with her long-limbs and beautiful eyes, her quick intelligence. The star of Ralph's English class.

Clara's big sister. My best friend's daughter.

A searing pain in my stomach. I bent double, struggling to breathe.

No, please not her.

She was only seventeen. She was still a child.

A memory fell into place. No wonder she'd seemed so subdued, so embarrassed when she came to see me just before she left for her big travelling adventure, funded by the cheque I'd given her. My thank you for coming over to the house that night at zero notice to sit with Anna. Thank you for sending the text messages that covered my tracks. *Our* tracks.

Ralph, how could you?

I eased myself sideways to the floor, my knees drawn up.

Megan. Ralph, giving her extra coaching at lunchtimes because she was such a promising pupil. Helping her read more widely, to extend her knowledge, before her university interviews. Ralph's boyish excitement when Megan started writing her own poetry and sharing it with him.

He'd seen her after school. I'd sanctioned it. I'd even been pleased when he asked if I thought it would be okay to include her in one of his staff poetry events, just to make her feel respected, to feel like an adult.

'I'd give her a lift home,' he'd said. 'I'd look after her. Ask Bea if that's okay, would you?'

I'd been grateful. I thought he was proving himself to me, apologising for his affair with Laura Dixon, showing me the kind of man he'd be in the future, if I stood by him and went ahead with his plans.

I shuddered.

My mind leaped on. *Laura Dixon. She'd found out, she must have.* That was what she was threatening to tell. That he'd been harassing his underage pupil.

Ralph had raged when I told him that Laura's threats were just bluster. Why would she risk going to the Head, to the governors? We'd argued about it. After all, if they fired him, wouldn't she lose her job too? She was just as guilty as he was, if they called his conduct unprofessional.

She was crazy, he'd said. Vengeful, all because he'd broken things off.

She was out to ruin him, he kept repeating, raking his fingers through his hair. We had to disappear before she acted, before she made her delusions public and this whole madness blew up in his face.

Think of the shame, the humiliation. He had turned large, wild eyes on me. Not just for him. For me. For Anna.

And then he set out details of the fraud which would allow us to escape it all, to start again, together.

Now, I tried to focus on breathing, to ease the pain. *How could you, Ralph?* I didn't know what I'd do if a grown man, a married man, harassed Anna like that, when she was just a teenager.

I thought again about Megan. She'd looked haunted, her eyes hollowed. She'd trembled when I forced her to go through Ralph's books.

How can I tell you? she'd said. *I can't tell anyone.*

No wonder she'd struggled to concentrate, to revise for her exams. Every essay must have reminded her of Ralph. Every novel. Every poem.

I blew out my cheeks.

You'll blame me, she'd said.

I saw it, now. Megan had kept her mouth shut about Ralph's abusive behaviour, not because she cared about him but because she cared about me, her family's kind and helpful friend. And about Anna, her little sister's playmate.

I leaned forward and reached for a tissue, wiped my eyes, my nose.

I'd trusted him. I'd closed my ears to the voices that told me he'd never change, he'd always cheat on me, he'd always lie. *No,* I'd told myself. *Deep down, he loves me. He loves Anna. We really can start again.*

But this? He'd betrayed me in the worst way possible. Lies. Nothing but lies. Even now, he hadn't let go of his obsession with Megan. Maybe he never would, until his longing was satisfied.

She thought he was dead but by texting her now, he was putting everything at risk. Our secret. Our new identities. Our futures.

Not just his. Not just mine. But Anna's too.

That was something I couldn't allow.

CHAPTER 53

I barely slept that night. As day broke, I lay, silent, staring at the weak sunlight creeping in patterns across the ceiling. Sounds drifted in. Alien, country sounds.

My head ached. I hunched into a ball, frightened, stomach churning.

Once the sun was up, I padded through to Anna's room. She was lying on her side, her lips parted, her breath sounding in little puffs. She'd kicked off the duvet and her legs were bent and scissored, as if she were running away even as she slept.

I covered her again, then made myself a strong coffee and took it back to the bedroom. I sat at the window to drink it, looking out across the valley. The fields looked lush with dew. The sun, strengthening now, was burning off the mist. I sat very still and tried to feel its warmth, to take strength from it.

Once we'd had breakfast, I drove Anna to the nearest town to find a supermarket and stock up on food. We pretended to be explorers, searching the cobbled streets on foot, looking at postcards and stuffed toys, sweet shops lined with old-fashioned jars, outdoor equipment stores with tents and waterproof jackets and climbing gear. It was all a game to her, for now. We were playing at being here, not settling.

We held hands as we walked, swinging our arms. I tried to play along, not to let her see how frightened I was.

In the supermarket, I chose a marbled slab of steak for Ralph and a chocolate cheesecake, his favourite dessert. Anna chose a tub of chocolate ice cream. She skipped out of the supermarket back to the car, beaming, clutching a family-sized box of cereal to her chest, her spiky hair shining like a halo. Her happiness, her optimism, seemed so light against my own heaviness.

We unpacked the shopping and put it all away in the barn, then walked down the hill to the pub-hotel where we'd spent our first night. The heat was gathering. The sunshine burning now, glancing off the dry stones and shrivelling the grass. Sheep huddled under the trees or lay along the thread of shade thrown by the walls lining their fields.

The pub garden was crowded with holidaymakers: families with young children, cyclists and hikers in thick socks and heavy boots, crammed along the benches on either side of wooden table, shaded by umbrellas, or sitting in clusters on the grass.

Inside, the thick stone walls of the pub kept the interior cool. The main lounge was deserted. Shafts of sunshine fell across the faded armchairs and worn carpet, lighting columns of dancing dust.

Anna and I ordered from the bar, then went back to the lounge to wait for our sandwiches and soft drinks, away from the crowds. I found the remote and switched the television to the children's channel. Anna brightened and settled in front of it, ready to disappear, eyes glazed, into the programmes.

I watched her for a moment. She looked so young, so vulnerable, sitting cross-legged on a cushion, her shoes sloughed off. Buddy, her new toy, stood upright in her lap.

I leaned forward and kissed her on the top of her head.

'Are you okay for a minute, Anna, if I go outside to make a phone call?'

She was so wrapped up in the television that she didn't even stir.

I went back out to the garden and through the noisy crowd to a grassy mound on the far side. Two boys, three and four years old perhaps, rolled down it, then collapsed together, shrieking, at the bottom. They clambered to their feet and ran back up the slope on stubby legs to roll again. Their hair was speckled with pollen.

I sat, knees drawn up, at the top of the mound and drew out Ralph's new phone, the one I'd taken from his pocket the night before. I pressed the button and watched the screen spring into life. No new messages. Two missed calls. From Ralph, I suspected, trying to find out where he'd left it. I stared at the screen, trying to steel myself to make the call.

The two boys came racing up the mound again, the smaller one grasping at the older one's clothes to pull him down. They were breathless, laughing, slapping at each other, knocking into each other. Behind them, the hotel garden was vibrant with colour, from the blooming hanging baskets by the door to the red striped umbrellas, the bright cotton T-shirts.

I shook my head, wondering what these people would think of me if they knew what I was about to do.

My eye strayed to the lounge windows at the side of the building. They shone with sunlight. Anna was on the other side. I imagined her, sitting there quietly, waiting for me, trusting me. I remembered the sight of her asleep that morning, her limbs splayed, her face soft. My heart contracted and shortened my breath. *Oh, Anna.*

I hunched forward and punched a new number into the phone, then closed my eyes to shut myself off from the scene in front of me and waited as it rang.

CHAPTER 54

I let Anna fall asleep in my arms that night.

She was delighted, cuddled up in the crook of my elbow as I lay beside her in her narrow bed. She lifted her head now and then to check my face, to be sure of me, planting little kisses on the tip of my nose, my lips, my chin, then finally settled. I stroked her back, soothing her to sleep, the same way I had when she was tiny. In those days, I fell asleep next to her most of the time, from sheer exhaustion.

It was my need, not hers. I held her against me, feeling her thin ribs expand and contract, the smell of her skin coated with lavender oil from her bath and the remnants of strawberry shampoo. She'd kicked off the duvet and the heat rising from her body warmed me.

'I love you,' I whispered, once I was sure she was asleep. I withdrew my arm with stealth. The bed creaked as I eased away my weight. 'I hope you'd forgive me, if you knew. You've been through enough.'

I had a shower and dressed with care in a slinky dress, one of the few I'd kept. Perfume. Bare legs. Heels. I put on make-up in the bathroom cabinet and stood back in the doorway, craning to see myself. I looked like someone else. Like Mrs Mack.

In the kitchen, I prepared everything I could, setting out the frying pan, the garlic and oil, making a rocket salad. The kitchen knife flashed as I chopped peppers and tomatoes.

Afterwards, I went through to the settee and armchairs and sat in the window, looking out over the valley. I folded my hands in my lap, imagining unseen eyes watching me. This was my signal to them, to the world, that I was ready for what the night might bring.

Slowly, the light mellowed and thinned. The dying sun bled across the far valley, giving way at last to darkness. The thick, leafy foliage, drawing a curtain over every approaching path and track, turned black. I strained to see, to hear him approach.

A twig cracked, invisible but close to the barn. I jumped. The darkness rubbed against the windows. I crept back through the barn towards the front door and stood there, listening and waiting.

A tap on the wood, so light it could be a branch blowing against the gables. The low rattle of a key in the lock. The door opened.

He stood there, silhouetted against the night.

A whisper, 'Helen?'

'Hello.' I crept forward and reached my arms around him, pressed my body against his. He was leaner and fitter than I'd ever known him, his shoulders solid with muscle.

I stroked the back of his neck and he inclined his head, leaning his face towards mine. I kissed him.

'Miss me?'

'Oh, yes.' I smiled in the darkness. 'Shut the door. Come inside.'

Ralph found glasses and poured the wine he'd brought, then stood, leaning back against the spiral staircase, and watched me while I cooked. I fried the steaks in a haze of garlic and spitting fat.

His eyes followed the curves of my body as I moved around the small kitchen adding spices, black pepper, turning the meat, dressing the salad. The swaying of my breasts and hips was augmented by the high heels. He was interested, but wary about making a move. I sensed it all. I knew him. It had been such a long time since I'd dressed to please him. It was a dance the two of us had almost forgotten.

When the steak was almost ready, I threw him the matches.

'Would you light the candles?'

He moved down the dining table, lighting the row of candles I'd arranged between two place settings there. Once the candles flared and he'd replaced their stubby glass chimneys, I switched off the kitchen lights and brought our food across.

The room was eerie with shadows. We sat opposite each other together in the soft candlelight, knees touching.

He reached forward and cupped my cheeks with his hand.

'You look amazing, Mrs Mack.' His eyes were gentle. 'You are amazing.'

I gazed back at him. For a moment, in the low flicker of the candles, the years seemed to melt away. I saw again the younger man, the man I'd fallen in love with. The thoughtful poet. My love.

His expression changed. 'What's wrong?' He peered more closely at me through the gloom. 'Why are you teary?'

'I'm just happy,' I lied, pulling away from him and lifting my glass in a toast. 'Happy to have you home.'

I made a supreme effort during the meal, shooting him endless questions about his favourite topic, himself. His cleverness in finding and fitting out the barn. His poetry. His hopes for the future. Even, when the conversation lulled, his thoughts on a new four-wheel drive car. I listened with large eyes and moist lips, pretending to be enthralled.

Quietly, I checked the time when I could, willing it to hurry.

After the steak, I fed him chocolate cheesecake and refilled his wine glass whenever I could. I barely drank myself. I was almost there. Another half an hour, perhaps. The spoon trembled in my hand and I set it down and made fists in my lap.

When I cleared away the dishes, he got to his feet and headed to the downstairs toilet. Once he was inside, I snatched his phone from my bag and slipped it back into his jacket, hiding it as best I could in a deep pocket.

I checked the clock. Fifteen minutes. It was almost time. If I could trust him. If everything went according to plan.

I started to set up the coffee maker, shaking so hard that the packet slipped in my hands. Ground coffee scattered across the counter.

'Easy, there!' He was at my shoulder, his hands reaching for mine to take over.

I started. I hadn't heard the door, hadn't realised he'd come out. What if he'd been watching me, if he'd seen me returning the phone?

'You okay?' His breath smelled of garlic and red wine.

I nodded and turned away. 'Let's have coffee near the windows. Looking out at the valley.'

I leaned over the dining table and blew out the candles, one by one. Puffs of pungent smoke.

He was suddenly behind me, pressing me forward against the edge of the table. I shivered. He'd moved with speed and stealth and now he was pinning me there.

'I know what you're up to.' His breath flared hot against my ear.

I closed my eyes.

His large hands slid round to the front of my dress and cupped my breasts, then squeezed.

'You're trying to turn me on,' he said. 'And you're doing a damn good job.'

I put my hands over his. 'So are you.' I twisted round in his arms and he kissed me, urgent now and loosened by wine.

When he paused, I moved quickly and lifted his arms away.

'Wait.' I put a finger to his lips. 'I've been thinking.'

He frowned.

I wriggled against him and felt his body respond to mine. *Eight minutes to go, maybe. Seven.*

'Maybe it's been my fault, Ralph. At least, partly.' I kept my voice low. 'I've been so focussed on Anna all these years. I forgot to look after you the way I should. I'm sorry. I didn't pay you enough attention.'

His eyes were on mine, cautious, wondering where this was going.

I smiled. 'Don't look so stern, Mr Mack. I'm just saying, I want to make some changes around here. I want to have fun again. With you.'

'Sounds good to me.' He lowered his face, moving in again to kiss me.

I pulled away. 'Wait. I mean it. I want to wow you, Ralph. I want to be so good, you'll never want another woman again.'

I pressed my lips against his and parted them, teased him with the tip of my tongue.

'Can we try something new?' I whispered. 'Something we've never done before?'

It was his turn to tremble. The whites of his eyes glistened in the darkness.

Five minutes. Maybe four.

'Something a bit kinky. Outside.'

He moistened his lips.

'Close your eyes.'

I made him stand there, legs parted, hands on the tabletop while I slid open a kitchen drawer and took out belts and scarves and a small, stuffed envelope.

I fastened the scarf tightly round his head, binding his eyes. 'Do you trust me?'

He nodded. I kissed him lightly on the lips, then lifted his hands behind his back and fastened them with the belt, knotting it as hard as I could.

He flexed his fingers. 'That's tight.'

I bit his ear lobe. 'That's how I want it.'

He said, less certain now, 'Are you sure about this?'

'Oh yes.' I pressed myself against him. 'I want to surprise you. Let's take this outside.'

It was time. I picked up my car keys and the thick envelope from the counter and slipped them into my bag, slung it on my shoulder, then walked him towards the door, keeping my body close to his.

He said, 'Have you got a blanket? It might get cold.'

'Don't worry. I've got it all planned.'

He smiled, snaked his tongue round his lips.

I opened the front door and led him out, then unlocked the hire car and opened the back seat. I helped him inside, head first, my hands guiding him.

He shuffled onto his back, lying awkwardly on his bound wrists, his legs dangling. 'Like this?'

'Perfect.'

I bent up his knees and knotted a final belt as tightly as I could around his ankles. He squirmed, trussed.

'I'm not sure this is going to work, Helen.' He wriggled, trying to sit up in the cramped space and failing. 'Maybe if you undid my hands?' He was starting to sound worried.

I withdrew from the car and stood up, looking round.

A man stepped out of the shadows, as silent as a cat.

Mike Ridge didn't say a word. He just nodded at me, then took my place at the open back door, leaning in to Ralph. A sudden ripping noise, like a plaster being torn off a wound. Then another and another. Then all I could hear were muffled sounds of alarm.

Mike straightened up, shut the car door on Ralph and motioned me off to one side.

He put out his hand and I dug the envelope and the car keys out of my bag. He slit the top of the envelope with a neatly cut thumbnail and flicked over the cash there, mentally checking the amount. I added the car keys.

I whispered, 'How will you do it?'

He arched an eyebrow. 'You don't want to know.'

I bit my lip. 'But it'll be quick? Painless?'

He shrugged, as if to say, *if that's how you want it.*

'Call the cops tomorrow morning,' he said. 'Nine or ten o'clock, maybe. Not the emergency service, the local police station. They take longer. Report the car stolen overnight. You'll need paperwork for the hire car company.'

I blinked. 'What'll you do with it?'

He said, 'I'll burn it out, afterwards. Don't worry.' He raised his hands, showing me his gloves. 'Trust me. I know what I'm doing.'

He turned away. I grasped at his arm, pulling him back to face me again.

'You're sure about this? What if they find him?'

'They won't.' He looked as if he were struggling to be patient with me. 'Look, even if bits of him did surface someday, they'd have nothing to go on. So, it's his DNA? Who'd be surprised?' He sucked his lower lip, thoughtfully. 'That's the thing about dying. People only expect you to do it once.'

I hesitated. *Maybe it wasn't too late. I could say I'd changed my mind, call him off.*

He said, 'Okay?'

I thought about Laura Dixon and how close he'd come to murdering her. The way he'd failed to show the slightest remorse. I thought about Megan and his menacing messages. He'd wanted to keep pursuing her, to punish her for rejecting him. How could he take a risk like that, a risk that might put us both in prison, out of spite and wounded pride?

I thought about Anna. The grief and upheaval he'd forced on her, all because of his lies and selfishness. I shook my head.

Mike Ridge, watching me, seemed to read my thoughts.

'I'll tell you something for nothing, Mrs W. It might've been the other way round.'

I blinked. 'What do you mean?'

'He phoned me about a week ago. Anonymous, of course, but I'm not stupid. He'd seen me around, I expect, outside the house. Offered me cash.'

I frowned. 'For what?'

'To rub you out. No questions asked.' He pulled a face, as if to say, *see what I'm saying? Is that any way to behave?*

Then he opened the back door and motioned towards Ralph.

I leaned again into the car. Ralph was squirming on the back seat. His eyes were blinded by a thick strip of masking tape. Another covered his mouth. Tape was wound around his ankles and wrists too, sealing the work I'd begun with the belts.

I put my mouth close to his ear and, feeling my breath, he quietened to listen.

'Why were we never enough for you, Ralph?' I whispered. 'Anna and I.'

He tossed back his head and struggled to sit up.

'All those years. I put up with your lies, your affairs. I covered for you. I did everything you asked. I even lied to help you escape Laura Dixon and claim the insurance. I risked everything.' I paused and caught my breath, trying not to cry. 'Why didn't you just leave Megan alone?'

He bucked and struggled on the back seat and tried to shout, his words swallowed by the tape.

I whispered, 'And by the way, this Romeo and Juliet thing? You keep forgetting. Romeo? He ends up dead.'

I kissed him on the cheek, crying now. Kissed him goodbye.

CHAPTER 55

Two months later

'Ugh! I just touched something! It's alive!'

'What? Let me see.' Anna shoved Clara out of the way to look. 'Look, Mummy! A spider! It's *huge*!'

They were standing side by side on kitchen chairs, sorting through freshly picked blackberries piled high in bowls. Their hair, brushed and tied back just hours ago, was already falling free, straggly and studded with fragments of leaf. Their sleeves were pushed back to the elbow, showing a patchwork of scratches from the bushes. Their fingers and mouths were stained purple with juice.

Anna, fearless, caught the spider in her hands. 'Quick! Open the door!'

Clara followed, screeching and jumping, as Anna headed outside to release the spider back into the wild.

Clara was shouting, 'Mummy! It's Mummy!'

I wiped my hands on a towel and hurried outside to see. Bea's car was bouncing down the track, lurching from side to side in the muddy ruts. Her brow was furrowed, her knuckles white where she gripped the steering wheel.

She skidded to a stop next to my new car, switched off the engine, then, finally, looked up, waved and beamed as the girls went careering over to her.

She jumped out and enveloped them both in hugs. 'Had a good week?'

'Brilliant!'

'Fab!'

'Wow!' She raised her eyes to me. 'And how about you?'

I smiled. 'Splendiferous.'

We went for lunch at the pub at the bottom of the hill. Saturdays were usually busy and the outdoor tables were already taken. Bea and I found a patch of weak October sunshine in a corner of the garden and sat on a picnic rug, wrapped up in cardigans and coats.

The girls tore up and down the mound at the far end of the garden, making themselves dizzy with rolling races, then practising handstands and cartwheels, collapsing on each other in a heap of limbs.

'She's had a brilliant time.' Bea smiled. 'You are kind.'

I shrugged. 'So has Anna. She's really missed her.'

'Likewise. You dug me out of such a hole. I'd got used to falling back on Megan at half-term.'

'Where is she at the moment?'

'Northern Cambodia.'

I nodded. 'All going well?'

'She's having a ball. You were right.' She gave me a shrewd look. 'She deserved a break. She worked herself into the ground last year.'

We clinked glasses. The white wine was crisp and cold. Bea tore open a packet of crisps, set it between us on the rug and munched on one. I felt my shoulders relax, as if I were setting down a heavy burden, one I'd been carrying for a long time.

Bea twisted sideways to look me over. 'Anyway, how are you? How's your year away?'

'Is that what it is?' I laughed. 'Pretty good. Anna seems settled in school. It's tiny. She's got ten in her class. But it's a great school.' I hesitated, embarrassed. 'I'm helping out there, actually.'

Bea looked surprised. 'Teaching?'

'No! Sorting out a library for them. They didn't really have one. I've got plans for a fundraiser after Christmas so we can buy more stock.'

We sat quietly for a moment. The year was cooling, rolling towards winter, but here the sunshine fell warm on our faces.

Bea said, 'How's Anna doing, generally?' She felt her way forward. 'Does she talk about her dad much?'

'She came home upset the other day because kids at school started asking where he was.' She'd sobbed in my arms, curling into me. How could I comfort her? 'The teacher said he was probably safe in Heaven. I don't know if that helped or not.'

Bea said, thoughtfully, 'She looks well. Stronger. More her own person.'

I nodded. 'I think that's right.'

'You guys will come back eventually though, won't you?'

'I don't know.' I sighed. 'Maybe.'

Bea hesitated as if she were deciding whether to leave me alone or to pursue the subject.

'Mrs Prior says you will.' Bea raised her eyebrows. 'She says you needed closure but once you have that...'

'Oh, please.' I shook my head. 'Mrs Prior! That's a reason never to come back, right there.'

'I wouldn't let that stop you.' She leaned towards me and lowered her voice. 'Word on the street is that she's pregnant. And if she is, I bet she doesn't come back again. So, you might be okay.'

I raised my eyebrows. 'Who's giving you all this gossip?'

She shrugged. 'I've got to make an effort, now you've gone. There's no one else to tell me what's going on.'

'I'll take that as a compliment.' I took a sip of wine. 'Go on, then. What else do I need to know?'

She paused. 'Not much.' She watched the girls, who were back to rolling down the mound. 'Well, there is one thing.'

I stiffened. I knew exactly what she was going to say. Something about Ralph. Some incriminating evidence had been found.

She drank a gulp of her wine, then said, 'It's about Miss Dixon.'

'Miss Dixon?' I blew out my cheeks. 'What about her? Is she teaching again?'

She shook her head. 'Not yet. But she's moved. Gone to live near her sister in Kent.'

'Who told you that?'

'Jayne in the office.'

I nodded. She was a pretty reliable source. 'Any idea how she's doing?'

'Better, I think. Her sister's got kids and Miss Dixon is going to help out for a bit. Until she feels up to teaching again.'

I nodded. 'I'm glad.'

A lad from the bar came out with a tray of sandwiches, shouting our number.

Bea waved him down, then ran across to the girls to get them to come and eat. Their trousers were stained with soil and grass and purple splashes from squashed bilberries. I watched Bea as she bent over them, brushing them down, one by one, half-scolding, half-teasing.

My mind was far away, on Laura Dixon. I wondered if she missed Ralph. If she thought she still loved him. I remembered the sad shadow she'd become.

I was glad she had a sister. A kind sister, by the sound of it. She'd paid enough now, for what she'd done. I hoped she'd heal.

We ate. Anna and Clara sat cross-legged on the grass, spilling crumbs, giggling together.

Bea said, 'I'm glad you came here. Not Bristol.' Then, to Clara, 'Don't just eat chips. Have some sandwich too.'

I shrugged, avoiding her eye. 'I'm glad too. This place popped up at the last minute. Cheaper too.'

Bea gave me a narrow look. 'I thought we'd lost you altogether, for a while. That reminds me – why did you change your mobile number?'

I bit into a chip. 'Oh, I lost the old phone. I've just got a cheap pay-as-you-go now.'

Bea reached for another sandwich. 'Well, anyway, it's great to see you. Don't ever run out on us again, will you?'

'I won't.' I looked at the girls. Anna was feeding Clara a chip, pretending she was a dog. 'I promise.'

That evening, Anna and I snuggled in her bed while I read to her. When I put the book down, she wrapped her arms around me.

I said, 'It was fun seeing Clara and her mum, wasn't it?'

Anna squeezed me. 'Best. Day. Ever.'

I kissed her hair, breathed in her clean, soapy smell.

'We do all right together, you and me. Don't you think?'

She twisted round to kiss me, square on the lips.

'Mummy,' she said. 'Pretend I'm a baby fox and you've just found me and I can talk?'

She scrunched into a ball, pretending to have a fox snout and paws. I tickled her for a bit behind her long foxy ears, stroked her imaginary fur, until she was ready to go to sleep.

'I love you, little fox.'

'I love you too, Mummy.'

*

Downstairs, I made myself a cup of tea and curled in an armchair, looking out at the lazy curve of the valley. The nights were drawing in. The leaves, already orange and gold, were dying. The bare branches wrote a stark scribble across the darkening sky.

I tried to imagine winter here. Teachers at school said the village was sometimes snowed in for days, even weeks. Classes had to stop. Shops closed. The only moving vehicles were tractors. Just the thought of it made me shiver.

I'd been grateful to see Bea. She reminded me who I was. I was not a pretend Mrs Mack. I was Mrs Wilson again and I really was a widow now. Once enough time had passed, I'd be able to start the process of applying through the courts for my missing husband to be declared dead. Eventually, I'd have a lot of money coming to me.

And, if we wanted it, Anna and I, our old life still waited for us, down in the south. *A year away*, Bea had called it. Maybe that's what this was. A year out of time, to rest and recover and find ourselves again.

There were days I woke up, here in the barn, and, still half-asleep, time played tricks on me. I'd think that I was lying in our old bedroom, in the house we bought together. That if I stretched out my hand, Ralph would be there, sleeping quietly beside me. Later, I might potter downstairs and start to make breakfast, hearing the sudden explosion of Ralph's shower in the bathroom, before he came down, battered school bag in hand, sweeping the mess of floppy hair from his eyes.

Then I'd hear the sharp, bright songs of the birds in the copse behind the barn and the distant lowing of cows and I'd blink and open my eyes and find myself here, without him. With Anna.

I finished my tea and sat quietly, looking through the picture windows at the darkness and seeing my own reflection imposed on it, a ghostly outline of myself floating in the glass. The silence pressed down on me. Intense and eerie. The valley was veiled in black.

A sudden noise. A stick cracked. I jumped.

Something was there. Blood roared in my ears as I strained to listen.

Another noise. A barely audible scraping against the wall. *A fox, maybe, on the prowl? Or a person, creeping round the side of the barn towards the door.*

I set down my mug, as stealthily as I could, and crept the length of the ground floor, every nerve taut. The only lights I had on inside were the bright ones illuminating the kitchen. I didn't dim them, frightened of giving myself away.

A tap at the door. *Just a branch, blown against it by the wind? Or a knuckle?*

Was someone there?

I froze. I couldn't speak, couldn't call out. I just stood there, on my side of the door, my breath stopped in my mouth, and waited. My heart banged.

The silence buzzed. *Nothing.* Just the wind. I was being a fool, spooking myself over nothing.

I recovered enough to ease the handle of the front door and peer out.

Once I opened the door, light from behind me spilled out, drawing a fading cone across the ground. I shivered in the sudden chill. My eyes scanned the darkness, trying to read the moving patterns under the trees.

A night wind was blowing up, stirring the autumn leaves, setting them dancing in circles.

'Hello?' My voice sounded thin, vanishing on the breeze. 'Is someone there?'

My heart raced. Was that a person, moving between the trees, or just the shifting shadow of a moving branch? I took several steps into the darkness, then paused, trembling.

I took a deep breath, steadied myself and carried on, further into the copse. Above my head, the branches, carrying the last dry leaves of the year, swished and rustled. Every time a twig cracked underfoot, I started.

Nothing. I shook my head, trying to reassure myself. I was being absurd, creeping around outside at night, terrifying myself. *What was I thinking?* I turned and began to head back.

The cone of light from the open door bled into the darkness. As I reached the blurred edge, I stopped abruptly and stared at the ground.

There was something there, in the mud. Marks. Something the girls had drawn, perhaps, playing in the earth with sticks. But why hadn't I noticed them before?

I bent down to look, suddenly afraid. They weren't random scratches. They looked too definite.

I ran my eye along the marks, following the lines through the gloom, tracing the shapes.

In the weak half-light, they seemed almost to form two words, words which the blowing dust and mulch were already starting to erase.

Miss me?

A LETTER FROM JILL CHILDS

I want to say a huge thank you for choosing to read *The Mistress*. If you enjoyed it and want to keep up-to-date with all my latest releases, just sign up at the following link. Your email address will never be shared and you can unsubscribe at any time.

www.bookouture.com/jill-childs

When I was a teenager, and prone to passionate, moralistic judgements about the world, an older friend told me how having children had changed her attitude to marriage. Before children, she said, if she'd ever found out that her husband was cheating on her, she would have packed her bags and left him.

Now, with children to consider, she thought it more likely she'd stay, however hurt and humiliated she might feel, and try to weather the crisis.

That conversation happened decades ago, but it's stayed with me, partly because, at the time, I couldn't believe my feisty, strong female friend would contemplate accepting betrayal, however theoretical.

Now I'm married with children of my own and of course I understand far better what she was trying to say.

But, even with children, how far could forgiveness stretch, for the sake of keeping a family intact?

What if a husband wasn't contrite but persisted with his affairs? What if he preyed on someone vulnerable? What if he used emotional blackmail to pressure his forgiving wife into going along with something she knew was wrong?

It was out of these thoughts that *The Mistress* was born.

I hope you loved *The Mistress*. If you did, I would be very grateful if you could write a review. I'd love to hear what you think, and it makes such a difference in helping new readers discover my books for the first time.

I love hearing from my readers. You can get in touch on my Facebook page or on Twitter. Thank you!

All best wishes to you and yours,
Jill

 jill.childs.71
@author_jill

ACKNOWLEDGEMENTS

Thank you to my wonderful editor, Kathryn Taussig, and all the team at Bookouture.

Thank you to my brilliant agent, Judith Murdoch, the best in the business.

Thank you, always, to my family for all their love and support and especially to Nick, the still centre of my world. It's time you had another one, so this is for you.

CPSIA information can be obtained
at www.ICGtesting.com
Printed in the USA
BVHW040856140523
664122BV00017B/373

9 781838 889692